STAR WARS
THE FORCE AWAKENS

ALAN DEAN FOSTER

SCREENPLAY WRITTEN BY
LAWRENCE KASDAN & J. J. ABRAMS
AND MICHAEL ARNDT

BASED ON CHARACTERS CREATED
BY GEORGE LUCAS

arrow books

1 3 5 7 9 10 8 6 4 2

Arrow Books
20 Vauxhall Bridge Road
London SW1V 2SA

Arrow Books is part of the Penguin Random House group of companies
whose addresses can be found at global.penguinrandomhouse.com.

Penguin
Random House
UK

First published by Century in 2016
First published in paperback by Arrow Books in 2016

www.randomhouse.co.uk

A CIP catalogue record for this book is available from the British Library.

ISBN 9781784752910

Printed and bound in Great Britain by Clays Ltd, St Ives Plc

STAR WARS™

TIMELINE

I — THE PHANTOM MENACE

II — ATTACK OF THE CLONES
THE CLONE WARS (TV SERIES)
DARK DISCIPLE

III — REVENGE OF THE SITH
LORDS OF THE SITH
TARKIN
A NEW DAWN
REBELS (TV SERIES)

IV — A NEW HOPE
HEIR TO THE JEDI
BATTLEFRONT: TWILIGHT COMPANY

V — THE EMPIRE STRIKES BACK

VI — RETURN OF THE JEDI
AFTERMATH
AFTERMATH: LIFE DEBT
AFTERMATH: EMPIRE'S END
NEW REPUBLIC: BLOODLINE
THE PERFECT WEAPON (EBOOK ORIGINAL)

VII — THE FORCE AWAKENS

A long time ago in a galaxy far, far away. . . .

First comes the day
Then comes the night.
After the darkness
Shines through the light.
The difference, they say,
Is only made right
By the resolving of gray
Through refined Jedi sight.

—*Journal of the Whills*, 7:477

Luke Skywalker has vanished.
In his absence, the sinister
FIRST ORDER has risen from
the ashes of the Empire
and will not rest until
Skywalker, the last Jedi,
has been destroyed.

With the support of the
REPUBLIC, General Leia Organa
leads a brave RESISTANCE.
She is desperate to find her
brother Luke and gain his
help in restoring peace and
justice to the galaxy.

Leia has sent her most daring
pilot on a secret mission
to Jakku, where an old ally
has discovered a clue to
Luke's whereabouts. . . .

I

SHE NEEDED HIM. AND HE WAS NOWHERE TO be found.

There was no one else she could rely on. No one like her brother. No one else at all, now that the New Republic stood on the verge of implosion, of destruction, of complete collapse.

They had thought that with the fall of the Empire it would all be so easy. That people would understand the need for patience, that time would be required to rebuild that which the Empire had taken away. Cities, communications, trade: All these could and were well on their way to full restoration. It was the intangibles that proved so much more difficult to re-establish throughout galactic society.

Freedom, for example. The freedom to speak one's mind, to object, to dispute. She sighed. Those who had led the rebellion had underestimated the deeply buried desire of far too large a proportion of the population who simply preferred to be told what to do. Much easier it was to follow orders than to think for oneself. So everyone had argued and debated and discussed. Until it was too late.

Pacing the chamber, she caught a glimpse of herself

in a length of polished metal. She knew she looked tired. Sometimes she wished she had been born a commoner, an ordinary citizen, instead of planetary royalty. Such thoughts led her inevitably to memories of Alderaan. Her homeworld, now many years gone, reduced to ashes.

And her own father had been a party to it. It was a legacy she could not escape. She could not let something like that happen again, to any other world, to any other people. It was her responsibility, and the weight of it was heavy. Too heavy?

Easier if she had help. The kind of help only her brother was capable of providing. If he wasn't dead.

No. Surely not. Wherever he was, if he had passed on, she would have sensed his demise. Of that she was certain. Of that much she *had* to be certain.

There had come a hint, a clue. Not much, but better than any report that had found its way to her in some time. She would have followed up on it herself, for who better to search for clues to the location of a missing brother than his own sister? When she had proposed the idea, the shock of objection on the part of her fellow Resistance leaders could have been heard halfway across the galaxy. Reluctantly, she had conceded to reason. Someone would go in her stead.

The name of a particular pilot had been put forth. His record was no less than remarkable, and she could hardly argue that a pilot scouting solo would draw less attention than a perambulating princess. So she agreed.

"Finding one man should not, in the final analysis, be so difficult," insisted one of her colleagues. "Even on all the known worlds, there are only so many hiding places."

"For an ordinary man, yes," she had replied. "But

we're not trying to find an ordinary man. We're looking for Luke Skywalker."

There had been some further argument, especially
from other leaders who had remained convinced that
the pilot chosen to follow up on the slender lead was
too young for such a crucial task. In the end, har-
mony had triumphed.

Once again she caught her reflection in the metal. It
had been some time since she had not prevailed in the
course of such discussions.

A thin, knowing smile gleamed back at her. No
doubt her authority in such matters derived from her
shy, retiring nature. The smile faded. No time for sardonic reflection now, she told herself. No time for
extended, lengthy discussion. Times were desperate.
The ruthless First Order was on the march, threatening to overwhelm the shaky framework of the weak,
increasingly vulnerable, and still-developing New Republic.

Where was her brother?

The Star Destroyer *Finalizer* was massive and new. It
had been forged and assembled in the distant orbital
factories of the First Order, constructed in secret and
uninfected by the virus that was the New Republic.
Its devoted and fanatical builders had designed it to
be more powerful, more technologically advanced,
than anything that had come before it. Certainly there
was nothing in the possession of the new Resistance
that could stand against the vessel.

Almost invisible when they first dropped from a
port in the side of the immense *Resurgent*-class Star
Destroyer, the four transport vessels were of a proven
design. Their function straightforward and simple,
they had no need of the extensive redesign embraced

by their mother ship. For all that, the transports still performed their prescribed role with brute efficiency.

As they went about their mundane daily tasks below, the inhabitants of the glowing orb known as Jakku had no idea they were about to receive a visit from four elite squadrons of Imperial stormtroopers.

On board the quartet of transports, the eighty white-armored troopers prepared for touchdown in the manner of soldiers everywhere. Wisecracks alternated with nervous speculation about what might await them. Surging adrenaline generated nudges and the occasional comradely whack on a neighbor's arm. They knew one another well, had confidence in their team, and felt certain they could cope with anything the minor world toward which they were descending could throw at them.

Squad leaders barked commands. Weapons were armed, checked, rechecked. Flame troopers made certain their special weapons were loaded to capacity. Each trooper made a point of inspecting the armor of a neighbor, ensuring that joints were sealed and panels tight.

The ensuing silence was replaced by a deep rumbling, motionlessness by jolts and bangs, as the four craft entered Jakku's atmosphere. Someone made a particularly inappropriate comment and was immediately quieted by those seated across from him. After that, the only noise within each transport was the roar and thunder as they bucked their way down through thick air.

An automated electronic voice sounded the "Prepare for landing!" warning. Armored bodies tensed. There was a single sharp jolt, followed by the return of a silence so thorough it was shocking. Hands tightened on weapons, bodies tensed, and inside the bay all eyes turned to the transport's bow doorway. The

quiet was barely broken by the slightest of mechanical hums as the front of the ship started to lower toward the unseen ground.

There were smaller villages on Jakku. More primitive, more rural. No one passing over, or even through, Tuanul would have suspected that it held a secret. Even if they had, they would have found no reason to linger. The worlds of the galaxy were full of secrets, and there was no reason to suspect Jakku was any different. But this particular secret . . .

It was a peaceful place, as was the case with most small communities situated on desert worlds. Despite the desolation that was apparent at first glance, it boasted its characteristic assortment of indigenous life-forms. Regardless of the absence of much in the way of visible vegetation, the distant isolated hoots and mewlings of nocturnal native animals indicated that life was present even where none could readily be seen. A single wind chime yodeling in the occasional breeze provided a tinkling counterpoint to the yelps of hidden sand-dwellers.

With neither the place nor the motivation to hide, a creature that was decidedly non-native rolled eastward out of the village. Consisting of a rounded head floating above a much larger sphere, it was dull white with striking orange markings. Designated BB-8, the droid was, at the moment, very, very concerned.

Where a human would see only empty night sky, advanced calibrated synthetic optics saw a moving point of light. When the light resolved itself into four separate points, the droid commenced an agitated beeping. The phenomenon he was seeing might signify nothing, except . . .

The quartet of lights was descending in a controlled

manner, on what could only be described as a calculated path, and they were rapidly slowing. If they
continued in the observed fashion they would make a
controlled touchdown at . . . BB-8 performed an almost instantaneous calculation.

Too near. Too near for coincidence. One such light
was reason for concern. Four hinted at possibilities
dire to contemplate.

Beeping and whistling in something approaching
cybernetic panic, the droid spun and sped back toward
the village. That is, its head spun. Facing all directions simultaneously, the spherical body did not need
to turn, only to accelerate. This BB-8 did with alacrity. While it could have transmitted the conclusion
it had reached, it did not do so for fear of any such
message being intercepted, possibly by those it feared
might be inhabiting the source of the four descending
lights.

In addition to its motley group of mixed galactic
peoples, Tuanul was home to an assortment of used
but still valuable machinery. A fair portion of the village population eked out a modest living modifying
and restoring such equipment for resale in larger
towns and cities. As the droid sped past, the occasional human or alien worker glanced up from the
task at hand, frowning, bemused by the droid's apparently unwarranted haste as it raced through the
community. Then they returned to their work, shrug-
ging with the appropriate body parts.

Machines in various degrees of dismemberment
and disarray did not slow BB-8, who dodged effortlessly around and through them. The flocks of bloggins the droid encountered were not so easily avoided.
Whereas deconstructed devices tended to sit in one
place and not move, bloggins not only wandered where
they wished, but regarded whatever patch of land or

sand they happened to be occupying at the moment as exclusively theirs, and took raucous exception to interlopers. The birdlike creatures promptly objected to the droid's chosen path. The pecking he ignored, and he could have barreled on straight through them. But the domesticated flocks provided food for a number of the villagers, and their owners would not have been pleased to see them flattened.

So BB-8 was forced to dodge and avoid, which he did with skill and patience, beeping and shrieking at the shamble of pseudo-avians in order to clear a non-destructive path. Eventually the last of the annoying beasts was behind him. Deep within the village, there was far less likelihood of encountering anything domesticated that was worth eating: a biological process he understood from an objective point of view but for which he could never rouse much empathy. His goal was close, and there was not a nanosecond to lose.

Like most of the buildings in Tuanul, the residence toward which he was speeding was an odd amalgamation of the contemporary and the very primitive. Dwellings on many of the minor desert worlds were like that: designs dictated by necessity as well as the environment. Though BB-8's intended destination resembled little more than a primeval hut, it contained electronics and multiple concealed enhancements capable of making living in a harsh, dry climate more than merely tolerable.

Though he was fatigued, Poe Dameron tried not to let it show. He owed that much to his host. Besides, he had a reputation to uphold. He had come a long way through difficult and dangerous circumstances to be in this place, in this moment—all on behalf of the

Resistance and specifically on the orders of General Organa herself. He was not about to let a minor inconvenience like exhaustion tarnish a farewelling.

His visage, framed by dark, thick waves of hair, was a bit proud of countenance: something that others, not knowing him, might mistake for arrogance. Confident in his skills and in his mission, he sometimes displayed an impatience that arose only from a desire to fulfill the task at hand. His worn-down red-and-sand-hued flight jacket had been with him as long as he had been in the Resistance, rising through its ranks.

From the moment of Poe's arrival, Tuanul had struck him as somewhat less than imposing. This was in notable contrast to his host. While Lor San Tekka appeared physically capable of removing the heads from various unthinking carnivores, his manner was more that of a Soother, and a professional one at that. One immediately relaxed in his company. Provided one held no inimical intentions toward the hut's owner, of course. Though their visit had been brief, the pilot felt quite confident of his analysis.

Coming close, Tekka placed a small leather sack in Poe's open palm, then covered both with his own hand. He smiled softly and nodded.

"These days I can only do so much. Would that I could do so much more." He sighed heavily. "And there is so much more that needs to be done. But . . . this will begin to make things right."

As the older man's hand withdrew, Poe tightened his fingers around the leather bag. In size, it was small. In importance . . .

"Legend says this map is unobtainable," Poe noted. "How'd you do it?"

The older man just smiled, clearly not willing to give up all his secrets just yet.

Poe grinned back at him, accepting it. "I've heard stories about your adventures since I was a kid. It's an honor to meet you. We're grateful."

Tekka shrugged—an old man's shrug, slow and full of meaning. "I've traveled too far and seen too much to ignore the collective anguish that threatens to drown the galaxy in a flood of dark despair. Something must be done; whatever the cost, whatever the danger. Without the Jedi, there can be no balance in the Force, and all will be given over to the dark side."

Though Poe was reasonably secure in his knowledge of such things, he was also intelligent enough to know he could not begin to discuss them in depth with someone like Lor San Tekka. Rather than make a fool of himself by trying to do so, he prepared to take his leave. Besides, he had a delivery to make. Casual philosophical conversation could wait for a better time.

"The general has been after this a long time," Poe said, as a way of beginning to take his leave.

Tekka smiled at some secret thought. " 'General.' To me, she's royalty."

"Yeah, but don't call her Princess," Poe told him. "Not to her face. She doesn't like it anymore. *Really* doesn't like it."

He was about to elaborate when a frantic metal sphere rolled into the room, barely braking in time to avoid hitting the two men, and began to spew a stream of electronic chatter. The two men exchanged a glance before rushing toward the building's entrance.

Poe had his quadnocs in his hands even before he stopped running. Aiming them toward the general section of sky indicated by BB-8, he let the integrated automatic tracker focus on any targets in the vicinity. The device located four almost immediately. Lower-

ing it, he spoke without turning, his gaze fixed on the horizon.

"Not to be presumptuous, sir, but you need to hide."

Tekka didn't need quadnocs. He had already identified the incoming ships by the sound they made as they finished their descent. "Not to overstate the obvious, but *you* need to leave."

Despite the importance of his mission, Poe found himself conflicted. Not only did he respect Lor San Tekka, he liked him. How could he leave him here? "Sir, if you don't mind, I—"

The older man cut him off. "But I do mind, Poe Dameron. You spoke of your mission." Both his gaze and his tone hardened. "Now fulfill it. Compared to what is stirring in the galaxy, you and I are little more than motes of dust."

Still, Poe demurred. "With all due respect, some motes are of more importance than others . . . sir."

"If you wish to flatter something, flatter my memory. Go. Now! I must see to the defense of the village." Turning, Tekka headed off, not looking back.

Poe hesitated a moment longer, then whirled and raced toward the far end of the village, BB-8 pacing him effortlessly. As he ran, he was passed by armed, stern-visaged villagers. How the alarm had been raised he did not know, just as he did not pause to wonder at how or why such seemingly simple folk had come into possession of so many weapons. Doubtless Lor San Tekka would know. Poe resolved to ask him—one day.

The ship that was parked some distance from the village was well hidden beneath a high rock outcropping. That wouldn't shield the X-wing from sophisticated search gear, Poe knew. He needed to exit the atmosphere, and fast. Hurrying to the cockpit as BB-8

rolled into the copiloting position, he hurriedly activated the controls. Instrumentation flared to life. In the distance a swarm of bipedal shapes in glistening white armor could be seen approaching the village. Stormtroopers. The weaponry they unleashed confirmed their identification.

Those villagers who had armed themselves attempted to mount a defense. In this, bravery was a poor match for training and advanced equipment. As more and more of their number went down, the defenders had no choice but to pull back.

It was over almost before it began. Seeing the hopelessness of further resistance, the villagers began to give themselves up, surrendering in twos and threes. As penned animals panicked and broke free, several of the specially equipped flame troopers began setting chosen structures afire. To an outraged Poe there seemed no reason for it. But then, to those behind the First Order, sowing fear and terror was merely politics by another means.

His angry thoughts were interrupted by a stream of electronic anxiety from the droid. "We're going, Beebee-Ate, we're going! Almost there . . ." He thumbed another control.

Landing lights snapped on as engines whined to life. *Roll clear of the overhang and then punch it,* he told himself.

He was a second from doing just that when the ship was hit.

The pair of stormtroopers had come up on him unseen. Whoever had planned the attack was too smart to rely on a simple frontal assault. Perhaps these two were part of a preceding suit drop or had used a vehicle to circle around behind the village. If one of their bursts connected with the cockpit, their origin wouldn't matter.

On the other hand, they were either angling for a commendation or just plain stupid, because their line of approach put them right in front of the X-wing's weapons. Poe hit the control that deployed the drop-down pivoting gun from the belly of his X-wing, then fired. The resulting blasts cleared the ground of the enemy and every other living thing that had been un-fortunate enough to have been in their immediate vicinity.

Having dealt succinctly with the momentary inter-ruption, Poe returned his attention to the X-wing's instrumentation. An ascending whine rose from the rear of the ship. Shuddering slightly, it started to move out from beneath the protective rock. Strapped into the pilot's seat, Poe flinched in response to the unexpected vibration. There shouldn't be any shud-dering.

The X-wing stopped, but the rising whine did not. After quickly shutting down to prevent any further damage to the engines, Poe popped the canopy and climbed out. Moving to the back of the ship, he stared hard at the now inert engines. The two stormtroopers might not have been tactically sophisticated, but they had been good shots. The damage to the engines was severe.

BB-8 rolled up beside him. Nothing was said. Nothing needed to be said. Both man and droid could see that they were in big trouble.

In the village the fight continued as a die-hard group of its inhabitants, perhaps knowing all too well what the representatives of the First Order had in mind for them if they surrendered, refused to give up their weapons. While the battle was a mismatch, it was not

a slaughter, and those villagers who continued to resist gave as good as they got.

Shot straight on, a trooper went down in a mass
of shattered armor, shredded flesh, and blood. One of
his companions immediately rushed to his side and
knelt to render assistance. A torn, bloody glove lifted
toward the would-be rescuer, shockingly bare fingers
protruding from the torn protective covering.

Faces behind helmets stared at one another. With a
shock, the trooper who had arrived to render aid to
his fallen comrade recognized the one whose life was
now bleeding out inside his armor. They had trained
together. Shared meals, stories, experiences together.
Now they were sharing death together.

Combat was not at all like the would-be rescuer
had envisioned it.

A brief, final flailing by the downed trooper splat-
tered the newcomer's face mask with blood. Then
hand and arm fell, and movement ceased.

There was no assistance to be rendered here, the
second trooper realized. Straightening, he surveyed
the hell in which he found himself. His weapon hung
at his side—unfired. He stumbled off, away from his
dead comrade and that exposed, pale, pleading hand.

As madness ebbed and surged around him, he wandered through the village, feeling himself more a participant in a historical drama than in an actual battle.
The horrific and all too common red stains on the
ground contradicted his denial. This wasn't like his
training at all, he told himself numbly. Unlike in sim-
ulations, reality bled.

Smoke and dust rose from the devastated buildings
around him. His helmet's aural receptors picked up
the sounds of distant explosions as well as those close
at hand. Crackling flames did not rise from burning

sand; they rose from homes, small workshops, storage buildings.

As he turned the still-standing corner of a building, movement caused him to raise his weapon reflexively. Frightened and unarmed, the woman he found himself confronting inhaled sharply and froze. The expression on her face was one the trooper would never forget: It was the look of someone still alive who realizes she's already dead. For an instant they remained like that: predator and prey, each fully cognizant of their respective status. When he finally lowered the blaster's muzzle, she clearly couldn't believe it; she continued to stare at him for a long moment.

What could only be described as a thunderous *hiss* caused them to turn away from each other. When the trooper turned in the direction of the sound, his movement broke the woman's terrified paralysis. She whirled and fled.

The shuttle that was descending was far more imposing than those with which the trooper was familiar, boasting exceptionally high folding wings and a raptorish silhouette. When the bay door opened, it was to allow a single figure to exit. Tall, dark, cloaked, with its face hidden behind a metal mask, it ignored the still-swirling chaos of the battle to head unerringly in the direction of Lor San Tekka.

Struck by the new arrival's apparent indifference to the enveloping fray, the trooper was startled when a sharp nudge from behind momentarily threw him off balance. A glance found him locking gazes with a superior. The noncom's voice was curt.

"Back to your team. This isn't over yet."

The subject of his ire nodded in recognition and hurried off, wondering what the arrival of that singular figure might portend but not daring to inquire.

For an ordinary trooper like him, ignorance was not simply an abstract value. It was in the manual.

At least for now, Poe realized, the X-wing was not flyable. If he could scrounge certain critical components, find a machine-grade cutter, then maybe, just maybe . . . But first there was a far more important matter to attend to.

From within the leather bag he had received from Tekka, he removed an artifact. Its significance far exceeded its size. After a moment of fumbling with BB-8's exterior, the pilot inserted the artifact into the droid. A confirming beep indicated that it was securely lodged. Satisfied, he stood to eye the glow of the burning village.

"Get as far away from here as you can," he ordered his mechanical companion. "Any direction, so long as it's away from this place." When the droid's anxious electronic response indicated it was hesitant to comply with the command, Poe added emphasis to his voice.

"Yeah, I'm gonna take out as many of those bucketheads as I can. Beebee-Ate, I'll come back for you. *Go!* Don't worry—it'll be all right. Wherever you end up, I'll find you."

BB-8 continued to hesitate. But when the pilot remained indifferent to repeated queries, the droid finally turned and rolled off, accelerating across the sand and away from the village. It looked back only once, its head swiveling around to regard the X-wing and pilot rapidly fading from view even as it increased its speed in the opposite direction. Much to BB-8's regret, it could only protest a direct order, not reject it.

● ● ●

The tall, hooded figure whose arrival had so trans-
fixed the shell-shocked trooper made his way directly
to Lor San Tekka. He did not waver in his course or
objective, ignoring startled stormtroopers and armed
villagers alike. Seeing him approach, Tekka halted
and waited: The village elder recognized who was
coming toward him and knew there was no point in
running. Resignation slid over him like a cloud.

The passenger from the shuttle stared at Tekka, examining him from head to foot much as one would
a relic in a museum. Tekka gazed back evenly. The
black mask, with its slitted forehead and thick, snout-
like breathing apparatus, covered the face of the man
he knew as Kylo Ren. Once, he had known the face
behind the mask. Once, he had known the man himself. Now, to San Tekka, only the mask was left. Metal
instead of man.

Ren spoke first, without hesitation, as if he had anticipated this meeting for some time. "The great soldier of fortune. Captured at last." Though emanating
from a human throat, the voice that was distorted by
the mask had the sick flavor of the disembodied.

Tekka had expected no less. "Whereas something
far worse has happened to you."

Words had no effect on the mask or, so far as Tekka
could tell, what lay behind it. There was no reaction,
no outrage. Only impatience.

"You know what I've come for."

"I know where you come *from*." For all the concern he displayed, Lor San Tekka might as well have
been sitting atop a mountain ridge, meditating on the
sunset over the Sko'rraq Mountains. "From a time
before you called yourself Kylo Ren."

From behind the mask, a growl: feral, but still
human. "Careful. The map to Skywalker. We under-

stand you've acquired it. And now you're going to give it to the First Order."

At the point where he had entered the village, moving cautiously and keeping to what cover was available, Poe could now observe the confrontation. Tekka he recognized even from behind and in bad light. The tall, masked visitor was unknown to him. He strained to overhear what they were talking about, but without edging closer and exposing himself to wandering stormtroopers, he could only look on.

"You don't belong with them." Tekka spoke calmly, in matter-of-fact tones, and without any fear. Speaking truth to the lie that stood before him, striving to bring light to darkness. The hope was a faint one, but he had to try. "The First Order arose from the dark side. You did not."

Impatience on the part of the visitor gave way to exasperation. "How is it possible that a conversation becomes so tedious, so quickly?" A sweep of one long arm encompassed the boundaries of the village. "Don't turn a simple transaction into a tragedy for these people." A tincture of undiluted sadism stained the voice behind the mask. "Hasn't your presence here done enough for them already?"

"I made my peace with these folk and this place long ago. As to the other, to turn away from your heritage is the true tragedy."

Ren stiffened ever so slightly as he leaned forward. "Enough witless banter." He held out a hand. "Old man, give it to me."

From his vantage point nearby, analyzing the movements and gestures of both men, Poe could divine enough to guess what was being discussed. And to envision the eventual, inevitable conclusion.

"No," he muttered under his breath. "No, no, no . . ." Forgoing any further effort at concealment

and disregarding his own safety, he broke from cover and started toward the pair.

"You may try," Tekka responded with quiet defiance, "but you cannot deny the truth that is your family."

Kylo Ren seemed to grow before him. Rage flared behind the mask as reason gave way to fury. A lightsaber appeared in one hand, flaring to life, a barely stable crimson shaft notable for two smaller projections at the hilt: a killer's weapon, an executioner's fetish of choice. "So true."

Light, refulgent and cutting, ripped across and through the figure of Lor San Tekka.

II

POE SAW THE SABER COME TO LIFE. SAW IT start to describe its lethal arc. Time seemed to slow as he watched it descend. Thoughts raced through his mind, half crazed, wholly powerless. He heard himself yelling, sensed himself raising his blaster and firing. Too late, too slow, he told himself despondently even as he continued to fire.

Perceiving the threat, Kylo Ren reacted immediately. A hand rose sharply, palm facing toward the unknown assailant. The gesture was merely the physical manifestation of something infinitely more powerful and entirely unseen. It intercepted the discharge from the pilot's weapon, freezing it in midair as effectively as any solid barrier. From behind the mask, eyes of preternatural intensity tracked the attack to its source.

Initially driven by pure rage, Poe now found that he could not move. His heart pounded, his lungs heaved, but his voluntary muscles refused to respond. He was paralyzed as effectively as the blast from his blaster.

A pair of stormtroopers took hold of him and dragged him forward until he stood helpless before the impassive Ren. Had they not held on to him, Poe

would simply have fallen over. He attempted bravado even so. "Who talks first?" Poe asked, making his voice light. "Do you talk first? Do I talk first?"

Having deactivated his lightsaber and returned it to his belt, Lor San Tekka's murderer casually scrutinized the prisoner. Poe's nerves twanged as feeling slowly began to return to his arms and legs. Ren's gaze settled on the details of the pilot's clothing.

"A Resistance pilot, by the looks of him." He nodded curtly. "Search him. Thoroughly."

One of the troopers who had dragged Poe forward commenced a detailed and none too gentle pat down. Pulling a small device from his service belt, the other trooper slowly passed it the length of the prisoner's body, beginning at the pilot's head and ending at his feet. The examination did not take long.

"Nothing," declared the first stormtrooper, standing at attention.

Poe winked up at the trooper who had used his hands. "Good job."

Forgetting himself for a moment, the goaded trooper kicked the prisoner's legs out from under him. Poe went down hard on his knees, still defiant.

The other trooper gestured with the handheld instrument. "Same here, sir. Internally, this one is clean. Nothing but the expected food residue." He didn't hesitate. "Terminate him?"

Kylo Ren did not let his disappointment show. At such times momentary delays were not unexpected. All would be satisfactorily resolved, in good time.

"No. Keep him." A brief pause, then, "Intact and functioning."

Plainly disappointed, the two troopers dragged Poe away. Ren watched them for a moment, contemplating possibilities. *Later,* he told himself. For now, there were other details to attend to. He allowed his

thoughts to be briefly diverted, regretting the time
that had been wasting in dealing with necessary in-
consequentialities.

Awaiting his pleasure, the senior officer in overall
charge of the special squadrons drew herself up at
his approach, her black cape of rank hanging loose
around her. It stood in startling contrast to her armor,
which even in the poor light shone like polished silver.

"Your orders, sir?" she murmured.

Kylo Ren surveyed his blazing surroundings. He
had already spent too much time here, to only partial
satisfaction. He disliked such delays. "Kill them all,
Captain Phasma, and search the village. Every building, every possible storage facility and place of concealment. When your troops have razed it to the
ground, search the ground. Scanners, perceptors. You
know what to look for."

A single nod and she turned. A line of troopers
stood before the assembled surviving villagers. "On
my command!" Weapons were raised. The reactions
of the villagers were typical. Some stepped forward,
insolent to the last. Others fell to their knees. There
was whimpering and crying and shouts of defiance.
None of it lasted very long.

"Fire!"

It wasn't a massacre. In the lexicon of the First
Order it was nothing more than a prescribed chastise-
ment. Appropriate retribution for harboring a fugi-
tive of note. It was the nature of the tutorial that was
important, not the numbers involved. It took less
than a minute.

When it was over, and the only sounds were methodical chatter among the troopers mixed with a
variety of unholy crackling, they dispersed to carry
out a final survey and scan of the debris—inorganic
and otherwise. Standing by himself, one trooper with

a bloody face mask was startled when a hand came down on his shoulder. Though the hand belonged to a comrade, the first trooper did not relax.

"Notice you didn't fire. Blaster jam?"

Automatically, the trooper being questioned nodded in response. His comrade gestured knowingly and clapped him on the shoulder. "Turn it in when we get back to base. Let the tech boys deal with it and get yourself a new one."

"Thanks. I will."

No sooner had his helpful colleague departed to rejoin his own unit than the trooper found himself gaping at the tall, dark-clad figure striding purposefully toward the singular shuttle that had set down in the midst of battle. Though he willed himself to move, to turn away, he found he could not. He remained rooted in place, clutching his unfired weapon, staring despite himself.

And in response, the figure of Kylo Ren turned and looked sideways, directly at the soldier. The trooper saw only light reflecting off a mask, and his own fear.

He knows. He must know. And I'm . . . dead.

But he wasn't. The glance lasted barely a second. Then Ren resumed his pace, deep in thought as he strode toward the shuttle. In the course of returning to his ship he passed a blaster lying on the ground. It was Poe's, the one that had come within an arm's length of killing him. Once he was beyond its reach he touched it—but not with his hands. It rose, seemingly of its own accord, and flew free, smashing into a nearby structure and scaring the wits out of an idling stormtrooper unfortunate enough to be standing nearby.

The purification of the village extended to its outskirts, where a clutch of troopers had just finished searching the damaged X-wing that had been aban-

doned there. Having done all they could with the tools and equipment at hand, they prepared to return to their units. Specialized gear could have reduced the Resistance fighter to its component parts, but that was not how they had been ordered to proceed.

"Nothing there," declared the last of the quartet as he descended from the fighter's cockpit. "The usual Resistance trash; that's all. Deep scan shows nothing in the fuselage or elsewhere."

As soon as he was safely out of range, his companions activated the pair of heavy weapons they had brought to bear on the hiding place. A couple of bursts was all it took to reduce both ship and outcropping to rubble.

The sound of the exploding X-wing reverberated across the gravel flats and dunes. Far away now, a solitary spherical droid looked back even as it continued to flee. The fireball that rose into the sky suggested the detonation of something far more volatile than primitive buildings and scrapped mechanicals. If he could have rolled faster, the frightened droid would have done so.

Contrary to much popular thought, desert worlds are not quiet at night. In the absence of light, an entirely different ecology springs to life. Moving with greater caution, BB-8 tried not to pause at each howl, every *meep*, the sounds of clawed feet scraping against bare rock. There were things in the vacant, wild regions of underdeveloped planets that would gladly take apart a solitary droid just to see what made it tick. Or roll, he knew. His internal gyros threatened to send him tumbling wildly at the very thought of such an encounter.

Droids such as him were not meant for unpopulated places, and he desperately desired to find others like himself. Or, failing that, even people.

• • •

The shackles that Poe had worn on the troop transport were removed as soon as he and his captors disembarked. Aboard the Star Destroyer, there was no reason to physically restrain the prisoner. Apparently enjoying themselves, or perhaps merely impatient to get out of their armor, his escort chivvied him along with what he considered to be unnecessary roughness. Not that stormtroopers of any ilk were noted for their individual diplomacy. Considering whom he had tried to shoot, he knew he ought to consider himself fortunate that they had brought him aboard still attached to all his important appendages.

A physical state of being, he knew, that could be altered at any moment.

On the other side of the enormous and impressive receiving bay, other troopers were filing out, grateful that more of their number had not been lost on the expedition and looking forward to some rest and food. Intent on reliving the battle below, they paid no attention to one of their own who fell behind. When he was convinced no one was looking at him, the trooper turned and raced back into the open transport. He removed his helmet and proceeded to void the contents of his stomach into the nearest refuse receptacle. The terror in his expression was palpable. Fortunately, there was no one there to witness his disgrace.

There was, however, now someone behind him.

Terror gave way to cold fear as he found himself gazing back at Captain Phasma. How much had the senior officer seen? How much did she know? Too much, as it turned out.

Aloof yet commanding, she indicated the rifle he still carried. "FN-2187. I understand you experienced

some difficulty with your weapon. Please be so good as to submit it for inspection by your division's technical team."

"Yes, Captain." How he managed to reply without stammering he did not know. Instinct as opposed to training, he decided. Self-preservation.

"And who gave you permission to remove that helmet?"

He swallowed hard. "I'm sorry, Captain."

He could feel her disgust as he struggled to put the helmet back over his head. "Report to my division at once," Phasma said.

Worse, he knew miserably, was likely to come later.

It was where technology went to die.

Mountains of metal, cliffs of plasticene derivatives, oceans of splayed ceramics were jumbled together in a phantasmagoric industrial badlands that none dared enter, for fear of being poisoned, cut, or lost forever. None except a very few, for whom daring was as much a sense as sight or hearing.

One such individual clung insectlike to a dark metal wall pimpled with protruding sensors, manipulators, and other decaying mechanisms. Clad in light protective goggles with green lenses, face mask, gloves, and gray desert clothing, the busy figure was burdened with a substantial backpack. A multifunction staff strapped to her back made precision work in such tight and dangerous quarters difficult. Wielding an assortment of tools, the scavenger was excising an assortment of small devices from one metal wall. One after another, bits of booty found their way into the satchel that hung below the slender figure.

When the satchel was full, the scavenger secured it shut and commenced a perilous descent, avoiding

sharp projections and threatening gaps in the wall. Arriving at the bottom of the metallic canyon, the figure hefted a piece of larger salvage recovered earlier and then, laboring under the double load, headed toward a distant slit of sunlight.

Outside the metal caverns and at last clear of danger, the scavenger shoved the goggles up on her forehead and squinted at the blasted surroundings. She was nearly twenty, with dark hair, darker eyes, and a hint of something deeper within. There was a freshness about her that the surrounding harsh landscape had failed to eliminate. Anyone glancing at her would have thought her soft: a serious error of judgment.

It had been a respectable day's work, enough to ensure she would eat tonight. Pulling a canteen from her belt, she wiped sweat from her face and shook the remaining contents of the container into her upturned mouth. *There should be more,* she told herself as she began tapping the side of the canteen. The last few drops sometimes clung stubbornly to the insulated interior.

Concluding that she had drained the container of all its contents, she reattached it to her belt facing inward. The satchel and the larger piece of salvage were secured to a piece of sheet metal, which she sent sliding down the mountain of sand in front of her. Off to one side, shade was provided by one engine of a decomposing, old-model Star Destroyer. Too big to cut up, its technology obsolete, it had been left to molder on the hillside. In the desert climate, decay would take thousands of years. Being something less than portable, the great hulk of a shell was ignored while opportunistic scavengers such as Rey plundered its interior for saleable components.

A second shard of sheet metal served as a sled for the girl to follow the results of the day's labor down

the dune slope. Practice allowed her to manipulate the metal skillfully enough so that she neither fell off nor crashed into any of the scattered debris that littered the dune face.

At the bottom she stood and dusted herself off. Her dun-hued garb was desert basic, designed to protect the wearer from the sun and preserve body moisture. It was inexpensive, easily repaired, and unlovely. The same could be said for the clunky, boxy, beat-up speeder parked nearby. If the battered, rusty vehicle had a redeeming feature, it was the over-and-under twin engines. Since one or another tended to flare out and die at any given moment, their utility stemmed more from their redundancy than from any ability to supply speed or maneuverability.

After fastening her acquisitions to the transport, she climbed into the driver's seat. For an anxious moment it seemed as if neither engine would ignite. Then one, and finally the other, roared to life. That was her life, Rey reflected: a succession of anxious moments, interrupted only by the novelty of occasional panic. All part and parcel of trying to survive on a backwater world as harsh and unforgiving as Jakku.

Racing along the flat desert floor, she allowed the speeder's perceptors to guide her between endless rows and piles of ruined starcraft, obsolete or fatally damaged military equipment, civilian mechanicals that had outlived their prescribed lifetime, and even long-downed Imperial vessels. No one visited here. No one came to take inventory or write history. In these times there was no nostalgia for death: especially not for that of machines.

Instrumentation blinked. Barrier ahead: too much wreckage through which to maneuver. She knew the spot. Though going over would use more power, at this junction the only alternative was a wide and po-

tentially dangerous detour. At least at altitude, she knew, there would be the benefit of cooler air.

Lifting, the speeder rose over the crumpled metal before it, soaring to a necessary height. For the hell of it, she executed a barrel roll; a small moment of exhilaration in an otherwise humdrum existence. By the time she came out of it, Niima Outpost was plainly visible just ahead. Niima: center of the galaxy, repository of manifold cultures, offering to its myriad inhabitants a never-ending succession of entertainment, education, and enjoyable distractions.

Her smile twisted. Niima was a functioning armpit of a town and nothing more, a place where no one asked questions and everyone went quietly about their own business. It was just large and developed enough that if you dropped dead in the street, there was a fifty percent chance someone might go to the trouble of raking up your body and passing it along to a local protein recycler, or cremator, or burial tech, if either of the latter were part of your personal philosophy and so indicated on your identification, and provided there were funds available to pay for your chosen means of disposal.

Otherwise, the deserts of Jakku would take care of the remains in their own good time, and without rendering any opinions on the virtues of the deceased.

As long as she could work, Rey had no intention of suffering such a fate. No one does, of course. Death displays nothing if not variety in its methods, which are often surprising and sometimes amusing. She parked her speeder, then unloaded her salvage and hauled it toward the community structure that had been built for that purpose and was open to all. No one offered to help her with the heavy load. In Niima, youth and gender were no barrier to neighborhood indifference.

Once inside the tented, shaded structure, she un-

packed the results of the day's work, leaned her staff against a worktable, and began cleaning. When it came to salvage, appearance did matter. Compared to the strenuous work she had put into its recovery, a bit of polishing and buffing added little to the overall effort. Around her, other scavengers were doing the same. Humans and nonhumans communicated freely, commenting on one another's findings and exchanging gossip, mostly in the local patois. They filled a good deal of the available workspace. When not chatting amiably with one another, they strove to learn where their competitors were finding their best salvage.

Also, they were not above stealing from one another when the opportunity presented itself. Rey kept a close eye on her goods.

Glancing up from her work, her gaze happened to fall outside the tent. The biped whose movements had caught her eye was human. A woman, clad in wrappings of deep maroon that shaded to purple, a band of turquoise makeup across her eyes and forefingers indicating her clan. Standing on a ship's open ramp, she surveyed her surroundings. A moment later a similarly clad and decorated boy appeared and moved to join her. A domestic exchange ensued, during which the adult did something to the child's hair. Returning to her work, Rey was only partially aware that the brush she was using on a narrow piece of salvaged electronics had begun to imitate the same caressing, grooming movement of the woman's fingers.

Coming up beside her, one of Unkar Plutt's assistants barked at her and gestured in her direction with his staff, implying it would be in her best interests to focus on her work and not allow herself to be distracted. Without another glance in the direction of the mother and child, Rey returned to her own work.

Finishing sooner than she expected, she made her way across the tent to the exchange booth. Fashioned from a small salvaged sand crawler, dark brown from rust and age, it was surrounded by piles of recently purchased components. In contrast to the dominant tenting, it boasted a solid suspended ceiling in the form of another piece of salvaged metal. In Niima, the most disagreeable part of surrendering salvage was taking payment. This was due not to the quality of the food one received as payment but to the nature of the individual distributing it.

The lumpish shape seated slightly above and in front of her was not human. The Crolute's stout build terminated at the top in a thick, fleshy, hairless skull whose most prominent feature was a broad, flat nose. The nasal cavity extended all the way up and into the bald, metal-capped head. A separate layer of flesh flowed downward like a second neck. Loose black pants were tucked into heavy work boots, while the long-sleeved, dun-colored shirt struggled to contain additional layers of neck. Half a dozen bicolored metal plates hung from his neck and shoulders to just below the thick knees. Muscles were hidden beneath an additional layer of blubber.

While she knew he looked forward to their occasional business dealings, she could not say the same. Since that would have required not only listening to him but looking at him, she always strove to keep their encounters as brief as possible.

Unkar Plutt, on the other hand, was delighted to extend their encounters for as long as she could stand it. He always took his time when examining her pieces, letting his gaze rove slowly over everything she put before him, making her wait. Only when the bounds of common courtesy had been markedly surpassed did he deign to acknowledge her presence.

"Rey. A decent offering, if nothing remarkable. Today you get a quarter portion."

She did not give him the pleasure of seeing her disappointment, just took the pair of packets that appeared in the transfer drawer in front of him. One transparent package contained beige powder; the other, a more solid slab of something green.

"That's my girl," Plutt commended her.

Not replying, she turned and left, moving as quickly as she could without alerting him to the fact that his presence disgusted her. She could feel his eyes all over her until she exited the big tent.

Out on the salt flats of Jakku, the only place to shelter from the sun was inside something one had built oneself. Rey's speeder was an insignificant speck against the fiery, setting mass as she slowed on approach to her residence. Climbing down, she left it parked where it had stopped. There was no reason to secure it. Few came this way. Those who did, including the pirates and bandits who haunted the desert wastelands, wouldn't waste time trying to steal a vehicle as dated and banged-up as her transport.

Unloading, she gathered her belongings and headed for the makeshift entrance that led into the belly of the half-destroyed AT-AT walker. It might be an ancient, rotting, rusting example of now useless military might, but to Rey, it was home.

After carefully unloading her gear and supplies onto the homemade cabinets and shelves, she remembered to make a scratch mark on one interior wall of semi-malleable material. She had long since stopped bothering to count the scratches, which now numbered in the thousands.

Bits and pieces of homemade décor ornamented

isolated alcoves and corners: here a handmade doll fashioned from reclaimed orange flight suit material, there a cluster of dried desert flowers; on the far end of the bed insert, a pillow that had cost her a day's work. It wasn't much, but where such examples of defiant individuality had been placed, they softened the drabness of their surroundings.

Green slab-stuff sizzled in a makeshift cook pan. Opening the packet of beige powder, she dumped it into a tin half full of water. A brief stir activated the mixture, which promptly expanded and solidified into a loaf of something like bread. She slid the cooked meat off its pan and onto a plate, then slipped the loaf out of its container. Taking a seat, she dug into both as if she had not eaten in weeks. It seemed that these days all too many meals were like that.

When she had finished, she picked up the plate and licked it dry before setting it aside. Rising, she moved to a window that looked in the direction of Niima. The signature contrail of a single ascending ship streaked the flat dark blue of the evening sky like chalk on slate. Wiping her mouth, she turned to a shelf where an old, badly damaged Rebellion helmet rested. She stared at it for a moment, then picked it up and put it on.

Still wearing the helmet, she made her way outside into the cooling air. Nothing much to see tonight, she reflected. The sun going down. Tomorrow morning, the sun coming up. And so on to another day, not unlike its predecessor and the interminably repetitive ones that had gone before.

She tried to think of something else—something that had changed, something that seemed different—if only to keep her mind from atrophying. But there was nothing. Nothing new. Certainly nothing to daydream about. On Jakku, things never changed.

There *was* that occasional mention in the market of a rising new power in the galaxy. An organization that called itself "The First Order." Determined, relentless. Nobody seemed to know much else about it. Not something to worry about here, she knew. Whatever it was, whatever it represented, it wouldn't come to this backward, out-of-the-way world. Nobody came to Jakku.

She was alone.

Something squealed that was not shifting sand.

Rising quickly, she removed the helmet. The sound could not have come from within its long-dead electronics. Even as she inspected the headpiece, the noise was repeated. A hysterical, panicked beeping. Whirling, she ran back into the dwelling and emerged a moment later clutching her staff. The beeping was sounding continuously now, no less frantic for its frequency.

Reaching the top of a nearby dune, she found herself gazing down at a sight as curious as it was unexpected. Trapped in a net of local organic material, a small spherical droid was attempting to escape its prison, an effort rendered extremely difficult by the fearful mechanical's total absence of limbs. Mounted atop a squat, four-footed, square-helmeted lugga-beast, a native Teedo was struggling to constrain and reel in the legless but overactive and insubordinate droid.

When uncertain as to anything taking place on Jakku, Rey knew, it was always reasonable to assume that something untoward was happening. At least until she understood the particulars of the confrontation she was witnessing, it was only right to call it to a momentary halt.

"Tal'ama parqual!"

Motion ceased as both the Teedo and BB-8 stopped wrestling and turned to peer up at her.

"Parqual! Zatana tappan-aboo!"

Making an effort to simultaneously control both its heavy-headed mount and its captive, the Teedo yelled back through the mouthpiece of the goggle-eyed helmet that covered its reptilian cranium. Its attitude was decidedly unconciliatory, even threatening. Meanwhile the hovering head of the imprisoned droid swiveled rapidly back and forth, trying to watch both Teedo and human simultaneously.

Rey immediately took offense, not only at the Teedo's tone, but at its speech, which far exceeded the bounds of common courtesy that existed between fellow desert-dwellers and made difficult coexistence possible. The luggabeast rider knew better, and its intemperate words were enough to decide her on a course of action. Descending the far side of the dune, she drew her knife and began hacking at the netting.

"Namago!" she growled. *"Ta bana contoqual!"*

Observing that it was on the verge of losing its prize, the Teedo unleashed a stream of indigenous invective. None of it had the slightest effect on Rey, who continued cutting away at the mesh until the native promulgated a slur that would have been vile in any language. Pausing in her work, she turned to face the tightly clothed creature, gesturing with her knife and fairly spitting a reply.

"Noma. Ano tamata, zatana."

Long and drawn out, the Teedo's response to this would have been unprintable on any of a hundred civilized worlds. Turning the metal-enclosed head of its mount, the unpleasant scavenger departed in the opposite direction. As soon as the native was a safe distance away, BB-8 rolled clear of the netting and

began beeping loudly and challengingly in its direction.

"Shhh," Rey hastened to quiet the droid. "Don't tempt it. Enough insults can override anyone's common sense, even a Teedo's." BB-8 instantly went silent. Together, the two of them tracked the luggabeast until it and its rider had vanished from view.

An electronic query drew her attention. Rey knelt down beside the questioning droid.

"He's just a Teedo. A local. Not so unlike me, really." Her expression twisted. "Except this one was particularly impolite. Wanted you for parts." Leaning forward slightly, she studied the top of the droid's head. "Your antenna's bent." As she examined the scored markings on her softly beeping new acquaintance, her interest continued to deepen. "Where'd you come from?"

The droid beeped a reply. Pursing her lips, Rey shook her head.

"I don't know what that means." A string of beeps followed. This time, she smiled. "Oh. Classified. Really? Well, me too. Big secret." Rising, she started back toward her dwelling. "I'll keep mine and you can keep yours." Raising an arm, she gestured. "Niima Outpost is that way. Stay off Kelvin Ridge. Keep away from the Sinking Fields up north or you'll drown in the sand. Otherwise you should be okay. The closer you get to Niima, the less likely you are to run into a marauding Teedo."

Beeping softly, the droid started to follow, halting only when she turned on it sharply.

"Don't follow me. You can't come with me. I don't want anyone with me. You understand?" More beeping, distinctly anxious this time. She grew angry. "No! And don't ask me again. I'm not your friend. I don't have any friends. This is Jakku. Nobody has

friends here. Just fellow survivors." Turning once more, she moved off with longer strides.

The beeping that sounded now was laced with unmistakable desperation, poignant enough to make her stop. Turning once more, she looked back at the imploring droid. She didn't like it—him. Her fondness for most machinery extended to its trade equivalent in food. But she found herself feeling sorry for this small, helpless droid. At least, she told herself, this one seemed harmless enough. And notwithstanding her warning, there was no guarantee that the Teedo might not come back.

She nodded reluctantly in the droid's direction. Immediately, it rolled up beside her. Together, they headed for her abode.

"In the morning," she said firmly, "you go." A responsive beep acknowledged her decision. "Fine, you're welcome." Another beeping, which made her laugh. "Yes, there's a lot of sand here. Beebee-Ate? Okay. Hello, Beebee-Ate. My name is Rey. No, just Rey." Still more beeping, and her smile disappeared. "Look, you're not going to talk all night, are you? Because that won't work. You know how humans recharge. We don't plug in: We sleep." A second acknowledging squeal. "Good. Keep that in mind and we'll get along 'til morning. *Quietly.*"

A single beep left hanging in the dry desert air, they disappeared behind the dune.

III

THE HOLDING CELL HAD NO BARS. THEY WERE not needed. There was nowhere aboard the ship for a prisoner to go. Even had there been, the single occupant was shackled tightly to his chair, unable to do more than turn his head. Poe knew he should have been flattered. They were taking no chances with him. But all he could think about was how he had failed his mission.

So sunk was he in depression that he scarcely reacted when they beat him. Delivered with practiced skill, designed to hurt but not result in permanent damage, the blows fell intermittently, at different times of the day on different parts of his body. He did his best to shut out the pain, much as he succeeded in shutting out the questions. What he did not know was that they were merely a softening-up, an introduction to his principal interrogator.

That formidable individual arrived in due course. Recognizing him from the attack on the village, Poe threw himself against his bonds in a final, supreme effort to break free. Demanding the last of his strength, the failure left him completely exhausted. It was just as well, he consoled himself. Fighting against the fig-

ure now standing before him would be counter-productive at best. Fighting and resistance, however, were two different things, and he resolved to focus what remained of his energy on the latter. Doubtless his inquisitor could sense his determination. Was the masked figure smiling? There was no way to tell.

While his interrogator's greeting was far from challenging, the sarcasm underlying Kylo Ren's words was plain enough.

"I had no idea we had the best pilot in the Resistance on board. Revealing yourself through your futile attempt on my life was foolish. Revenge is little more than an adolescent concession to personal vanity. Even had you not been slow and ill-prepared, Tekka was already dead. Comfortable?"

Poe did his best to sound nonchalant. "Not really." He gestured as best he could with a shackled hand. "The accommodations leave something to be desired."

"I regret the necessity. They are gratuitous in my presence. But those others who have made your acquaintance possess only the most primitive abilities, and further defiance on your part would demand their unnecessary exertions." He bent toward the prisoner. "None of this unpleasantness need be necessary. We both wanted the same thing from the old man. Perhaps he was more forthcoming with you than he was with me."

Poe made a show of seriously considering the proposal before replying phlegmatically, "Might wanna rethink your technique. Hard to get cooperation from a dead man."

Ren stood back, looming over the prisoner. "A truism on which you might personally wish to reflect. It is pathetic, though. Is it not? You and I, both in pur-

suit of a ghost." His tone darkened. "Where did you put it?"

Poe stared up at him innocently. "Where did I put what?"

"Please. All time is transitory, and mine especially so. This will go more quickly and less awkwardly if we dispense with childish nonsense."

Poe readied himself. "The Resistance will not be intimidated by you."

"As you wish, then. There is no 'Resistance' in this room. Only the pilot Poe Dameron. And I."

A hand extended toward the shackled prisoner. Silent agony followed soon after.

"Tell me," Ren murmured. "Tell me."

General Hux was waiting for him. As expected, the interrogation had not taken long. The senior officer did not have to ask if it had been successful. No matter how determined the prisoner, no matter his or her individual resolve, Ren's questioning invariably produced the same results.

The metal-covered face regarded the general, the voice that emanated from behind it dispassionate. "The pilot does not have it. The map to Skywalker's location is in a droid. An ordinary BB unit."

Hux was plainly pleased, though that meant nothing to Ren.

"That makes it easy, then. The directions are in a droid, and the droid is still on the planet."

"Even a single planet offers innumerable places for concealment," Ren pointed out.

Hux did not dispute this. "True enough, but the world below us is primitive. A simple droid will gravitate toward support facilities for its kind. Of these, Jakku has few enough." He turned away, planning.

"With any luck we may not even have to search for it ourselves."

Even to a droid, Niima Outpost was unimpressive. BB-8 took it all in, recording every visual in detail for possible future reference. Nothing the droid saw was encouraging.

Having unloaded him from her speeder, Rey once more hefted the satchel that bulged from a new day's scavenging. Eying the indecisive droid, she nodded toward one part of town.

"There's a trader in Bay Three name of Horvins. Don't be put off by his appearance—he's actually a pretty decent sort. Might be willing to give you a lift, wherever you're going. So . . ." She paused a moment, considering, and then shrugged. "Good-bye."

She had only taken a few steps when a series of beeps caused her to look back and laugh. "Oh, really? Now you can't leave? I thought you had somewhere special to be."

Plaintive and anxious, the electronic response was nothing like what she expected. Retracing her steps, she knelt to stare into the droid's dark eye.

"Don't give up. He still might show up. Whoever it is. Classified. Believe me, I know all about waiting."

The droid beeped questioningly.

"For my family. They'll be back. One day." She tried to smile and failed miserably.

BB-8 moved as close to her as protocol permitted and beeped softly. It caused her to rise suddenly, plainly annoyed by the query.

"*What?* No! I'm not *crying*." This time when she started off she did not look back.

She didn't have to. Ignoring her admonitions, the

droid tagged along, beeping continuously, irritating her with distressing consistency.

"I was not!" she continued to insist. "Just because a little water flows from a human eye doesn't mean it's crying. Check your info dump." She rubbed at the eye in question. "Nothing but a piece of grit. This whole world is nothing but a big piece of grit." The droid's comment on this left her not knowing whether to laugh or cry.

"No, Beebee-Ate. I don't have a world in my eye."

But her eyes continued to water as she made her way deeper into town, and she gave up trying to persuade the droid to leave her alone.

Maybe one day things will change, she told herself absently as she waited her turn in the line. Like the hot, dry desert wind, reality cut in as she stepped up to the front and unloaded her goods. She hid the wave of revulsion that swept through her. Maybe one day, before the universe died, Unkar Plutt would take a bath.

The merchant made his usual show of inspecting her salvage, but his attention was actually on the rotund droid that had parked itself behind her and slightly to one side.

"Two interlifts. I'll give you one quarter portion. For the pair."

She reacted immediately. "Last week they were a half portion each, and you said you were looking for more." She indicated the two devices. "Here's two of 'em."

Plutt's flesh rippled. "Conditions have changed." He hefted one of the components and squinted at it. "Besides, this one is missing a membrane. I don't like paying for incomplete equipment." Before she could object further, he leaned forward. "But what about the droid?"

"What about him?" she asked guardedly.

"Is he with you?" Plutt smiled. Which, if anything, was worse than his usual expression of indifference. "I'll pay for him. He looks functional."

Behind her, BB-8 began to beep apprehensively. Rey ignored him, intrigued.

"He might be."

"Why then didn't you offer him up together with the interlifters?" Plutt was drooling. Normally that was a cue for her to flee while she still had control of her stomach. This time she ignored the bile.

"As you say, he's functional." She spoke with studied indifference. "I can always use a functioning droid around the house."

Plutt begged to differ. "This one? Of what use could it be to someone like yourself? It has no service limbs."

"Maybe I enjoy the company. You said you'd pay. How much?"

His pleasure apparent, Plutt could not contain himself. "Sixty portions."

Somehow she managed to restrain her reaction to a single muscular twitch. Sixty portions would feed her for . . . for . . . for a very long time. Time enough to do other work that had been long neglected. Time enough to relax and rest her bones. Time enough for— *leisure* was a word that had long ago been dropped from her vocabulary.

Beeping furiously, BB-8 nudged her from behind. The droid had been following the conversation from the beginning and was not liking the turn it had taken, not at all.

"Quiet," she muttered.

Either the droid didn't understand or else he was willfully ignoring her instructions. Having little patience with obstreperous mechanisms, she reached over

and thumbed a sequence on his head. Immediately, that portion of the droid slid sideways until it made contact with the ground. No further beeps issued from its speaker. Artificial consciousness was absent now, and it was just a quiescent piece of machinery, a spherical piece of junk.

But apparently one that held some value, she told herself. How much value? Before agreeing to anything, it behooved her to find out.

"One hundred portions."

Plutt was patently surprised by the counterdemand, and just as obviously unhappy. Not that he was a stranger to argument. Scavengers wouldn't be scavengers if they didn't frequently dispute the value of their finds. It was just that he had not expected it from this one, especially considering what he had already offered. It didn't matter. Nothing mattered right now except gaining possession of the droid. So he smiled anew.

"Your audacity always has exceeded your size, Rey. I've always admired that about you."

"Yeah, yeah. I'm wonderful. Do we have a deal or not?" She stayed expressionless.

"How can I resist the force of your personality?" he replied in mock alarm. "One hundred it is." Atop his battered throne, he turned. "As you can imagine, it will take me a moment to assemble your payment. Please be patient."

Rey could hardly believe it. He'd accepted the counteroffer! She had only made it to see the expression on his face, never dreaming he would readily accede. A hundred full portions! Eagerly, she opened her satchel in preparation for receiving the expected bounty. This was one heavy load she was not going to mind toting. Her elation extended as far as making small talk with the detested Plutt.

"What are you going to do with the droid? He travels well, but as you pointed out, he doesn't have any service limbs."

"Oh, I'm not going to keep him for myself." Plutt spoke absently as he continued to stack full nutrition portions beside his seat. "Certain parties have been asking around about a droid like that. None of my business what they want it for. Smart traders don't delve deeply into their customers' motivations." He glanced over at her. "If I find out, I'll do you the courtesy of letting you know. Meanwhile, I'd like to think this exchange'll be good for both of us. That's the best kind of business, after all." As he started placing packets into the transfer drawer, she moved to take them.

"That's my girl." His tone oozed something more than false possessiveness. There was an eagerness in his voice that was something new even for Unkar Plutt. An eagerness that all but translated into triumph.

It took a real effort for her to let go of the first pile of food packets and draw her hand back. She glanced down at the inert droid, thinking hard. At last she looked back at the merchant.

"Actually—the droid's not for sale. I made a mistake." Willing herself to do so, she shoved the brace of food packets to the back of the transfer drawer.

Plutt was beside himself, any thought of restraint gone. As his voice rose, other scavengers in the room looked up from their work. Even for the irritable merchant, the outburst was exceptional.

"Sweetheart," he bellowed, his tone belying his choice of words, "we already had a deal!"

Grinning tightly, she echoed his earlier observation. "Conditions have changed." Reaching down, she reactivated the droid. BB-8's head immediately swung

up into its natural dorsal position. Had the droid possessed eyelids, it would have blinked.

"Conditions have . . ." Plutt looked like he was going to explode. "You think you can be snide with me, girl? You think you can play games here? Who do you think you are?"

She drew herself up with as much pride as she could muster. "I am an independent operator, scavenger of the metal lands, free of debt and beholden to no one. Least of all to a small-time trader named Plutt."

"You are . . . you are . . ." The merchant tried to control himself. "You have nothing. You *are* nothing!"

"On the contrary," she shot back, "I just told you who I am. As to what I have, that would be my freedom and my pride." Murmurs of assent rose from behind her, from the vicinity of the worktables. She had said aloud what her colleagues and compatriots, regardless of species, all wanted to say but dared not. At least not to Plutt's ugly face.

All pretense of deference gone, Rey took a step toward the chair and shot the merchant behind it so steely a glance that he visibly flinched. BB-8 reacted with a beep of admiration. Resisting the urge to give the sphere a reassuring pat, Rey concluded the day's dealings with Unkar Plutt.

"The droid is not for sale."

With that she turned and headed toward the big tent's exit, the excitedly beeping droid pacing her effortlessly.

Plutt watched her go. He was starting to calm down, his mind working systematically. The confrontation had almost escalated beyond repair. Such loss of control was not like him. In the course of negotiations he would often shout, yell, occasionally pound the service shelf in front of him. But all the time, he

was calculating. It was all about the business, all about the profit. Never personal. Not even now, when it involved the lovely but disrespectful Rey. That was something of a pity, he mused as he picked up a communicator.

A voice answered. Ignoring the newly arrived scavenger who had tentatively approached, Plutt turned away and lowered his voice.

"I have a job for you." With a free hand he slammed the service portal opening shut, leaving the scavenger holding his bag of goods and staring blankly at the merchant's back.

Slumped and shackled in the seat, Poe was still breathing. Beyond that, he no longer cared much what happened to him. It wasn't his fault, he kept telling himself. For an ordinary person, no matter how strong they thought themselves, resisting the probing of a creature like Kylo Ren was simply not possible. He had tried. There was no shame in the failure.

He didn't much care what they might do with him now, though he could guess. Having given up what little of value he had possessed, he was no longer of any use to them. There was nothing about X-wing weapons systems the First Order did not already know, and as a mere pilot, he would not be expected to know anything about military movements or tactics. He had rendered himself expendable. No, not expendable. Less than that. He was now extraneous. As such, he doubted they would keep him alive. He would not receive food, but he might become it.

His head came up as the door to the holding cell whooshed open and a stormtrooper entered. At least, Poe mused, it would be over soon. He could look forward to freedom from any further tormenting

thoughts. The trooper's words to the room's single guard surprised him, however.

"I'm taking the prisoner to Kylo Ren."

Poe sagged in his seat. What more did they want from him? Everything, anything of value that he had known was now known to them. Had they over-looked some line of questioning? He could not think of one. But then, at the moment, his mind was not functioning properly.

The guard wondered, too. "I was not told to expect you. Why would Ren wish to question the prisoner outside the cell?"

The new arrival's voice darkened. "Do you dare to question Kylo Ren's motives?"

"No, no, that's not what I meant! I . . ." Without another word, the guard proceeded to release the prisoner from his shackles. It took twice as long as it should have, since in his sudden nervousness he kept fumbling the task.

Procedure demanded that the trooper keep his weapon trained on the prisoner at all times as to-gether they made their way down the corridor. An-other time, another place, Poe might have considered making a grab for it. But he was far too weakened to contemplate such a likely fatal effort. In any case, the trooper seemed as competent as all his kind and gave no indication of relaxing his vigilance.

A rough prod with the weapon's muzzle caused Poe to stumble and nearly fall. So exhausted was he that he could not even raise an objection or mutter a curse.

"Turn here," the trooper commanded sharply.

The passageway they entered seemed unusually narrow and poorly lit. In contrast to the one they had just left, they encountered no personnel. No troopers, no techs, no general crew.

A gloved hand clutching his shoulder brought him

to a halt. Poe took in his claustrophobic surroundings. An odd place to carry out an execution, he thought resignedly. Apparently they were not going to make a show of him.

The trooper's words came low and fast. "Listen carefully and pay attention. You do exactly as I say, I can get you out of here."

Within Poe's wounded brain something like cognizance stirred. He turned and gawked at the trooper's mask. "If . . . *what*? Who are you?"

In lieu of reply, the trooper removed his helmet—a helmet that had been cleaned of the blood that had been smeared across it by the flailing hand of a dying trooper far below, in the course of a minor battle on an obscure corner of the planet Jakku.

"Will you be quiet and just listen to me? This is a *rescue*. I'm helping you *escape*." When a stunned Poe didn't respond, the trooper shook his shoulder firmly. "Can you fly a TIE fighter?"

Poe finally stopped gaping at the dark-skinned young man and found his voice. "What's going on here? Are you—with the Resistance?"

"*What?*" The trooper indicated their surroundings. "That's crazy! How long do you think anyone with Resistance sympathies would last on a ship like this? You're under continuous observation. You so much as wink the wrong way and before you know it, the psytechs are all over you. No, I'm just breaking you out." He cast a nervous glance up and down the narrow, dim corridor. "Can you fly a . . ."

Having long since surrendered anything resembling hope, it took Poe more than a moment to begin regaining it. "I can fly anything. Wings, no wings, push-pull echo force, in or out of lightspeed—just show it to me. But why are you helping me?"

The trooper spoke while staring nervously down the corridor. "Because it's the right thing to do."

Poe shook his head, not buying it for a second. "Buddy, if we're gonna do this, we have to be honest with each other."

The trooper stared at him for a long moment. "I need a pilot."

Poe nodded. A wide grin broke across his face. "Well, you just got me."

FN-2187 was taken aback by Poe's quick agreement. "Yeah?"

"Yeah," Poe insisted. "We're gonna do this. If you can get me into something that flies, that is."

The trooper slipped his helmet back over his head. For an instant, the whole enterprise teetered on the edge of believability. Was he being set up? Poe wondered. No longer needed, was he being made the subject of some cruel psychological trial, only to be thrown away at the conclusion? Yet there was something about the trooper that made Poe feel he could trust him. His manner, his look: There was something that said "throw in your lot with this one and you won't be sorry that you did."

The trooper pointed back in the direction they had come. "This way. And stop looking so positive. Optimism doesn't fit a prisoner's profile."

Poe obediently lowered his head and adopted as morose an expression as possible. Once, as they re-entered the main corridor, a hint of a smile broke through, to be quickly quashed.

The longer no one intercepted them and no one questioned their passage, the more Poe dared to allow himself to hope. What they were attempting bordered on the insane. Escaping from the custody of the First Order, much less from inside a Star Destroyer, was nearly impossible.

Nearly.

The very unfeasibility of it worked in their favor. He could not be a prisoner trying to escape, because prisoners simply did not escape. Just as stormtroopers did not desert their posts to facilitate such flight.

Ordinary troopers were one thing; the group of officers coming toward them as they entered the hangar was quite something else. Face still resolutely aimed downward, Poe tensed and fought not to meet their eyes. Beside him, the trooper nudged him gently with the end of his blaster and muttered tightly.

"Stay calm, stay calm."

Poe swallowed as the officers drew near—and walked on by.

"I am calm," Poe whispered.

"I was talking to myself," the trooper explained as they maintained their methodical tread toward the far side of the enclosure.

"Oh, boy," Poe whispered, this time to himself.

"Act nervous," the trooper advised him. "As if you're being sent to your doom."

Poe swallowed. "Thanks for the tip."

The craft they were approaching was a Special Forces TIE fighter. Poe couldn't help it—raising his gaze, he raked the ship with his eyes. If one discounted its origins, its dark angles took on a deadly beauty. No one stood near it: no techs, no maintenance workers, and no guards. What reason could there be to have to post a guard beside a ship inside a Star Destroyer? The entry hatch was open. Open and inviting: He had to will himself not to break into a run. There was no telling if the fighter was functional, or if it was being monitored by automated hangar security. The hangar's atmosphere was contained, of course. Otherwise he wouldn't be able to speculate about such things, since he would be a cold, dead

protein crisp floating in space. How to get the massive access portal open?

One thing at a time, he told himself. Get to the ship first. Then get on board. Find out if it was operational.

A tech droid came toward them, trundling along the open floor. He could sense the trooper at his side tightening up. They maintained their pace and direction. So did the droid. It was very close now, its optics easily able to resolve the fine details of prisoner and escort. What would they do if it started to ask questions?

Questioning a prisoner and guard not being a part of the tech droid's protocol, it continued on past without beeping so much as a casual query.

IV

THE INTERIOR OF THE TIE FIGHTER WAS SPOT-less. Droids and techs had done their work well, leaving it ready for pilot and gunner. It was a true pilot who now settled himself into the cockpit command seat. As to the other missing crew member, that remained to be seen.

Slipping free of his bloody, confining jacket, Poe examined the controls laid out before him. Some were familiar from his professional studies of First Order ships, others from perusing details of Old Imperial craft. What he didn't recognize immediately, he felt sure he could work around. A modern fighter like this one would be naturally forgiving, its computational components engineered to compensate for pilot miscues and oversights. He was relying on the likelihood that the ship itself would automatically correct for any minor mistakes in judgment.

Minor mistakes. He still had to fly the damn thing.

Movement behind him caused him to glance back over his shoulder. Having shed his helmet, the trooper who had freed him was settling himself into the gunner's seat and struggling to make sense of his surroundings. Poe tried to project reassurance as he

punched instrumentation. A whine began to rise from the ship's stern.

"I always wanted to fly one of these things," Poe said. "Can you shoot?"

"Anything designed for ground troops, I can. Blasters."

Poe reflected that his companion sounded less than confident. "Same principle! Only the results are a lot more expansive. The toggle on the left should be to switch between cannons, missiles, and pulse. Use the instrumentation on the right to aim—let the auto-targeting help you—and triggers to fire!"

Leaning slightly forward, the trooper tried to absorb what he was seeing as well as what the former prisoner was telling him. There were far more controls than those he was hearing about. Which were the ones he really needed to worry about?

"This is very complicated," he confessed, "and I'm not sure where to start. Maybe if we waited a moment or two so you could clarify a few things?"

Freed from his shackles, then freed from captivity, Poe was not in a mood that allowed for a period of leisurely instruction. For one thing, he doubted he was going to have the opportunity. Any second now, someone was going to wonder why the Special Forces fighter was lighting its engines with the hatch closed.

"No time," he yelled back. "Consider this on-the-job training!"

Working only semi-familiar controls, he persuaded the ship to lift. Unfortunately, it was still tethered to support lines. Cables twanged as they went taut, holding the TIE fighter to the deck.

Inside the main control room for Hangar Six, a confused tech turned from his console to the officer passing close behind him.

"Sir, we have an unsanctioned departure from Bay Two."

The First Order colonel halted, turned, and stared out the sweeping port that overlooked the hangar floor. At the far end, a fighter could be seen struggling to decouple from its support cabling. Neither the apparent preflight movements nor the fact that cabling was still engaged made any sense. That they were occurring simultaneously suggested a serious miscarriage of duty—or the inconceivable.

"Get me communications with that vessel. Alert ship command, notify General Hux, and stop that fighter!"

Throughout the *Finalizer,* confusion expanded exponentially. Departments were alerted that normally went unexercised while the ship was in orbit around peaceful planets. Off-duty personnel were roused to the sound of alarms ringing on their personal communicators. Contradictory commands flew back and forth between bemused sections. A large majority of those alerted responded slowly and reluctantly, confident that what they were responding to was nothing more than a drill.

No such illusions afflicted the hurriedly assembled troopers who were struggling to push the heavy weapons platform into position on the hangar deck. The musical *spang* of cables snapping away from the TIE fighter pressed them to move even faster. The officer in charge was shouting, but no command could ready the weapon any quicker than its energizing program allowed. It would take another moment or two to fully power up.

Seeing the threat that was being prepared on the other side of the hangar, Poe proffered his companion some urgent advice. "Okay—now would be a good time to start shooting."

Behind him, the defecting trooper's gaze wandered desperately over the plethora of controls laid out before him. "I'll do my best. I'm not sure I can . . ."

A massive wave of blasts from the TIE fighter's primary arsenal filled the hangar. Internal weapons emplacements shattered. Troopers and mobile cannon were obliterated. Parked TIE fighters were reduced to rubble, fragments of fuselage and wings bouncing off the deck, ceiling, and walls. One collective burst demolished the hangar control room. Where moments before there had been calm, now there was bedlam, alarm, and fire.

The latter was extinguished when the fighter lifted, spun on its axis, and Poe activated the TIE fighter's departure mode. It had been locked down by the hangar controllers, but when FN-2187 imploded the operations center, all electronics that were usually controlled from there had gone neutral. The Special Forces TIE fighter had no trouble resolving the problem, automatically issuing the necessary directives.

"Sorry, boys!" the trooper seated in the gunner's chair yelled, even though there was no one save Poe to hear him. Accelerating, the Special Forces craft blasted clear of the Star Destroyer's flank, leaving in its wake a splay of smashed TIE fighters, dead troopers, and an assortment of ruined accessory material.

Poe was becoming more and more comfortable with the vessel's instrumentation. In a very short period of time, his mood had swung from fatalistic to exalting. Not only was he alive, not only was he free—he had a ship! And what a ship: a Special Forces TIE fighter. He was certain of one thing as he maneuvered around the immense destroyer: Nobody was going to make him a prisoner of the First Order ever again.

"This thing really moves." He shook his head in

admiration. Fine engineering knew no politics. "I'm not going to waste this chance: I owe some people in that ship a little payback. We'll take out as many weapons systems as we can."

The trooper had expected to run as far and as fast as the TIE fighter would take them. "Shouldn't we go for lightspeed as soon as we can?"

A tight, humorless grin crossed Poe's face. "Someone on that ship called me the best pilot in the Resistance. I wouldn't want to disappoint him. Don't you worry. I'll get us in position. Just stay sharp and follow my lead." He paused only briefly. "How about this? Every time you see the destroyer, you shoot at it."

Still unhappy with the direction their escape had taken, FN-2187 relaxed ever so slightly. "I can do that."

It wasn't a ship, Poe told himself as he gleefully manipulated the manual instrumentation. It was a part of him, an extension of his own body. As fire began to lance out toward them from the immense starship, he whirled and spun the TIE fighter, utilizing predictors as well as his own skills to avoid the blasts. Taking them underneath the mother ship, he danced back and through gaps and openings, executing maneuvers beyond the abilities of all but the best pilots. Several skirted the edge of believability. Poe didn't care. He was free and he was flying.

Behind him, the renegade trooper unleashed blast after blast, triggering explosions in a frenzy of random damage that could only panic and confuse those on the vast vessel above them. A brace of cannons loomed ahead—but the trooper seemed content to fire indiscriminately at their surroundings. That needed to change, Poe knew, or they would never get the chance to jump to lightspeed.

"Dammit, a target is coming to you. My right, your left. You see it?"

Targeting controls brought the major weapons emplacement into bold view on one of the trooper's screens. "Hold on. I see it." He readied himself, then unleashed fire at the precise moment when aptitude interlocked with instrumentation.

The whole gun emplacement erupted in a rapidly shrinking fireball. Debris spun around them as Poe took them through the devastation, the fighter's shields warding off whatever he could not directly avoid.

Unable to restrain himself, the trooper let out a yell that echoed around the cockpit. "*Yes!* Did you see that?"

Poe whipped the TIE fighter around to the side of the *Finalizer*. "Told ya you could do it! What's your name?"

"FN-2187."

"FN-whaa?"

"That's the only name they ever gave me."

The longing in the trooper's voice was all too human. That, and something more. Something that had driven him, among his hundreds, his thousands of colleagues, to step outside the comfort zone of training and regimentation, something that had ignited some exceptional spark of individualism within him. Poe knew that spark was present in the man behind him, and he now made it his task to see that it did not fade away. But where to start?

"If that's the name they gave you, then I ain't using it. 'FN,' huh? I'm calling you Finn. That all right with you?"

Behind him, the trooper considered. A delighted smile spread slowly across his face. "Yeah, 'Finn.' I like that! But now you're one up on me."

"Sorry?"

"I don't know your name. If you tell me it's RS-736 or something like that, I'm going to be seriously confused."

The pilot had to laugh. "I'm Poe. Poe Dameron."

"Good to meet you, Poe!"

"Good to meet you, Finn!" Settling on a line of attack, he prepared to dive once more into the heart of the Star Destroyer, a bug attacking a bantha.

But it was a bug with a very nasty bite.

On the main bridge of the *Finalizer*, General Hux peered over the shoulder of Lieutenant Mitaka. While there could be no single central command station on a vessel as enormous as the Star Destroyer, Mitaka's console approximated such a position as effectively as anything could.

Hux could hardly believe what he had been told. Not only had the prisoner escaped, he had managed to find his way to an operational hangar, slip aboard an outfitted and ready-to-fly fighter, and blast his way free. And not just any fighter, but a Special Forces TIE fighter. If the proof had not been right in front of him, making a treacherous nuisance of itself as the ship's perceptors strove to keep track of the stolen fighter, Hux would not have believed such a thing possible.

A very slight shudder ran through the deck. Mitaka's voice was even, but Hux could tell that the dark-haired lieutenant was shaken by what he was seeing. "They've taken out an entire bank of defensive weaponry. And they continue to attack. They're not running."

Hux didn't understand. It was beyond comprehension. Prisoners *ran* from prisons, they didn't stick around to assault their jailers. The action smacked of an unshakeable wish to commit suicide. What he

knew of the escaped prisoner strongly suggested a desire to live. What had happened to change him? Or, Hux thought, was the profile that had been drawn up by the psytechs simply wrong?

Formal profile or not, of one thing he was now certain: They had badly underestimated what had seemed to be a Resistance pilot on the verge of physical and emotional collapse.

"Engage the ventral cannons," Hux ordered.

"Bringing them online," Mitaka said.

No matter how close a flight path the escaped pilot took, Hux knew that sensors would prevent the guns from firing adjacent to the ship's structure itself. Exceptional pilot that he was, the escaped prisoner would know that. Probably he was counting on it, which was why he continued to fly so close to the destroyer's surface instead of bolting for empty space. Now Hux was counting on the pilot sustaining the same strategy. The longer he remained within the destroyer's sphere of armed influence, the more forces could be brought against him, and the less chance he would have to make a second, more permanent escape.

A voice sounded behind him: unmistakable, controlled, and plainly displeased. "Is it the Resistance pilot?"

Hux turned to face Kylo Ren. Unable to see past the metallic mask, unable to perceive eyes or mouth, one had to rely on subtle changes in voice and tone to try to descry the tall man's mood. Hux knew immediately that mood equaled if not exceeded his own consternation.

"Yes, and he had help." Though Hux was loath to admit it, he had no choice. "One of our own. We're checking the registers now to identify which stormtrooper it was."

While the all-concealing mask made it difficult to tell the focus of Ren's attention, it was plainly not on the general. "FN-2187."

It unnerved Hux that Kylo Ren had managed to ascertain the identity of the rogue trooper before the ship's own command staff. But then, Ren had access to a great many aspects of knowledge from which ordinary mortals like himself were excluded, Hux knew. He would have inquired further, but the taller figure had already turned and headed off. Ren's indifference was far more unsettling than would have been anything as common as a straightforward insult. Shaking off the encounter, Hux turned his attention back to the lieutenant's console.

"Ventral cannons hot," the lieutenant reported.

"Fire," Hux commanded.

One detonation followed another as the *Finalizer*'s weapons systems struggled to isolate the darting TIE fighter from the debris among which it danced. Poe was constantly changing his flight path, never doing anything predictable, utilizing the destruction he and his companion had already wrought to confuse the predictors that were an integral part of the big guns' operating systems. Though more debris provided more cover, Poe knew he couldn't keep up such maneuvering forever. Ultimately, the damage he and Finn had caused would be reduced to fragments, and then to powder, by the efforts of the destroyer's weapons. Bereft of anywhere to hide, the TIE fighter would eventually catch a powerful laser pulse. That would be the end of the game. Before that happened, they had to get clear.

No doubt every gunner, every weapons system operator on the destroyer, was just waiting for the stolen

fighter to break outsystem preparatory to making a jump to lightspeed. Their attention would be focused in those directions, away from the ship and toward the great darkness. The last thing they would expect someone escaping from the vicinity of the planet Jakku to do would be to—head for Jakku.

As he sent the TIE fighter roaring toward the desert world below, a hand reached forward and down to rap him on the shoulder. "Wait—this isn't right! Where are you going?" Behind them, a few desultory blasts erupted from the Star Destroyer's weapons. It would take very little time for the great ship to bring all its power to bear on the fleeing fighter. But very little time was all a pilot like Poe needed.

"You mean, where are *we* going. Back to Jakku, that's where." As if, he thought, the brown and yellow globe expanding rapidly in front of them wasn't indication enough. But he could sympathize with Finn's confusion. What they were doing made no sense. Always, he knew, the best way to avoid predictability. Even if it was a little mad.

"*What?* Jakku? No, no, no! Poe, we gotta get outta this *system*!" The TIE fighter rocked crazily as one near-miss after another reached them from the destroyer and Poe fought to confuse any automatic trackers. Finn's voice grew calmer, but only slightly. "Oh, okay, I got it. We're gonna go sub-atmosphere, circle the planet, and strike for lightspeed on the other side, out of the big guy's range, right? *Right?* Tell me I'm right, Poe."

Poe didn't bother to shake his head, focusing on the fighter's wonderfully responsive controls. "I got to get to my droid before the First Order does!"

Finn gaped at the back of the pilot's head. "Your *droid*? What does a droid have to do with escaping?"

"It's not about escaping. This whole business isn't about escaping."

"Could've fooled me." Feeling slightly numb, Finn slumped back in his seat. "You must really, really, *really* like this droid."

"He's a BB unit. One of a kind. Orange and white. Utterly unique and utterly invaluable."

Finn's voice rose anew. "I don't care *what color it is*! I don't care if it's capable of invisibility! No droid can be that important!"

Poe let out a private, knowing grunt. "This one is, pal."

"Okay," Finn countered, "you say that it's important. I'll tell you what's important, *pal*. Getting as far away from the First Order and its representatives as we can, as fast as we can! *That's* what's important. To me, anyway." He lowered his voice. "I saved your life, Poe. At the very least, you owe me mine. We go back to Jakku, we *die*."

"That's a chance we've got to take." The pilot's stance was unshakeable. "This isn't about my life, or yours. I'm sorry, Finn, but there are far greater things at stake. Forces are in motion that must be dealt with. Unfortunately, I seem to be at the center of them. It's a responsibility I can't—I won't—forgo. I'm sorry you've become caught up in the middle of it, but I can't do anything about that."

"I don't care how important this droid of yours is, or what you and it are involved in. For you and me, Jakku is another word for death."

Poe could not dispute Finn's logic, so he ignored it—just as he had set aside reason when he had rushed into the village in a futile attempt to save the life of Lor San Tekka.

Of course, he reminded himself, that hadn't turned out so well, either. But he was being nothing if not

truthful. He had sworn an oath to the Resistance, and he had no intention of breaking it now. No matter how bad the odds. He took a deep breath. Although it meant breaking protocol, Finn deserved to know.

"My droid's got a map that leads to Luke Sky-walker."

It took Finn a moment—a long moment—for the full impact of the pilot's declaration to hit home. "You gotta be *kidding* me! Skywalk— I never should have rescued you!"

Even as he spoke, a burst from the destroyer intercepted Poe's latest evasive effort. Sparks flew within the cockpit, followed by an eruption of acrid smoke and fumes. The fighter's engines flared wildly, sending it out of control. And since it was headed straight toward the surface of Jakku, that was where it continued to race—out of control.

Finn quit looking for something to shoot at because his instrumentation had gone completely dead. Coughing, fighting for breath, he yelled in the pilot's direction. "All weapons systems are down! My controls are neutralized! You?"

There was no reply, save for the now continuous shrilling of the fighter's alarms. Finn waved at the increasingly dense smoke as he strained forward toward his new friend—and drew back in horror.

Poe was not moving. His eyes were shut. Blood streamed down his face.

"No—noooo! *Poe!*"

No response came from the unconscious pilot. Eying him in the closed, smoky confines of the cockpit, his own eyes filling with tears in response to the increasingly bad air, Finn couldn't even tell if the other man was still alive. The blackness of space was gone now, completely blotted out by the increasingly proximate surface of Jakku. Even if he could some-

how take Poe's place, Finn knew he could not safely set down an undamaged fighter, much less one in this condition.

He did, however, figure out the location of his seat's eject control. Equipped with a manual override in the event of total electronics failure, it was clearly marked. Gripping the handle, he wrenched on it as hard as he could. Neither the extra muscle nor additional adrenaline was necessary. The handle moved smoothly and without resistance. A moment later, he felt his body being ripped away from the TIE fighter. The universe spun wildly around him, and for a brief moment his sight was filled with alternating visions of yellow planet, black space, and white clouds.

Then he passed out.

On the *Finalizer* command deck, General Hux had moved away from Mitaka's station. Wandering from console to console, he proceeded to question a succession of technicians and fire-control officers. The anxiety that had been building in him but which he had managed to keep restrained was greatly lightened when one tech looked up at him to report.

"They've been hit."

Hux's expression did not change, but inside he felt considerable relief. He studied the tech's console, his gaze flicking rapidly from one readout to the next. The details coming in appeared conclusive, but in this matter there was no room for mere ninety-nine percent certainty; no room for analytical equivocation.

"Destroyed?"

The tech's response as he studied his instruments confirmed the general's circumspection. "Disabled only, it would appear."

Hux leaned closer. "He could be trying to throw us off."

"If so," the tech reported, "he's going to grave extremes. Sensors show pieces of the fighter are becoming detached and flying off. Such actions could not be carried out by the operator of the fighter itself and must be the result of the craft having suffered serious damage." He paused a moment, added, "I hew to my original opinion, sir. No one would choose to voluntarily engage in a descent such as the one the fighter is currently taking."

"Very well, then," Hux conceded. "They are disabled, perhaps fatally so. Given that and what you can divine of their present vector, what is the projected location of touchdown?"

Once more the technician analyzed his readouts. "The fighter is projected to crash somewhere in the Goazon Badlands. At this range and given the nature of the topography in question, it is impossible to predict the exact angle and velocity with which it will strike."

Hux nodded thoughtfully. "They were going back for the droid. That's the only explanation that makes any sense. Otherwise they would have tried to hit lightspeed as soon as the pilot had had enough of teasing us." He shrugged slightly. "It doesn't matter now. Or at least it won't once termination of this regrettable interruption is confirmed. Send a squad to the projected crash site and instruct them to scan not only the wreckage but the surrounding area. If they can't find bodies, then have them vac the debris. I won't accept that the pilot and the traitor are both dead until I have tangible biological proof." His tone darkened only slightly, but it was enough to cause the tech to wish the senior officer would resume his wandering.

"Biological traces are acceptable," Hux murmured, "but a couple of skulls would be better."

It felt to Finn as if it took him longer to escape from the confines of the encapsulated, ejected gunner's seat than it had to travel from plunging fighter to planetary surface. The clips and buckles, braces and foam that were intended to set him down in one piece now seemed designed to prevent him from ever emerging onto his own two feet. There was a sequence that had to be followed—first this control, then this button, then slide this to unlock—before the gear could be convinced to let him go. Or rather, he thought frantically, to let go of him.

Eventually he succeeded in freeing himself from the tangle of safety tackle. Staggering clear, he took in his surroundings. His spirits fell. He was alive, but if the environment in which he presently found himself was anything to go by, not for long.

The dusky dune field stretched in all directions, to every horizon. Somehow blue sky and sand now seemed more forbidding than the blackness of space. The warships that had largely been his home were sealed, environmentally controlled little worlds. Anything one needed was readily available, right at hand. Food, water, entertainment, sleeping facilities: All were no more than a few steps away. It was more than a little ironic that someone comfortable in the vastness of space should suddenly find himself suffering from a touch of agoraphobia.

Glancing skyward, he expected to see a landing craft or two dropping out of the clouds in hot pursuit. But his gaze was rewarded only by the sight of a pair of native avians soaring southward. They looked, he decided uncomfortably, too big to be herbivores. At

least they were not circling the spot where he had landed—or him. Yet.

Something else manifested over the eastern dunes. Smoke. The wind had dropped off, allowing it to rise in a column instead of being blown sideways and dispersed. Otherwise he would have noticed it earlier, despite his distress. Someone was making a fire in this forsaken place, or . . .

He started toward it, struggling in the remnants of his armor. Logic insisted no one could have survived the fighter's crash without ejecting beforehand, as he had done. But logic also insisted that it was impossible to escape from a First Order spacecraft, and they had done that. Not that it would matter if he was found here, wandering alive among the dunes. Of one thing he was certain: His former colleagues would not understand, no matter how hard he tried to explain. No one fled the First Order and lived.

The sand sucked at his feet as he stumbled toward the rising smoke. "Poe! Say something if you can hear me! *Poe!*" He did not expect a response, but he hoped for one.

Flame had joined smoke in enveloping the wreck of the TIE fighter. Built more robustly than the typical ship of its class, the Special Forces craft had survived the crash landing, although hardly intact. Debris from the impact was scattered over a wide area. Careful not to cut himself on twisted shards of metal and still-hot composite, he pushed through the heat and haze until he reached the cockpit. It lay crushed and open to the desert air. Trying to shield his eyes against the smoke, Finn moved in closer. Something—there was something sticking out of the wreckage. An arm.

Ignoring the heat and the licking flames, Finn reached in until he could get a grip on it. First one hand, then both, then pull—and it came free in his

hands. No arm, no body: just Poe's jacket. Frustrated, he threw it aside and tried to enter the ruined cockpit. Increasing smoke and heat made it impossible for him to even see, much less work his way inside.

"*Poe!*"

He felt his legs start to go out from under him. But they hadn't buckled; the ground had. Looking down, he saw sand beginning to slide beneath him. His feet were already half covered. He was sinking. In front of him, the ruins of the ship began to slide into the hollow in which it had come to rest. Sand was crawling up the wings and reaching for the open cockpit. If he didn't get away from the quicksand, it was clear he was going to join the TIE fighter in premature internment. He began backpedaling frantically, yelling at the disappearing vessel.

"*POE!*"

Going. Down, down into the sand, to a depth that could not be imagined. Maybe just below the surface, he thought as he scrambled to find safe footing. Maybe much, much deeper.

The more the sand covered the fighter, the faster the vessel sank, until in a few moments it was completely gone. Joining it was most of the debris that the hard landing had thrown aside. There was nothing. Nothing to show that—

A violent explosion erupted almost beneath his feet, sending him staggering backward. For an instant, the substantial fireball that blew skyward flared an angry black and red before dissipating into the atmosphere. Regaining his footing, he stumbled forward. In place of the vanished TIE fighter there was some scattered debris and fused sand. Nothing more, and certainly no sign of another human being. Unlike the fighter, in the case of his companion there were no surviving fragments.

Drained of energy and overwhelmed, he started kicking at the sand, as if exposing a lower layer might reveal something, anything, familiar or encouraging. But each kick exposed only more sand. Looking around wildly, he saw only the silent dunes. It was as if nothing had ever touched this place; certainly not the hand of civilization.

He had escaped. He had survived. He had landed intact and apparently unharmed. And by the looks of things, he was just as dead as if none of it had ever happened. He inhaled deeply, then screamed at the empty planet, knowing as he did so that there was no one around to hear him.

"I DON'T . . . KNOW WHAT . . . TO DO!"

V

IT SEEMED IMPOSSIBLE THAT THE DAY COULD grow any hotter. This being a day filled with one impossibility after another, however, Finn felt no surprise as the heat continued to intensify. Squinting into the glare, he saw nothing in front of him but sand. Sand interrupted by the occasional salt flat followed by more sand. Nothing but sand off to his left, sand off to his right, sand behind . . .

A shape was coming toward him, sharp outlines resolving themselves out of a distant mirage. Nor was it silent. A rising, unsteady whine accompanied the rapidly expanding vision. A vehicle! Some kind of craft out here, in this blasted nothingness, and it was coming straight toward him! Staggering, he raised his arms and began yelling as loudly as his parched throat would permit.

"Hey! Here! Over here! *Hey!*" At this point he didn't care who was in the vehicle, not even if it was occupied by followers of the First Order. Anything, anyone, as long as they could spare some water.

The speeder was large, battered, and packed with an assortment of scoundrels representing several different species—none of them noted for their compas-

sion. Yelling down at him and making rude gestures, they rocketed on past without so much as slowing down, leaving in their wake only dry dust and derisive laughter.

"Thank you!" To the vocal sarcasm he added a mock bow. "Oh, yes, kind fellow travelers, thank you so very much! Thanks a lot!" He continued muttering under his breath, utilizing words and phrases from a half dozen worlds that would have seen him busted in rank had he employed them in the presence of an officer.

No need to concern himself with anything like that anymore, he knew. He was no longer a trooper in the service of the First Order. Should he ever again find himself among its adherents, the last thing he would have to worry about was censure for the use of bad language.

Where was he? This wandering among and between dunes was taking him nowhere. He needed a goal, a destination. His gaze rose. To find that, he needed to acquire a more thorough view of his surroundings.

There are physical tasks more daunting than climbing a steep sand dune, but few that are as frustrating. One step sliding backward for every two up, and that assuming the climber didn't lose his footing and roll all the way back down to the bottom of the sand hill. Determined to make it to the top, Finn kept fighting, legs churning, until at last he stood on the crest of the small, sandy mountain. His first glimpse of his surroundings was as disheartening as he had feared: more sand, piled into slightly lower dunes. But in the distance off to his left, was that . . . could it be . . .

Yes! A settlement! What kind he did not know, but a settlement would have water and food and shelter from the sun. If he was exceptionally lucky, it might even be the destination of the cacophonous crowd that

had callously passed him in the speeder. He wouldn't mind meeting a few of those boastful travelers again—after he had refreshed himself and regained his strength, of course. He started carefully down the far side of the dune he had so painfully ascended. At least now he had a destination.

He was not yet willing to allow himself any hope.

The three-dimensional imagery was mundane: standard-issue trooper personal history and training records. Nonetheless, Hux reviewed it carefully. When analyzing a psychological profile in search of an anomaly, one looked for small clues. A bit of correspondence, a favored quote, even the posture of the individual in question: Any of these might suffice to point to an explanation for the trooper's inexplicable behavior. He did not expect to find a picture of FN-2187 holding up a sign that read "I am going to go berserk and free a prisoner and steal a TIE fighter." If there were any indications of mental imbalance or Resistance sympathies in the trooper's records, Hux expected they would be subtle, not blatant.

But so far, there was nothing. Nothing to suggest that FN-2187 might one day go rogue. Nothing to indicate he was anything other than a representative of his kind, no different from his comrades. Nothing to distinguish him as a person, as a soldier, as an exception.

When he thought about it, Hux mused, the fact that FN-2187 came across as mind-numbingly ordinary was more unsettling than if his history had been full of semi-traitorous rants and near psychotic episodes. It suggested that the ranks might harbor others like him. They could not be permitted to know what he had done. Psytechs were already hard at work

counseling those who had come into contact with him, whether through unremarkable everyday interaction or in the course of his violent flight. The whole incident had to be tamped down, obscured, and buried lest the germ of an infection spread through the ranks.

If there was one thing a competent fighting force did not need, Hux knew, it was unforeseen outbursts of individuality.

Light from the holos reflected off the chrome-clad figure standing beside him.

"Nothing noteworthy," Phasma said. "FN-2187 was assigned to my division, received some additional specialty training, was evaluated, and sent to reconditioning."

Hux shook his head slowly as he continued to scrutinize the records. If anything stood out in the history of stormtrooper FN-2187, it was his exceptional banality. "No prior signs of nonconformity. Not so much as talking back to a superior. He appears so ordinary as to be invisible."

"This was his first offense." Phasma betrayed nothing other than professional interest in the episode or in the man. "It is his only offense."

Entering the room, Kylo Ren moved to join them. "Finding the flaw in your training methods won't help recover the droid." Although his mask concealed his facial expression, the rage simmering below his calm demeanor was almost palpable.

"And yet, there are larger concerns," Hux insisted. It was evident from both Hux's tone and body language that he held no love for the newcomer. The feeling was mutual; neither took pains to hide his contempt.

"Not for me."

Typical Ren, Hux thought. *Self-centered, arrogant, indifferent to the interests of others.*

"The Supreme Leader made it explicit that the Resistance not acquire the map to Skywalker. Capture the droid if we can. Destroy it if we must."

Ren paused to consider the general's words. "A simple enough task, or so it would seem. Find one droid. Just how capable are your soldiers, General?"

Hux turned away from the trooper's holofile. He respected Ren and his abilities, but he was not afraid of him. One did not rise to the rank of general in the forces of the First Order by showing fear.

"I won't have you questioning my methods."

"What methods would those be, General? Those that allow a single common trooper to free an important prisoner from confinement, escort him to an operating hangar, and assist him in fighting his way to freedom? What methods teach such expertise? Obviously, at least some of your troops are skilled at high treason. Perhaps Leader Snoke should consider using an army of clones."

It was with great difficulty that Hux restrained himself. "My men receive exceptional instruction. They are programmed from birth to be loyal to one another, to their officers, and to the Order. The appearance of a single abnormality does not give you the right to question methods that have been refined through long—"

Ren interrupted the general's impassioned defense. "Keeping the map out of the hands of the Resistance shouldn't be a problem, then. Yes?"

"Again, this map. Which for all I know may or may not even exist."

Ren's voice darkened to a degree that caused Phasma to take a step backward. "I do not think I care for your implication, General. You would be wise

to keep such thoughts to yourself. You would be wise not to think them."

Hux held his ground. "My duty is to fight for the First Order with every iota of information, every scrap of material, and every functioning trooper at my command. That was in the oath I took. That is the oath I have sworn to uphold." His gaze did not flinch from the mask. "There was nothing in it about accommodating the ancillary interests of individuals, no matter how high their rank or how exalted their perceived importance. Careful, Ren, that your *personal interests* do not interfere with direct orders from Leader Snoke."

If Kylo Ren was affronted by the general's boldness, he did not show it. As if nothing untoward had passed between them, he continued. "Have you and your techs reviewed the close-in scans of the area where the stolen TIE fighter was forced down? That region is home to only one settlement of consequence: Niima Outpost. If the droid is still functioning, it would instinctively try to hide there."

Glad of the opportunity to change the subject as well as to report something positive, Hux replied in a more amenable tone of voice. "I concur. Furthermore, we found the traitor's armor. It was strung out along a single trail in the desert, where it had been abandoned. While the viewable footprints were interspersed among the dunes, they form a consistent pattern heading toward Niima." He smiled thinly at Ren. "A strike team is already en route."

"Good. I am pleased to see that you are personally in charge of this, General. Of retrieving the droid—preferably unharmed."

Before Hux could object again, Ren turned and departed back the way he had come. If he felt the hate

flowing in his direction from the senior officer behind him, he chose not to respond to it.

Jakku's sun had burnt him, dehydrated him, and tormented him—but it had not beaten him. Not yet. What was a little sunburn, Finn told himself, to someone who had defied the First Order, freed its prisoner, and wreaked havoc on a Star Destroyer? That was what his brain said.

His body begged to differ, shouting its displeasure at its recent treatment and threatening to collapse at any moment as he finally stumbled into Niima Outpost. Old ship parts towered around him; relics of better times, heralds of space travel past. Merchants and traders eyed him speculatively. Finn carried nothing of value save his organs, and judging by his exterior, his insides were not likely to be in very valuable condition, either. Some scavengers pointed and joked. Others, having suffered similarly from blowing sand and grit and sun, expressed murmured sympathy. That was all the help the stranger was offered. Niima Outpost did not coddle the weak.

Something flat, fat, and ugly was drinking from an open water trough. Gaping at it, Finn could not imagine what such a creature could possibly offer that would induce someone to provide it with drink. It looked neither friendly nor edible. He didn't care. It was the water he was interested in, and it was to the water he ran.

Cupped hands dipped, drew the dingy liquid to his mouth, and held it there for him to sip. It felt wonderful against his lips. It tasted awful going down his throat. He spat, revolted. It was the turn of his body, however, to override his brain. Fighting down the urge to gag, he drank. The unsightly lump of four-

legged flesh, which he would later learn was called a happabore, eyed him owlishly but otherwise ignored him. For all Finn knew or cared, the squat quadruped found him equally disgusting.

As Rey knelt beside BB-8, the excitable droid beeped madly.

"Easy, easy—you're going to drain your cells!" She patted the curving metal flank beside her. "You're welcome for not selling you." She saw no reason to add that she had come very, very near to doing exactly that. "Okay, stop thanking me. Now as to this other matter: You're going to have to calm down and speak slowly." More frantic beeping caused her to reply irritably. "That's not sufficient information, Beebee-Ate. I can't help you if you don't tell me who you're waiting for."

The droid paused. Thinking? she wondered. Or as she had warned it, running low on power? When it finally did speak again, her exasperation was palpable.

"Can you *trust* me? What do you think?" She started to rise, frustrated and not a little angry. "Tell me or don't tell me. I don't have time for games."

The droid moved closer, bumping her gently. She made a brief show of ignoring its entreaties before bending once more. "Yes, yes, I understand. You're waiting for your master. Who? Say again?" The droid repeated the name. "Poe." She shrugged diffidently. "The name means nothing to me. Should it?"

Unable to properly voice his own frustration, BB-8 settled for spinning several times on his axis. When he stopped, he began to explain. Despite her studied indifference, Rey found herself listening closely to the steady stream of carefully composed beeps and squeals.

"Yes, I know what the Rebellion was, and yes, I've heard of the Resistance." Her expression grew more serious as the droid continued. "The First Order. They're horrible. Rumor has it an attack squadron of theirs destroyed a sacred village right close to here, over near Kelvin Ravine." BB-8's next series of beeps caused the mask of indifference to fall from her face. She stared at the spherical droid in disbelief.

"You were *there*?"

She would have queried the droid further if not for the interruption. She recognized the approaching pair as two of Plutt's thugs. Halting, they towered over her: twin masses of mobile meat swathed in cheap desert clothing, even their faces completely covered. Plutt wouldn't send such as these to deliver a polite message. With a glance at BB-8, the nearest was quick to confirm her suspicions.

"Plutt wants droid. We take droid. Female don't interfere."

"The droid is mine," she shot back. "I didn't sell him. Plutt knows that."

"You right," agreed the other thug. "Plutt knows that. You didn't sell. So he take." His companion was already pulling a sack over BB-8. When Rey moved to stop him, the other speaker grabbed her arm.

Finn didn't know if the happabore was tired of sharing his space with the biped or was simply being friendly when it pushed him over. So indistinct was the gesture that Finn couldn't tell if it was a deliberate butt or just an amiable nuzzle. Whatever the creature's motivation, it knocked him right off his feet.

This new perspective gave him an excellent view of the confrontation that had started up in the nearby marketplace. He frowned. The young woman who

was being accosted by two far larger individuals was fighting back. Rising, he impulsively moved to help her. However, the nearer he drew, the less concern he felt.

Despite the difference in size between the girl and her assailants, it was looking as if she was not in need of any outside assistance.

A twist and flip, and suddenly the brute who had been holding her arm found himself on the ground. When his companion rushed to assist his downed associate, he found himself on the wrong end of a ferocious assortment of kicks, punches, and blows delivered by the staff the girl was wielding. In short order, both ruffians found themselves prone and unconscious.

Impressed but still wanting to lend a hand, Finn took it upon himself to pull the half-closed sack off the property that was the apparent source of the dispute. What he saw was nothing like what he expected. From a distance he had been unable to tell, but this close there was no mistaking the identity of the spherical mechanical.

Poe's droid.

As the girl spoke to it reassuringly, it shook itself, turned its head, and saw Finn. Whereupon it twitched to one side and began beeping like someone had pulled its rationality chip. This cybernetic disputation did not unsettle Finn half as much as the expression that came over the girl's face. She ought to have been pleased by his attempt to offer assistance. Instead, he sensed as well as saw nothing but rising hostility.

"Hey, what's wrong? I just came over to help. Not that you needed my help." He indicated the pair of insensible thugs. "That doesn't mean that I wouldn't have . . ."

Wordlessly raising the staff she carried, she came at him.

He dodged, barely, and began to run, trying to find a path through the marketplace, wondering what he had done to set her off, and more than a little bewildered at the turn of events. All he had done was move to render aid. Then the droid had seen him, had said something to upset her, and now he was running. Again.

As he bumped into displays and knocked over goods, he drew the ire of one merchant after another. His flight finally came to an end when, after turning several corners and thinking himself in the clear, he ran into the end of that staff. It collapsed him to the ground. Not that it took much of a blow to bring him down. He was completely drained from his trek through the desert.

Lying on his back, out of breath, and not much caring if he passed out, he looked up at her. She held the staff over him, ready to strike again if necessary.

"What's your hurry, *thief*?"

Blissful unconsciousness would have to wait, so shocked was he by the unexpected accusation. "*What . . . ?*" Before he could elaborate, BB-8 rolled up fast alongside him, extended a telescoping arm, and transmitted a sizable electric shock. It was powerful enough to sit Finn bolt upright.

"*Ow!* Hey, what . . . don't do that, woman!" He looked up at the girl.

"Stay down or I'll have to hit you again. The jacket!" She prodded him with the business end of her staff. "This droid says you stole it!"

Badly in need of food and clean water, Finn was forced to settle for taking a deep breath. "Listen, I don't want to fight with you. I've already had a pretty messed-up day. So I'd appreciate it if you didn't ac-

cuse me of being a th—*Ow!*" He glared at the droid, who had zapped him a second time. "*Stop* it!"

"Okay then." Rey was both unimpressed and unwilling to give the traveler the benefit of the doubt. "Prove it. If you didn't steal it, how'd you get it?" She gestured at BB-8. "It belongs to his master."

It took Finn a long moment to process what he was hearing. As he did so, he found it meshed perfectly with what he was seeing. The girl, the agitated droid, the jacket he was wearing . . . They deserved an explanation. He considered embroidering the news, or somehow softening it. In the end he made a hard decision: to tell the truth. He stared evenly at the distressed droid, then up at the unyielding girl.

"His master's dead."

By their reaction, it was plain that neither the droid nor girl had expected quite so blunt a response. Nor one so definitive. When Rey lowered the tip of her staff, Finn continued.

"His name was Poe Dameron." He focused his attention on BB-8. "Right?" Not a single argumentative beep came from the now-silent droid. "He was captured by the First Order. I helped him escape." Finn spoke dispassionately, evenly. "Broke him out of his holding cell. Together we stole a TIE fighter, did some damage to the Order."

He gestured at BB-8. "We couldn't flee outsystem, he said, because he insisted he had to find you." A soft, almost mournful beep issued from the droid. "We got shot down, crashed. I ejected safely. I know Poe didn't, because I found his jacket still inside the fighter. I tried to help him, but I couldn't get to him. This rotten sand sucked the ship right down. Would've taken me with it if I hadn't scrambled clear. I tried to help him. I'm sorry . . ."

The only difference in depression between an or-

ganic and a droid is the lack of flexible expression on the part of the latter. Saddened, moving slowly, BB-8 rolled off to one side. Rey watched the little droid go, then turned her attention back to Finn. Her hostility had given way to subdued admiration.

"You escaped a First Order ship *and* stole a TIE fighter?"

Finn nodded vigorously. "A Special Forces fighter. Poe was a pilot. I handled the gunnery."

She studied him more intently. "So—you're with the Resistance?"

Taking into account the way she gripped that lethal staff and how her dark brown eyes were burning into him, it was easy enough to know how to reply: This time he lied.

"Obviously," he told her, drawing himself up. "I'm with the Resistance, yes. I am. I'm with the Resistance. Who else would have helped a Resistance pilot escape the First Order except another member of the Resistance? I'm surprised you have to ask."

She relaxed, leaning lightly on the staff. "Most visitors to this part of Jakku are traders and trouble-makers. I've never met a Resistance fighter before."

It was difficult to strut in place, but Finn managed it. "Well, this is what we look like. Some of us. Others look different. Now that you have met one, what's your opinion?"

Rey pursed her lips. "You may be great behind the guns of a TIE fighter, but your hand-to-hand skills need a lot of work."

He slumped slightly. "I'm out of practice."

Though she thought that strange, she let it pass and gestured in the direction of the mourning droid. "Beebee-Ate says he's on a secret mission." The droid promptly pivoted on its axis and beeped at her. "Says he needs to get back to the nearest Resistance base."

That much, at least, Finn could understand. "Yeah. Apparently he's carrying a map that leads to Luke Skywalker, and everyone's insane to get their hands on it."

A frown crossed her face as she pondered this explanation. She eyed him dubiously.

"Luke Skywalker? I thought he was just a myth."

VI

FINN GAPED AT THE GIRL. WAS SHE SERIOUS?
It was true that Jakku was a backwater world, but
still . . .

"Really?" was all he could think of to say. He might
have added more if not for the sudden interruption
from a stream of excited beeps.

Rey turned to the droid. "What is it?" She looked
up, past the now concerned Finn. "Over there?"

Trailing her gaze, he was able to make out in the
distance the hulking forms of the two thugs who had
attacked the girl and tried to steal the droid. They
were not alone. The sun gleamed off the bright white
armor of two stormtroopers. One of the banged-up
hooligans was pointing in Finn's direction.

Grabbing Rey's hand, he started backward into the
maze of tents and temporary structures that formed
the marketplace.

"Hey!" she protested, but allowed herself to be
pulled along. "What do you think you're doing?"

"Beebee-Ate, come on!" Finn yelled. Unlike Rey,
the droid needed no urging.

A moment later a pair of blaster explosions obliterated the spot where they had been standing. A third

struck a cleaning unit, which immediately began spewing smoke and corrosive fumes. Still holding tight to Rey's hand, Finn darted in and out among the flimsy structures, dodging outraged owners and piles of goods alike. By now Rey was struggling with his grip.

"Let go of me!"

"We gotta move! I know how they . . ." Mindful of what he had told her, he backed up and began anew. "I mean, as a Resistance fighter, I'm familiar with stormtrooper procedure. We in the Resistance have to be knowledgeable about such things." As he ran, he nodded toward the way they had come. "Those two would rather identify us from smoking bits and pieces. Saves the trouble of having to ask questions."

"I'm not disputing that!" She finally managed to free her fingers from his. "I know how to run without you holding my hand!" Skidding to a stop, she gestured sharply to her left. "No! *This way.*"

Another blast from behind just missed them. By now a general panic had seized the denizens of the marketplace. Those who weren't scattering in every direction were doing their best to shield their stock. Their efforts slowed but did not halt the pursuing stormtroopers.

Rey and her companions hunkered down inside a larger tent crammed with machine parts, crates of salvage, and other mechanical detritus. Peeping cautiously through a gap in the scrap pile behind which they'd taken cover, she muttered urgently at Finn.

"They're shooting at both of us! Why are they shooting at *me*? I haven't done anything!"

Finn knew exactly why they were shooting at her, and he felt terrible about it. But there was nothing he could do. Not now.

"They saw you with me. You're marked."

Her lips tightened. "Thanks for that. Marked as what?"

He didn't respond directly. "I'm not the one chasing me around with a stick!" While staying hidden, he tried to scan their surroundings, searching desperately for something useful. "Anyone sell blasters around here?" A trained stormtrooper, he felt naked without a gun. Though he had been on the receiving end of the girl's staff, as far as he was concerned, it qualified as a local curiosity and not a proper weapon.

Behind them, BB-8 was quivering slightly. Both antennae were fully extended and inclined slightly eastward. Rey frowned at the droid. "Are you okay?"

While Finn's sensory equipment was less sensitive than the droid's, it was no less sophisticated. Man and machine were both listening to something that escaped the girl. Puzzled, she shifted her attention from one to the other.

"What is it? What's going on? I don't hear anyth—"

Finn shushed her with a gesture, listening intently. She started to object, thought better of it and went quiet. Behind him, BB-8 was growing increasingly agitated. Without a word, the droid spun and raced toward the rear of the storage area. Finn responded almost as quickly, grabbing Rey's hand and pulling her after him. As before, when she tried to pull away, he maintained his grip.

"Hey! Not again! *Stop taking my hand!*"

The explosion ripped up the storage area, its contents, and the ground just behind the fleeing trio as one of the two diving TIE fighters BB-8 and Finn had heard coming in unleashed its weaponry in a low pass over the town. The concussion threw Rey hard to the ground. She came up fearful and spitting out grit. The desert was full of dangers, and scavenging had its own risks, but she was used to those. An occasional

encounter with thieves was an occupational hazard. So was dealing on a recurring basis with the hostile and hungry creatures of the wastelands. The realization that First Order TIE fighters might be sent to locate and eradicate a single Resistance fighter suggested that she was well and truly out of her depth. This Finn must be more important than he seemed, she decided.

Where was Finn, anyway?

She found him nearby, unconscious. Getting a grip on his jacket, she rolled him over. The spherical white and orange droid joined her a moment later.

Should she shake him? Use her emergency bio-injector? She was no physician: Her medical training was restricted to what she had learned during a life of having to take care of herself. The wrong application, she knew, could leave him worse off than he was now.

She was saved from having to make a decision as he came to, blinking at his surroundings before his attention settled on her. Swallowing, he managed to gasp out, "Are you okay?"

It struck her that in her entire short life, this was the first time anyone had asked that question. "Yeah," she murmured. Her attention flicked between the fallen figure beside her and the blue sky that had turned abruptly deadly. "I'm okay. You?"

He peered down at himself as he sat up. Everything of consequence appeared to be intact and in place. "Think so. Too close."

She stood and extended a hand. He glanced at it, his dark gaze rising to her face, then gratefully accepted her offer of assistance.

"Follow me," Rey said. She turned and broke into a run, the grateful Finn allowing himself to be guided.

Around them, Niima Outpost was in complete disarray. Explosions had torn tents and other build-

ings apart, scattering merchants, traders, scavengers, maintenance workers, and every other innocent bystander in a panicky search for cover. Staff strapped to her back now, Rey led her companions onto the sand-scoured clearing that served as the town's port. Looking back, Finn saw the pair of TIE fighters bank and turn. He had no doubt what they were looking for.

"Isn't there any shelter around here?"

As she continued to lead him on, Rey shook her head and yelled, "Nothing strong enough to withstand TIE fighter weapons!"

"We can't outrun them!" *That's right,* he told himself. *Boost her confidence in you by stating the obvious.*

She pointed to the four-engined craft toward which they were running. "We might in that quadjumper!"

Finn shook his head. "I'm a gunner. We need a pilot!"

"We got one!"

He gaped at her. *"You?"* While her youth and probable lack of experience troubled him, he knew he was in no position to argue. Anyway, what was the worst that could happen? That they would crash on takeoff instead of being pulverized by the pursuing ships of the First Order?

They were still dangerously far from the quadjumper and terribly exposed on the bare landing area. Another craft loomed off to their right, nearby.

"How about *that* ship, it's closer! If nothing else, we can get out of sight!"

Rey scarcely glanced in the other vessel's direction. "That one's garbage! We need something that'll *move,* not just get off the ground—if we're lucky!"

They ducked simultaneously as the two TIE fighters roared past overhead. But instead of firing at the tiny

figures, their gunners directed bursts of energy at the fugitives' destination. The quadjumper came apart in a ball of flame, flinging bits and pieces of itself in all directions as the detonation scorched the landing area. Throwing up their hands, Finn and Rey shielded their faces from the heat and flying debris. When they lowered them, nothing was left to be seen of the quadjumper but a smoking pile of rubble. Rey's reaction was immediate and realistic.

"Okay—the garbage it is!"

Changing direction, they raced for the other craft. Though it was partially covered by several protective sand tarps, the loading ramp was down. Finn paused only briefly to glance at the ident plate sealed flush inside the airlock wall.

"*Mi con,*" he read aloud. "What the hell does that mean?"

Ahead of him, Rey yelled without looking back. "Some con man's private craft, probably. That might be a good thing. It might be built to travel faster than a crippled skimmer!"

"If we're lucky," Finn muttered, echoing her early observation as he and BB-8 followed.

Rey hit a wall panel even before her companions were safely aboard. To her great relief, it responded. The ramp behind them rose and the lock sealed. The vessel's layout was straightforward and they found the cockpit immediately. Tossing her staff to one side and throwing herself into the pilot's seat even as she was scrutinizing the instrumentation, Rey activated several controls. Much to her surprise, the console in front of her immediately came to life. She tapped a visualization.

"Gunner's position is down below!"

Turning, Finn headed for the indicated area. "You ever fly this thing? Or anything like it?"

As BB-8 looked on, she shouted back to him, "I've piloted all kinds of craft, but nobody's flown this old crate in years!"

"Then what makes you think it'll get off the ground?" he called.

Her reply was grim. "If you prefer, we can leave and try running across open tarmac while being shot at!"

Having no comeback for that, Finn slipped down and buckled himself into the gunner's seat. To his shock, it responded to his weight by whipping to the left. Hastily he grabbed hold of the controls.

"Whoa, easy!" Manipulating the intuitive controls allowed him to quickly take full control of the turret's movements. "I can do this, I can do this." If anything, he saw quickly, the track and fire controls were simpler and more primitive than those he had handled in the Special Forces TIE fighter.

Rey rapidly ran through a standard pre-lift sequence, activated the full panoply of relevant instrumentation, and sat back. A low whine rose from the rear of the craft. She reached for the control that would, she hoped, bring all her hurried preparations to fruition. One of three things would occur when she thumbed it, she knew: They would lift off, the ship would blow up, or nothing at all would happen. Not good odds, but the only ones they had. She took a deep breath and punched the control. "I can do this, I can do this—"

At the stern of the old ship, long quiescent engines flared to brilliant life. Fully powered up now, it soared into the bright blue sky of Jakku—but not efficiently. Shedding tarps as it rose, it spun and careened wildly, nearly crashing back to the ground. Wrestling with the unfamiliar controls, Rey managed to level off just in time to crash into and through the town's entry

archway: Niima Outpost's sole example of architectural pride.

Below, the puffy-faced figure of Unkar Plutt emerged from a collapsed structure to scream at the sky. *"Hey! That's miiiiine!"*

Finding the oddly named craft surprisingly responsive to manual control, an increasingly optimistic Rey spun it around and accelerated, blasting away from the port. The pair of TIE fighters that had been shooting up the town immediately gave chase.

Rey headed skyward, relieved to feel the ship's increasing power as they soared away from the surface. Trying to interpret the weapons systems, Finn yelled to her, hoping either his straining voice or the turret's audio pickup would permit at least a modicum of inflight communication.

"Stay low! It's our only chance! If we go extra-atmospheric, they'll outmaneuver us and run us down before we can make lightspeed—assuming this thing can still do lightspeed. And put up the shields—if they work!"

"Shield controls are on the other side of the console," she shot back. "Not so easy without a copilot!"

Below, Finn continued to struggle with the highly responsive, wildly swinging turret. "Try sitting in *this* thing!"

Realizing it was impossible to reach the necessary instrumentation while seated in full pilot's position, Rey momentarily let go of the controls. She'd have to do this manually, she knew. Put any ship on autopilot and the vectoring would immediately be sensed by a pursuer, who could then lock on and blow you out of the sky. In contrast, there was just enough wild wobble in their flight path as she leaned to her right to confuse any electronic predictors. Her stretching,

however, caused the ship to cant sharply as she tried
to activate the shield instrumentation on the copilot's
side while maintaining some semblance of flight control.

"Beebee-Ate, hold on!"

Her warning came too late for the droid. Beeping
madly, he rolled ceilingward as the ship spun.

Fingers straining, she just managed to reach the shield
controls and flick them to life, in the process having to
brush away several clumps of excessively long, rough
yellow-brown hairs that had become caught in the console. Relieved, she straightened in the pilot's seat and
resumed full command, stabilizing the vessel.

"I'm going low!" she shouted, mindful of Finn's advice.

Driving the ship surfaceward, she pulled up at the
last possible moment and sent them screaming across
the ground, clipping the crests of at least two dunes.
Trying to match the maneuver while pursuing at high
speed, both TIE fighters shot past, unable to slow in
time. They did, however, each manage to get off suc-
cessive bursts from their weaponry. Had the vessel's
shields not been up, the twin blasts might well have
brought them down. Just like its engines, the stolen
vessel's shields proved unexpectedly robust.

Tougher than it looks, she thought as she strove to
accelerate and dodge. The original owner had plainly
had some serious, and probably illegal, modifications
made to his vessel that on numerous worlds were
worthy of fines and possible imprisonment. She resolved to thank that individual profusely if she ever
had the occasion to make that acquaintance. Provided she survived the next hour.

A blast rocked them, and she barely managed to
hang on tightly enough to avoid a looming sandstone
monolith. Swallowing, she yelled as loud as she could.

"Could use some offense down there, you know? Maybe before our body parts are scattered all over the desert? Y'ever gonna fire back? Hold on, Beebee-Ate, hold on!"

Within the cylindrical corridor, the droid was beeping madly as he rolled up the walls, across the ceiling, and everywhere except where he wanted to be. Capable of comprehending the causes of nausea, the droid was fortunate it was not a condition his kind were subject to, but his internal gyros were being forced to work overtime.

"Working on it!" Finn called back to her. A moment later the weapons systems finally came to life beneath his hands. Spinning the turret, he began firing back at their pursuit. The primitive targeting system was clumsier than anything he had trained on or studied, and his blasts missed.

Another detonation rocked the ship. If not for their shields, he knew, they would have been debris by now. His mouth tight, he continued firing. The pursuing fighters came on, almost disdainful of their quarry's defensive efforts.

"We need cover!" he yelled even as he kept firing. "Quick!"

"We're about to get some!"

While she knew little more than theory when it came to maneuvering and fighting in free space, Rey had plenty of experience defending herself on the desiccated surface of Jakku. At least in the vicinity of Niima Outpost, she was familiar with every dune field, every canyon complex, every crater and escarpment. Keeping as close to the ground as possible, she rose and darted over rocks and dunes, grazing one upthrust ridge so closely that she took a chunk out of it. Unwilling to sacrifice distance to gain altitude in

order to attack from above, the two TIE fighters stayed close.

Just a little farther, she told herself as she clung grimly to the controls. *Just keep them off a little longer.* She was heading for her favorite scavenging spot: the ships' graveyard. Let them try to follow her in there! She banked hard, low enough to cut a crease in the sand.

Half wild, a burst from the craft's guns crossed the flight path of one of the tailing TIE fighters and happened to catch it where its shields were momentarily unpowered. Part of the craft crumpled instantly, causing it to trail wreckage as its pilot strove to keep it aloft.

"Whooooo!" Finn allowed himself a triumphant shout without letting go of the firing controls. To himself he added, more softly, *"Damn, that was lucky."*

"Nice shot!" Rey's praise reached him from above. He accepted it silently, without wasting time explaining that his success was due as much to her wrenching the ship around unpredictably as to any innate targeting ability on his part.

As she sent them snaking into the enormous field of derelict spacecraft and other industrial waste, the damaged TIE fighter slammed into one of the metal mountains and came apart. Out of nowhere, a brace of scavengers appeared to begin claiming portions of the remains. No one bothered to check the cockpit of the downed craft to see if the pilot might somehow have survived the crash.

Trailed by the surviving fighter, the ship slalomed through the colossal debris field. Sparks flew as she grazed towering metal walls and fallen station sections, but the hull of the borrowed craft held together. As he was banged around in the gunner's seat, Finn tried to keep track of their remaining pursuer while

peering out at a trash-paved surface that frequently came entirely too near to where he happened to be sitting.

Likewise, the next blast that erupted in his vicinity also came too close. The concussion set the turret spinning. When it finally stabilized, its rattled occupant was horrified to find that it had been jammed facing forward. He could not rotate it in any direction. At the same time, alarms began to sound throughout the ship, indicating that more than just the gunner's position had sustained damage.

"Guns are stuck in forward position!" he yelled upward. "I can't move 'em! You gotta lose our pursuit!"

Yet another blast rocked their craft. Much more of this, Rey knew, and modifications aside, one of the TIE fighter's bursts was going to overwhelm their shields. The vessel they had commandeered was a small freighter, not a warship.

Ahead lay the bulk of a downed Super Star Destroyer, its mass inconceivably large where it rested on the sand. Pulling on the controls, she drove the ship downward—and into the gaping breach that was the center of a ruined engine thruster. If she hoped this maneuver might dissuade their remaining pursuer, she was wrong. Unwilling to give ground, the pilot of the surviving TIE fighter took his craft in after her.

As he sat gawking out the turret's transparent canopy, a disbelieving Finn gauged the proximity of the metal walls that were racing past on either side of them.

"Are we really doing this?"

Sparks continued to flare from their ship's sides as Rey negotiated one increasingly narrow passage after another. Even a former crew member would not have

been as familiar with the corridors she chose. But she had not merely familiarized herself with them from a diagram: She knew them intimately, having inspected them individually and on foot or with climbing gear.

"Get ready!" she yelled to him.

Finn nodded energetically. "Okay, okay! I'm ready!" Then he frowned. "Ready for what?"

Have to time this just right, Rey told herself as she prepared. And if Finn wasn't ready, the maneuver she was about to try wouldn't matter. They would be shot down as surely as Unkar Plutt underpaid his scavengers. Finn was relying on her skills; now she had to rely on his.

Uninterrupted light appeared at the far end of the service corridor down which she was flying. Another blast from the unrelenting TIE fighter pilot nearly sent their craft crashing into the corridor's ceiling, and she only managed to correct at the last instant. There was no time to check readouts to see if any critical part of the stolen ship had been damaged. All that mattered was that they were still airborne and the controls continued to respond to her touch.

Then they were out, flying in bright sunlight. The instant the ship emerged from the decaying guts of the old Super Star Destroyer, she cut the power just so and swung the ship completely around.

Fortunately, as a trained stormtrooper, Finn was used to wild swings of his personal cosmos. So where such a tight aerial twist and turn might cause another, less experienced passenger to lose the contents of his or her stomach, Finn retained not only those but his wits, as well.

Now heading directly back *toward* the immense relic, he once more found the surviving TIE fighter directly in his sights, and he reacted accordingly. Whether it was their vessel's sudden and unexpected

reappearance just outside his own targeting instrumentation or the shock of what seemed to be a suicide plunge, the fighter pilot's fire missed.

Finn's did not.

Rey turned the ship hard away from the hulk of the Super Star Destroyer as the remaining TIE fighter burst into flames, lost speed and altitude, and crashed to the surface in their wake. Working the controls, a jubilant Rey sent the ship accelerating into the clouds. Those, and the sun-blasted surface of Jakku, soon fell astern, giving way to the cold yet comforting blackness of space.

Feeling confident that she could now entrust temporary control of the ship to its autopilot without fear of being tracked, she slipped out of her harness and hurried out of the cockpit. In doing so she passed BB-8, who after the acrobatic aerial contortions of the past few minutes was only now able to steady himself.

"You okay?" she inquired in passing. Several short, curt beeps avowed that he was, while also communicating that the experience they had just gone through had been less than pleasurable.

She found Finn in the lounge, trying to regulate his breathing while coming down from an adrenaline high. Turning to her as she slowed, he gave her a wide, disarming grin.

"That was *some* piloting!"

"Thanks." She shrugged. "I've been flying every kind of junk you can imagine almost since I could walk." It was her turn to smile. "Speaking of which, that was some shooting! I was worried you wouldn't have time to react."

"You could have told me what you had in mind. Might've saved me a heart palpitation or two."

She shook her head. "No time. I had to pull the

turn almost as soon as I thought of it. I just had to rely on your ability to react to the maneuver."

He nodded. "Good thing my hands were frozen to the track and fire controls. When all of a sudden he showed up in my sights, all I had to do was twitch my fingers."

"You got him on the first blast!"

His smile gave way to a touch of self-satisfaction. "It *was* a pretty good shot, wasn't it?"

"It was perfect!" Rey told him. It was silent in the lounge for a long moment before he murmured, "Why are we . . ."

"Staring at each other? I don't know . . ."

The need for possibly uncomfortable answers was obviated by a series of insistent beeps from BB-8, who had rolled in to join them. Rey knelt beside the agitated droid.

"Hey, calm down! You're okay, we're all okay. For the moment, at least." She indicated Finn. "Everything's going to work out fine. He's with the Resistance and he's going to get you home. We both will." She slid a hand along the droid's curving flank. "I'm not going to abandon you now. Not after turning down the kind of payment Plutt was offering." More beeps, to which she responded, "I'm just kidding. The amount wasn't what mattered. I just got a huge charge out of being able to deny that bloated bastard something he wanted so badly."

Having calmed the droid, she returned her attention to the room's other occupant. "I don't know your name."

Startled, he realized that on that score he was equally ignorant. "FN-2—Finn. Name's Finn. What's yours?

"My name is Rey." This time when she smiled, all trace of the hardened, desert-dwelling scavenger melted

away. It was a sweet smile, he found himself thinking. Warm. He repeated the name, enjoying the way his lips parted as he murmured the single syllable.

"Rey . . ."

He would have said much more, but this time it was the ship itself that interrupted. On the far side of the lounge, a section of decking broke loose, shot upward, and banked off the ceiling before coming to rest on the floor. Hissing vapor was starting to fill the room, threatening to overwhelm the ability of the atmospheric scrubbers to cleanse it.

Rey didn't hesitate. Ignoring the emission spewing from beneath the deck, she raced over to peer down past the ragged edge of the opening. Finn joined her. He suspected the venting gas had to be nontoxic; otherwise they would have been sprawled out on the floor by now, unconscious or dying. Standing alongside her, he tried to see past the raging mist and down into the depths of whatever had blown.

She tried to see while simultaneously shielding her eyes. "I don't know. Just hope it's not the motivator. Ship of this age and class is bound to have one." Sitting down, she slid both legs into the opening.

Finn stared at her. "You're going down there? Without even knowing what the problem is?"

They locked eyes. "The only way to know what the problem is *is* to go down there. Unless you've got a better idea?"

He gave a reluctant shake of his head. "I'm real good at blowing things up. Not so good at putting them together. You sure there isn't anything I can do?"

She tried to smile but couldn't. "While I'm down there, don't touch anything whose function you don't understand completely—and if you hear a lot of screaming and cursing, stand by."

He considered. "You'll want me to pull you up?"

This time she did manage the smile. "Only if there's just screaming and no cursing." With that she slipped over the edge and down. Her slender form was quickly obscured by the roaring vapor.

VII

THE GREAT SWEEP OF THE EXTERNAL OBSER-
vation portal on the Star Destroyer *Finalizer* allowed
anyone standing before it an uninterrupted view of
the vastness of space. Suns and nebulae, mysteries and
conundrums, all were laid out before the viewer. It
was a view intended to awe and inspire, hence the
presence of the portal where visual pickups and monitors would have sufficed just as well.

Kylo Ren regarded it in silence. He had been trained
in contemplation, was skilled in deliberation, could
remain meditating just so for hours at a time.

But he was losing patience.

Approaching from behind, all Lieutenant Mitaka
could see was a tall, caped figure silhouetted against
the spray of stars. He did not look forward to having
to make the report. It was his responsibility and he
had no choice. Nor was it the first time he had been
compelled to deliver bad news to a superior officer.
But Kylo Ren was different. Not precisely a superior
officer but something else. At that moment, Mitaka
would rather have been anywhere else in the civilized
galaxy than alone in a room with Kylo Ren.

The caped figure did not turn. He did not have to.

Mitaka knew Ren was as aware of his arrival as if he had watched him approach. He was tracking the lieutenant with something other than eyes.

"Something to report, Lieutenant? Or have you come, like myself, to marvel at the view?"

"Sir?"

A gloved hand rose to take in the sweep of light and energy arrayed before them. "Look at it, Lieutenant. So much beauty among so much turmoil. In a way, we are but an infinitely smaller reflection of the same conflict. It is the task of the First Order to remove the disorder from our own existence, so that civilization may be returned to the stability that promotes progress. A stability that existed under the Empire, was reduced to anarchy by the Rebellion, was inherited in turn by the so-called Republic, and will be restored by us. Future historians will look upon this as the time when a strong hand brought the rule of law back to civilization."

Mitaka forbore mentioning that the Republics had developed their own codes of law. To do so would have been . . . indelicate, and he doubted that Ren was in the mood for a political discussion of any kind. Standing at attention, he presented his brief report.

"Sir. Despite our best efforts, we were unable to acquire the Beebee-Ate droid on Jakku."

Now Ren did turn. Mitaka would have preferred it the other way. He always found it unsettling to have to gaze at the metal mask beneath the cowl.

"It was destroyed? Do not tell me, Lieutenant, that the droid was destroyed."

Mitaka swallowed hard. "No, sir. At least, not as far as we are able to determine. Reports from the ground indicate—"

He was interrupted. "No aerial survey results?"

"Two TIE fighters accompanied the recovery party.

Contact has been lost with both and it is assumed . . . it is assumed they encountered unforeseen difficulties."

Ren sneered softly. "You equivocate like a senator. Go on."

"Reports from our troopers on the ground indicate that the droid escaped capture by taking flight aboard a stolen Corellian freighter, a YT model. An older craft but in the hands of a competent pilot, a capable one."

Atypically, a touch of uncertainty colored Ren's response. "The droid stole a freighter?"

"Not exactly, sir. Again, according to these preliminary reports, it had help." Mitaka was starting to sweat. "We have no confirmation, but brief glimpses by our troopers correlated with the location of an earlier crash site lead us to believe that trooper FN-2187 may have been—"

He broke off as Ren reached for the lightsaber at his belt, activated the weapon, and raised the intense red band high. Expecting a swift judgment, Mitaka closed his eyes. After a moment, finding his head still attached to his neck, he dared to open them once more. Ren was slashing at the console nearby, at the walls, at the deck, rending and ripping, slashing long lines of bleeding metal into the very fabric of the ship. His rage was terrible to behold. Mitaka strove to remain perfectly still, to control his breathing, to become as invisible as possible lest he become nothing more than an inadvertent recipient of Ren's fury. Whether by chance or design, Ren spared him.

Shutting off the lightsaber, the taller man turned to the wretched bearer of bad news. He spoke calmly, as if his mad, destructive rampage had been nothing more than a brief interlude: an illusion.

"Anything else?"

At least the worst of the report had been delivered, Mitaka knew. And he was still alive. He allowed himself to relax ever so slightly.

"The two were accompanied and likely abetted in their flight by a third party, presumably local. A girl."

Reaching out, a black-gloved hand clutched the startled lieutenant and pulled him violently forward. That metallic visage was now close, closer than Mitaka had ever been to it. As the officer struggled to breathe in that remorseless grasp, Kylo Ren's voice took on a timbre lower and more menacing than any the lieutenant had ever heard.

"What—*girl*?"

Kneeling by the opening in the deck, Finn struggled to peer down into the depths. The constant hiss of escaping vapor made it difficult to hear or see anything. He badly wanted to shut off the blaring emergency alarm but didn't dare move away while Rey was still below and out of sight. Nor did he trust the droid to do it, fearing the worried mechanical might hit the wrong control. While a BB-8 model contained a lot of storage, he doubted the schematic for an old freighter was among the information on tap. Furthermore, this particular vessel had undergone a considerable number of modifications, not all of which might be hospitable to uninvited visitors. Booby traps, for example. As Rey worked out of sight below, he wondered if she had considered the same possibility.

Make the wrong adjustment and they could blow up the ship. Or the ship, responding on its own to unknown preprogramming, could blow them up. He hoped they hadn't escaped the clutches of the First Order only to eliminate themselves.

A head popped up, surrounded by vapor. Perspira-

tion streamed from Rey's face. "It's the motivator. Grab me a Harris wrench!" She pointed behind him. "Check in there."

Turning, he unlatched the storage container she had pointed to and began rummaging through the contents. As a stormtrooper, he was trained to deal with certain emergencies. These included but were not limited to troubles of a mechanical nature, such as how to do basic repairs on a speeder and other ground transport vehicles. So he knew what he was looking for. He only hoped he could find it.

"How bad is it?" he yelled back at her as he continued to sort through the container's jumbled contents, silently cursing the unknown owner of the ship. Whoever it was, he was no genius at organization. The tools and replacement components filled the container in the most haphazard, disorganized manner possible. "If we wanna live," Rey's voice echoed from below, "not good!"

The ship gave a nasty jolt, reminding Finn of their rapidly degrading situation. "Look, they're out hunting for us *now*; we gotta get out of this system *now*! The longer we stay sublightspeed, the more certain the chance that their sweep scans will pick us up. I don't want to have to try and outrun a Destroyer!"

Rey ignored him and glanced at the nearby droid. "Beebee-Ate said the location of the Resistance base is on a 'need to know' basis. If I'm going to take you two, *I need to know*!"

She disappeared below, once more leaving Finn and the droid alone in the shuddering, alarm-filled lounge. Busy as she was attempting to make the necessary repairs, he felt he could try to stall her. But that would only postpone the inevitable reckoning. Or he could ignore the query. Same inescapable result. He could lie, invent something—anything. Blurt out the name of

any system, any realistic destination. Anything to get away from this world and the attention of the Order. A quick sideways glance showed that the droid was watching him. That wouldn't work, either, since if nothing else BB-8 would contradict him. The only reply that would suffice was the true one, and he didn't have it. He edged over toward the droid.

"Okay, look—we have to know the location of the Resistance base. You heard Rey. She thinks she can get us there—*but you have to tell us where it is.*" The droid emitted a flurry of rapid, soft beeps. An impatient Finn waved them off.

"I don't speak that, but I think I got the gist. You just accused me of not being with the Resistance, didn't you?" The droid's body inclined forward slightly: a mechanical acknowledgment. "Right. Okay, just between us—no, I'm not. I'm a regular trooper who's gone rogue. By my actions, I've renounced my oath. In the eyes of the Order, that makes me something worse than a Resistance fighter. I don't know from the Resistance. All I've heard are stories and rumors and Order propaganda. But I do know what's right from what's wrong. That's why I've done the things I've done. That's why I find myself in this mess here and now." He paused for breath.

"All I want, all I'm trying to do, is get away from the First Order. I don't care where I end up as long as it's clear of their influence. But you tell us where your base is and I'll help you get there first, before I do anything for myself or on my own." He gazed straight into the droid's visual pickup. "Deal?"

BB-8 cocked his head to one side and said nothing. Finn felt no shame in pleading.

"Droid, *please.*"

He held the stare until a weary Rey appeared again. "Pilex driver, hurry!" As Finn returned to the storage

container and began searching anew, she took the moment to query him once more. "So, I didn't hear. Where's your base? Where's our destination?"

Searching through the pile of tools and odds and ends, he murmured tersely to the watching droid, "Go on, Beebee-Ate. You tell her."

Nothing from the droid. Not a sound, not a hum. Finn was on the verge of despair when the spherical mechanical finally uttered a short sequence of beeps. Rey looked surprised.

"The Ileenium system?"

Locating the requisite tool, a relieved Finn passed it to her. "Yeah, the Ileenium system." Where the hell was the Ileenium system? he wondered. "That's the one. Let's get this crate fixed and head there as fast as we can, huh?"

"Doing the best I can down here." Rey vanished again. As soon as she was out of sight, the grateful Finn gave BB-8 a thumbs-up. The droid responded by shooting out a welding torch in imitation of the human's gesture.

She wasn't gone long, nor was her attitude any more relaxed when she reappeared. "Bonding tape, hurry! If I get the ship working again, I'll drop you two off at Ponemah Terminal, but that's as far as I can go. Ponemah's still neutral territory. You should be able to make contact with Resistance representatives from there."

For the third time, Finn found himself plowing through the disorganized tool container. "What about you? What are you going to do? If anyone besides those two TIE fighter pilots saw you with us, your likeness is gonna be plastered all over this quadrant! If the Order doesn't haul you in for questioning, reward-seekers and bounty hunters will be scouring every port in hopes of picking you up. Better for you

if you stick with us." He threw BB-8 a quick glance. "The Resistance will protect you."

She shook her head. Vapor continued to geyser upward around her, though not as much as before, Finn noted.

"I gotta get back to Jakku!"

"*Back* to Jak— Why does everyone always want to go back to *Jakku*? There's nothing there! Sand and junk and rocks and sand and quicksand and sand— I don't get it!" Picking up what looked like a sealer, he turned to toss it to her.

"No, that one!" She pointed, but her stance was none too steady and her hand kept weaving around. Doing his best to follow her directions, he hefted another instrument. "No! The one I'm pointing to!"

"I'm trying! And you're not pointing real well, you know?" His exasperation nearly overcame his fear.

"*That* one! If we don't get a patch on down here, the propulsion tank will overflow and flood the ship with poisonous gas."

He tried another device.

"No."

Another.

"No—that one, to your left! No!"

Sidling up alongside Finn, BB-8 used his head to indicate the appropriate sealer. Hopeful, Finn picked it up. "This?"

By now he was surprised when instead of bawling "No!" again, she replied with an emphatic "Yes!" He tossed it to her, watched as she caught it easily and once more disappeared below. Leaving the tool container, he returned to the opening in the deck and called down to her. "You're a *pilot*. You can go anywhere. Why go back? You got a family there? Back on Jakku? Boyfriend? Cute boyfriend?"

As the flow of vapor finally slowed and then ceased,

so did the interminable alarm. Rey's reappearance co-incided with the return of comparative silence within the lounge. She broke it immediately.

"None of your business, *that's why.*"

The sudden dimming of lights put a halt to any incipient argument. They flickered but did not go out. All three of the lounge's occupants regarded their newly altered environment. BB-8 beeped nervously.

"That can't be good," Finn murmured.

"No, it can't be," Rey agreed as she climbed out of the opening. Together, they headed back toward the cockpit.

This time Finn settled into the copilot's seat. Looking back at him was a dead console. One did not have to be trained as a pilot to infer that a dead console did not bode well for future voyaging.

"It's the motivator, isn't it? That's the component you were so worried about." When she didn't reply, his heart rate increased. "It's worse than the motivator?"

Focusing on the console in front of her, Rey replied without looking up from the instrumentation. "I fixed that; this is something else." Without much hope, she tried several controls before sitting back, defeated. "Someone's locked onto us. All our controls are over-ridden. They've taken control of life support, too, for that matter. Easiest way to get us to cooperate."

"Who's taken control of us?" Tapping the scanner to remind him that it was useless, she could only shrug helplessly.

Nothing being visible through the front port, he left his seat and headed for the overhead observation dome.

"See anything?" she called back to him.

"*Yeah.*" There was no need for elaboration. She would see for herself all too soon. Oddly enough, the

sight allowed him to relax finally. There is no point in overexerting oneself when all hope is gone.

The other ship was gigantic, an enormous bulky freighter. The cargo bay door was open, and against the open hangar that loomed above, their stolen vessel appeared no bigger than an escape capsule. Its instrumentation frozen, its engines powerless, and its weapons systems dead, the paralyzed ship was drawn inexorably upward into the cavernous opening.

Returned to the cockpit, a defeated Finn slumped into the copilot's seat, his gaze fixed forward as he spoke. "It's the First Order. They've got us. It's all over, Rey." Behind them, BB-8 beeped querulously. Having nothing encouraging to say, Finn did not reply.

They weren't going to the Ileenium system, he knew. Not now. The likelihood of them even returning to Jakku was infinitesimal. Their fates would be decided on board the ship that was presently pulling them in. Decided and expeditiously carried out. The First Order was nothing if not efficient.

So *close*. In spite of what he had done, in spite of his own personal rebellion nearly succeeding, it had all come to nothing. Useless. Poe Dameron was dead. Soon he, and this poor girl, would join the Resistance pilot. Whatever map or other information BB-8 held would be forcibly extracted from the little droid, after which his memory would be wiped, his AI circuits removed, and the remainder probably recycled as scrap. Finn grunted softly. That was more than he and Rey could hope for. All he could do for her now was apologize for having inveigled her into a mess that was a consequence of his own making. He might relay that truth to the individuals presiding over his disposition. Plead on her behalf. But as an ex–First Order stormtrooper he knew that his words, however

eloquent, would buy Rey only as much time as it took for him to speak them. He was bitter and resigned.

He also knew that if given the chance he would have done the same all over again. The only thing that separated him from his comrades, the only thing that defined him as an individual, was his unshakeable sense of what was right. That much, at least, he could take with him.

"What do we do?" Rey was saying beside him. She kept trying the controls, to no avail. "There must be *something*."

He still could not look in her direction. "We can die."

She refused to accept it. *"There have to be other options besides dying!"*

He sighed heavily. "Sure. We could run—if the engines could be powered up. We could try and fight—if the blasters would function. We could step into the matter transporter—if such a thing existed." He shook his head dolefully. "No, we're dead. We don't even have hand weapons to try and hold off a capture te—" He stopped abruptly. Now he did turn to her.

"Earlier, when you were working below: You said something about volatile chemicals? Mixing to create poisonous gases?"

She eyed him uncertainly. "Yeah, but I fixed that. There's no blending now."

His tone was deliberate, his stare unflinching. "Can you unfix it?"

It took her a moment to realize what he was driving at. When understanding came, her expression brightened. Together, they left the cockpit and headed back toward the lounge, BB-8 trailing close behind.

The emergency masks they removed from their storage stations were designed to protect against loss of atmosphere. They most emphatically were not in-

tended to substitute for the environment suits that were employed during extravehicular excursions. But for the plan Finn had in mind, they should do just fine. Working together, they succeeded in wrestling the droid down into the service area below the deck. Once all three had safely managed the short descent, Finn pulled the blown section of decking back into place over his head. Fortunately, it had come loose in one piece and was unlikely to be noticed by preoccupied intruders. At least, not right away. It would have to suffice.

Next to him, Rey was working hard to undo the results of her earlier repair.

"This'll work on stormtroopers?" she wondered as she manipulated the tools she had used earlier and left behind.

"Standard issue helmets are designed to filter out smoke, not toxins. To cope with the latter, a trooper needs to engage one of several special filters, depending on the specific contaminant. Identification is the province of one or two squad leaders. Having brought this ship on board theirs, I doubt anyone will think to check for airborne pollutants. It's not like leading a ground assault, or forcing entry to an enemy warship. This is just an old freighter. Any kind of internal defense, much less something as nebulous as a gas counterattack, would be the last thing a squad sent to take its crew into custody would expect."

Rey was plainly impressed. "You Resistance guys really know your stuff."

He smiled uneasily. "You know what they say: Know your enemy."

Abruptly, the ship's internal illumination returned full strength. Even concealed within the service corridor, they could hear the muted sound of the ship's ramp lowering.

"Here they come," Finn whispered. "Hurry!"

"I am hurrying!" Her fingers worked nimbly at the seal she had applied.

"*Really* hurry!"

"I put this seal in place to keep us alive, not counter a hostile boarding," she hissed back at him as her hands flew. "I made it to *last*. Don't expect me to take it apart in a couple of minutes! Does this look like I'm *taking my*—"

"Chewie, we're home," Finn heard a man say. Then the covering in the deck above them was ripped away. Hands raised in surrender, hoping that the least they could expect was not to be shot out of hand, they found themselves gazing up at . . . not a stormtrooper.

The man holding the blaster on them was not wearing a helmet; not even a protective visor. There was nothing to interfere with his angry expression. It filled a face scarred with know-how, aged by experience, and world-weary—characteristic of someone who had set foot on dozens of worlds. His eyes were hazel, his gray hair tousled, and he wore the look of a man who had seen too much, too soon, and been forced to deal with idiots all too often. His evident age notwithstanding, the hand holding the blaster neither shook nor wavered. Eying him, Finn felt he knew the type if not the man. His only fear then was that the man might shoot first and ask questions later. Thankfully, he did not.

"Where are the others?" While there might be cracks in the man's countenance, there were none in his voice. "Where's your pilot?"

Hands still raised, Rey gulped. Who was this hard-faced intruder, and where were the First Order stormtroopers? "I—I'm the pilot."

Unblinking eyes regarded her with obvious disbelief. "*You?*"

She nodded. "It's just us." She nodded once to her left. "Us and a droid."

A second shape appeared above and beside their inquisitor. It was likewise most definitely not a stormtrooper. It was also much, much bigger than its blaster-wielding companion. A battery of sounds issued from between thick lips, something halfway between a moan and a question.

"No, it's true," Rey responded. "We're the only ones on board."

Finn gaped at her. "Wait—you can *understand* that thing?"

Beating Rey to a response, the man holding the blaster on them warned, "And 'that thing' can understand you, so *watch* it." Still aiming the weapon in their direction, he stepped back. "Get outta there. Come on up. No funny stuff. We're watching you." His attention focused on Rey, he almost smiled. When he did, there was a hint of something half playful in his demeanor. But only a hint. And there was nothing whatsoever lighthearted about the blaster he kept pointed in their direction.

As he emerged from the service corridor, Finn found himself looking up at the man's companion. And up, and up.

Impatiently, their captor gestured ever so slightly with the muzzle of his blaster. "Where'd you find this ship?"

"Right here." She saw no reason not to tell the truth. "I mean, down on the surface. Niima Outpost, to be specific."

Dropping his lower jaw to signify his disbelief, he stared back at her. "*Jakku?* That junkyard?"

"*Thank you!*" Finn said. "Junkyard!" His original opinion confirmed, he shot Rey a look that was pure I-told-you-so.

Looking away from them for the first time since they had emerged from below, their captor addressed his towering cohort. "*Told* ya we should've double-checked the Western Reaches! Just lucky we were in the general vicinity when the ship powered up and its beacon snapped on." He turned back to Rey. She was trying to make sense of the mismatched pair standing before her and failing utterly.

"Who had it?" he continued. "Ducain?"

Again, she thought: no reason to prevaricate. "I stole it from a salvage dealer named Unkar Plutt."

Brows narrowed as the weathered visage wrinkled even more. "From who?"

"Look." Taking a chance, Rey lowered her hands so she could spread her arms wide. "I don't know all the details for sure. I'm not privy to Plutt's private accounting. But talk says that Plutt stole this ship from the Irving Boys, who stole it from Ducain."

"Who stole it from *me*!"

In addition to anger, their captor's voice was filled with righteous indignation. To Rey, it sounded a little forced. Definitely this man was not now and never had been a stormtrooper or anything like it. What he had been, maybe, was someone not unlike herself. A bit of a businessman, a bit of a con man, a bit of an adventurer. And since he was older, it was only reasonable to assume that he had been a bit more of all of those things than herself. What his intentions toward them were she could not yet guess. But the fact that he didn't know who Unkar Plutt was was definitely a plus on his side. He would be unlikely to immediately turn them over or try to sell them to someone he didn't know. Where he stood in relation to the First Order remained to be seen. Thus far, at least, he didn't strike her as someone overly interested in politics.

Her hurried speculation as to their captor's possible motives was interrupted when he took a step toward her. Finn tensed, but neither the blaster nor the man's free hand came up.

"Well, you tell him when you see him again, you tell him that Han Solo just stole back the *Millennium Falcon* for good!"

Whirling, he holstered his blaster and headed for the cockpit, his lofty associate at his side. Either he was satisfied with her answers, Rey thought, or else he didn't care. With his back to them as he headed in the opposite direction, neither Finn nor Rey caught the change of expression from the suggestion of a smile that had threatened to crack his heated glare to a wide, contented grin. Not that it mattered. It wasn't his countenance that awed them: It was his name.

Han Solo.

A legend of the Rebellion against the Empire. Trader, pirate, con man, and fighter extraordinaire. It was hard to believe he was real, Finn thought. Solo was history come to life.

No longer under the gun, or even restrained, and abandoned in the lounge as if their presence was less than insignificant, Rey and Finn exchanged a look.

"What now?" Finn gestured in the direction of the corridor that led to the cockpit. "He—he just left us here."

"We could wait for one of them to come back," she suggested.

He nodded slowly. "Yes, we could do that. Just sit here and wait."

Without another word they broke for the cockpit.

VIII

FINN AND REY CAUGHT UP TO THE UNLIKELY pair in the corridor. Wanting desperately to confront their captor—if captor was what he was, considering that he wasn't acting much like one—Finn struggled to get past the hairy bipedal mountain that was blocking his path. Said mountain ignored Finn's feeble efforts to push his way past.

Having managed to sidle past on the other side, Rey could hardly contain her incredulity. "This is *the Millennium Falcon*? I didn't—I didn't make the connection when we stole—when we came on board." She could not keep herself from staring at the pilot. After all, it wasn't every day in the galaxy that one met a living legend. In point of fact, it was her first living legend. For a living legend, a part of her mused, his appearance was more than a little disheveled. Almost as much as that of his companion.

"*You're* Han Solo," she said, looking askance.

This time instead of a smile, a grin: part amused, part knowing, and maybe a little bit bitter. "I used to be."

Finn found himself equally dumbstruck. Here right before him, close enough to touch, was a celebrated

figure from the ancient past. Well, he corrected himself, from the fractious past, anyway. He doubted the individual who had angrily confronted them with blaster in hand would take kindly to being referred to as *ancient*. And the looming mass of wailing hirsuteness who was his companion . . . what was his name? He searched his memory and what he knew of history. *Slew*—something, that was it. No, he corrected himself. That didn't fit as a name for a—what was the species called? Ookie? Again he fought to recall.

Chewbacca. Chewbacca the Wookiee. And Han Solo. *The* Han Solo. Or else a pair of extremely accomplished liars. Though if what he could remember was accurate, accomplished liar would fit *the* Han Solo as well as anything else.

No harm in probing further, Finn told himself. It wasn't as if he and Rey were going anywhere. Not now.

"Han Solo?" he queried hesitantly. "The Rebellion general?"

"No," Rey broke in, half accusingly, half admiringly. "The smuggler!"

"Huh?" If he had been bemused before, Finn was now thoroughly bewildered. Without thinking, he addressed the shaggy mass lumbering along in front of him. "Wasn't he a war hero? In the fight against the Old Empire?"

Though the Wookiee uttered something guttural and incomprehensible, Finn thought he managed to catch the gist of it. Something along the lines of "Yeah—I guess—kinda . . ." Of course, the giant could equally have been confirming what Rey had said. Having no way of knowing whether his intuition or the girl's identification was correct, he trailed along in confusion. It did not occur to him that both might be equally accurate.

Rey could not keep from looking around, seeing the ship she had stolen in an entirely new light. No wonder it was crammed full of modifications! No wonder it had demonstrated unusual speed and maneuverability.

"*The Millennium Falcon.*" She could not keep the wonder out of her voice. "This is the ship that made the Kessel Run in fourteen parsecs."

"*Twelve* parsecs." Entering the cockpit ahead of the others, Han scanned the console. A wave of something washed over the *Millennium Falcon*'s rightful owner. Not nostalgia. That wasn't part of his makeup. But there was definitely something. Possibly remembrance of old friendships, or adventures long past, or exotic destinations once visited. Most likely the financial opportunities missed. Moving forward, he let his hands rest on the main console as his eyes continued to rove from instrument to monitor to . . .

What the devil was *that*?

Moving slightly to his right, he touched a couple of contacts and was rewarded with a readout that was anything but pleasing.

"Hey! Some moof-milker installed a compressor on the ignition line!"

"Unkar Plutt did." Rey saw Finn shoot her a look and she glanced away, abashed. "I'd spent some time poking around all the ships parked at the outpost. Mostly at night. It was a way to learn some things. I was careful, and nobody much cared anyway, since I never took anything or tried anything." She brightened. "Made it a lot easier when we filched this one. Though it wasn't my first choice."

Han nodded knowingly. "I can relate to that. What halfwit puts a compressor on an ignition line?"

She nodded in agreement. "I thought it was a mis-

take, too. Puts too much stress on the hyperdrive flow."

". . . Stress on the hyperdrive flow," Han echoed, reaching the same conclusion at the same time. For an instant he looked puzzled and just a tad curious. Who was this girl, who spoke so knowledgeably of flow rates and ignition pressures? His curiosity didn't last long. Too many other matters of greater consequence were on his mind.

"Chewie, put 'em in a pod and send them back to Jakku. Or anywhere else local they want to go."

"Wait, no!" Rey moved toward him. A stern stare halted her in her tracks but could not silence her. "We need your help!"

His brow wrinkled. "*My* help . . ."

Holding her ground, she indicated the silently watching BB-8. "This droid has to get to the nearest Resistance base as soon as possible. He's carrying a map that leads to the present location of Luke Skywalker!"

The strangest look came over the *Falcon*'s owner. In an instant and in response to Rey's distressed request, all the hardness seemed to drain out of him. For a moment he was no longer on the ship. He was not even in Jakku's system, but somewhere else. Unable to stand the lack of response, Finn spoke up.

"You *are* the Han Solo who fought with the Rebellion? If so, then you knew him."

"Knew him?" The flinty stare had gone hazy, the strong voice soft. "Yeah, I knew Luke."

"Well, then," Finn continued, "maybe you could—"

He broke off as a distant but distinct metallic *thunk* reached them inside the *Falcon*. Snapping back to the present, Han was all business again as he scowled in the direction of the ship's loading ramp.

"Well, that tears it. Don't tell me a rathtar's gotten

loose." Without another word he vacated the cockpit, hurrying back the way he'd come. Everyone else followed, with BB-8 bringing up the rear. Neither Rey nor the droid had the slightest idea what was going on. Finn did, and wished he didn't. Though he'd never seen a rathtar, he knew a little something about the species. A little, he knew, was more than enough. He had to struggle to keep up with the *Falcon*'s owner, who moved with surprising speed. Not unlike his ship, the trooper realized.

"Wait, wait," he implored the older man.

Ignoring him, Han exited the *Falcon* onto one of the service decks of the enormous freighter and headed directly for the nearest control panel.

"Hold up now. I need to be sure what you said. A *what's* gotten loose?"

"Rathtar," Han replied curtly.

"No." Finn was shaking his head. "You're not hauling rathtars."

Han spoke without breaking stride. "I'm hauling rathtars."

Materializing within and above the console, a host of images revealed both the interior and exterior of the hulking freighter. One of the latter revealed the approach of a nonmilitary transport. The sleek craft nudged its way along the hull, like a parasite hunting for an easy way into a potential host. Not recognizing the ship's design, Finn focused on Han instead. The pilot's expression showed that he was not pleased.

"You recognize the arrival," Finn said. It was not a question. "From the look on your face, I can tell that you wish you didn't."

"You could say that," Han replied. "It's the Guavian Death Gang." He looked over at the Wookiee, who moaned confirmation. "Yeah. They must've tracked us from Nantoon. You'd think traveling through hyper-

space you could throw people off. Not these guys. That's never good. They're persistent. I hate that."

"Hate what?"

Han didn't look at him. "When someone who wants to kill us *finds* us." Abandoning the cockpit, he and the Wookiee headed off toward a circular corridor opening. Once again, Finn and Rey found themselves reduced to following.

"What's a rathtar?" Rey asked Finn. They were now hurrying down a passageway that had, like the rest of the lumbering freighter, seen better times. Splashes of paint and old stain substituted for more efficient indicators, while unidentifiable crates and piles of gear were piled haphazardly in corners and against the walls.

It was Han who replied first. "You want the scientific description? They're big and dangerous and ugly."

"O-kaaay," she responded. "Why would anyone want something big, dangerous, and ugly? *Who* would want something big, dangerous, and ugly? And be willing to pay for it?"

Where the hell was that accessway? Han wondered. Girl sure had a lot of questions. "People have funny hobbies," he explained as he kept moving fast. "Some are collectors. There are those who collect different kinds of galactic currencies, some who collect old liquor containers, a few who like to accumulate holos of famous entertainers. Seems like the more money they have, the bigger the things they like to collect. There are even a handful who like to collect biological specimens. Those with money collect live ones. Those without money become scientists." He gestured and they turned a corner.

Finn moved closer to Rey. "I know of a perfect example that explains everything you'd ever want to

know about rathtars." She eyed him expectantly. "Ever hear of the Trillia Massacre?"

She shook her head. "No."

"Good," he replied. And that was the extent of his explanation, briefly referencing an incident so vile and depraved that he wished only to assure himself she knew nothing about it.

"So," she continued, turning her attention back to Han, who at least seemed willing to explicate a little, "you're carrying these rathtars to a collector?"

He nodded. "I got three going to King Prana. Kings not only like to collect, they like to boast about their collections. Seems Prana's in competition with the regent of the Mol'leaj system. The regent doesn't have a rathtar in his private zoo. Neither does anybody else."

"There's a reason for that," Finn muttered.

"So I got this contract to get some for Prana. Three. It was difficult work. I'm expecting a bonus, and I'm not ready to give it all up just because of the Guavian Death Gang."

"Three!" Finn could hardly believe what he was hearing. "How'd you get them on board?"

Han looked over at him. "I could tell you that Chewie and I got a bunch of their favorite food, tied it to a stick, and led them into the holding bay. But that would be a lie. Let's just say I used to have a bigger crew."

Striding effortlessly alongside, Chewbacca groaned assent. Behind Finn, BB-8 beeped a question to which the Wookiee readily replied. Droid and Wookiee then entered into a rapid-fire conversation, the sound of which made Finn's head hurt.

He was wondering why Han called a halt in the middle of an unremarkable section of corridor until their guide activated a hidden wall control and a

hatch opened in the floor. He gestured for them to descend.

"Get below deck until I say so. Don't go wandering around: This ship is big enough to get lost in, and there are areas you don't want to go." He smiled thinly. "Some of the cargo would be glad to see you, but you wouldn't want to see it. And don't even think about trying to take the *Falcon*."

Rey indicated the waiting droid. "What about Beebee-Ate?"

"He'll stay with me. If he's that important to you, that'll ensure you don't try anything funny. I'm still not sure I buy your story."

Finn felt a little chill. Fooling the girl had been easy enough, but this was *Han Solo*. Make one mistake, say one wrong thing, and he was liable to find himself not just challenged but dumped outside—without an atmosphere suit. He was going to have to watch his words more carefully than ever. If Han found out that he had a stormtrooper in his midst . . .

No, Finn corrected himself. Ex-stormtrooper. FN-2187 was dead. He was *Finn,* and no longer a fighter for the First Order. Why, the best pilot in the Resistance could testify on his behalf! If only he were alive . . .

Halfway down the hatch stairway, Rey paused to look back. "What happens now?"

Han's attitude softened slightly. "When I get rid of the gang, you can have your droid back and be on your way." He glanced across at BB-8. "I'm used to dealing with droids."

"The rathtars." Finn couldn't keep from asking. "Where are you keeping them?"

A thunderous *wham* sounded behind him and he jumped, stumbling toward the open hatch. Behind an oversize, triple-reinforced port, an orange orb ap-

peared. Finn assumed it was just an eye of some kind, but it was still big, dangerous, and ugly. Finn's heart slammed against his chest.

"Well, there's one," Han said nonchalantly. "Or part of one, anyway." For a second time something massive rammed against the opposite wall, and the deck shuddered under their feet. "Not real bright, rathtars. You'd think by this time they'd have figured out they can't break out of their holding compartments, but they've been banging away at the walls ever since Chewie and I got them on board. They don't seem to get tired."

"Maybe they just want food." Finn had managed to calm himself.

Han cocked an eye at him. "You volunteering?"

For an instant, Finn wondered if their guide was being more than half serious. Then Han smiled. "Don't worry. I don't think a rathtar would eat you anyway. You're not their natural prey. Take you apart piece by piece and stomp on the pieces, yes. But not eat you. Now get below. And keep *quiet*."

"What are *you* gonna do?" Rey asked from the opening. "I've never heard of a Guavian Death Gang, but it doesn't sound like something one man can handle." She nodded toward Chewbacca. "Not even one man and a Wookiee."

Han shrugged. "Same thing I always do. Talk my way out of it." At this his towering companion uttered a series of short, sharp moans and grunts. Han frowned up at him. "That is *so* unfair! Come on." Again the countervailing moaning. "Of course I do— so far." They started down the corridor back the way they had come, arguing all the way.

"Yes, I do," Rey and Finn heard Han saying as he and Chewbacca turned the far corner. "Every time."

They were alone in the sub-deck accessway. Except,

Finn reminded himself uneasily, for the ravening monstrosity on the other side of the near wall. Thankfully, it had ceased its fruitless attempts to break free.

"What now?" he heard himself asking.

Standing in the hatch opening, Rey peered downward. "We follow his instructions. After all, he's Han Solo. He must know what he's doing."

Han's thoughts were working overtime as he and Chewie headed toward the cargo bay where the Guavian ship was most likely to have gained entrance. On a warship, or even on the *Falcon,* controls could have been activated to keep them out. But the lumbering freighter presently in his charge had thoughtfully, and unfortunately, been equipped with instrumentation allowing unhampered access from the outside. It was a safety measure, designed and installed to ensure that in the event some fool crew locked themselves outside the ship, they could always get back in. A useful abettor that at this particular moment he deeply regretted.

Not that the Guavians, if denied entrance, would have hesitated to blast their way in. At least this way the big freighter wasn't damaged. As for that happening to him and Chewie, it remained to be seen.

No problem, he kept repeating to himself. *You've done this a hundred times before, with everything from helpers to Hutts. Just stay calm and collected and baffle them with space dust.*

They never made it to the cargo bay. In fact, they didn't have to look for the gang, because the gang found them. He and Chewie had hardly left Rey and Finn behind when a circular portal opened in the corridor ahead to admit six figures, all humanoid: five members of a helmeted, red-uniformed security team

and one man in a suit. Han recognized Bala-Tik immediately: confident, experienced, and, at the moment, all but bursting with barely controlled anger. Inclining his head slightly toward his companion, Han whispered confidently.

"I got this. Leave it to me."

Chewbacca coughed something not repeatable in polite Wookiee company.

"Han Solo," came the clipped voice of the gang leader, "you are a dead man."

Not a very promising beginning, Han had to admit. Not that he had expected anything else. The gang leader wasn't one to waste time on false pleasantries. Smiling broadly, he nodded back.

"Bala-Tik! Welcome aboard. Always good to see an old business associate. What's the problem?"

His visitor was not amused. "The problem is we loaned you fifty thousand for this job."

Peering through the grated hatch cover, Finn strained to hear what was transpiring down the corridor.

"Can you see them?" an anxious Rey asked.

. He shook his head. "No. They're too far away. I can hear that they're talking, but I can't make out the words. At least they aren't shooting at each other. Yet."

Rey considered. "If they found Han and Chewbacca this quickly inside a ship this big, that suggests they've got at least short-range life-form detectors. Which means if one of them starts wondering about the possible existence of other crew members, they might find us." She looked around. "We'll be safe enough here because we're close to one of the rathtars, but if they start parsing readouts, they'll separate us out from the cargo." She nodded up the service crawl space. "I'm not gonna sit here and wait to be

pried out like a mithuk in a burrow. The *Falcon* is this direction." She started moving.

Finn hesitated. "Han specifically said not to think about taking the *Falcon*."

She looked back at him. "He's talking to a Guavian Death Gang. It's not inconceivable that polite conversation might turn into uncontrolled blaster fire. If that happens and Han is on the losing end, I'd like to have a chance to avoid the consequences. Like maybe being fed to the rathtars. Coming?"

"Right behind you," he replied with alacrity. Together they started moving fast along the crawl space.

Han smiled while spinning a ready response, having already anticipated Bala-Tik's likely reaction. "Sure, right. Fifty thousand. A modest investment on which you're going to make a big, fat profit. Don't all my business enterprises pay off?"

"No," the Guavian gang leader replied curtly.

Han spread his hands wide. "Sure they do! I've never lost money on a single venture."

"Yes, you have." Bala-Tik was relentless.

"Hey, everybody who does business with me gets their money back even if I lose."

"No, they don't." Relentless *and* cold. Cold as only the head of a Guavian Death Gang can be.

Han responded with an exaggerated shake of his head and looked up at the Wookiee. "Can you believe this, Chewie? Out of the goodness of my heart and respect for everything this person represents, *I* bring to *him* the investment of the year, and all he can do is mock me!" He returned his attention to the silent Bala-Tik. "I expect thanks and all I get are insults. I didn't have to come to you, you know. I could have gone to anyone with this deal and they would have jumped at

the chance to get in on it. But no: I offered it to *you*. And this is my thanks?" His tone turned challenging. "What is it, Bala-Tik? Don't you want your cut of the proceeds?"

"I want my fifty thousand back," the gang leader snapped.

Han rolled his eyes. "Fine, fine! If that's the way you want it."

"Kanjiklub also wants their fifty thousand back."

Han gaped at him. "What?"

"Kanjiklub," Bala-Tik repeated calmly. "You also borrowed fifty thousand from them."

Han strove to remain calm, though he could not prevent a bit of the color draining from his face. "That's a lie! Who told you that?"

"Kanjiklub," Bala-Tik replied without twitching so much as an eyelash.

Han turned a disbelieving circle, his voice filled with outrage. "Oh, come on! You can't trust those little freaks!"

Quiet crawling up the corridor serviceway had brought Finn and Rey to a position below and dangerously close to the intruders. At least, Finn told himself, they could now see and hear what was going on.

"They have blasters," she whispered.

Finn nodded. "A lot of 'em."

Above, Han continued the dialogue. "C'mon, Bala—how long have we known each other?"

The gang leader was not about to be inveigled by smooth chatter. Especially not when large loaned sums were involved. "The question is how much longer *will* we know each other? Not long, I think. Unless we get our money back. And we want it back *now*."

"The rathtars are here, on board this ship," Han shot back. "I know it's taken a little longer than I promised—"

"Way longer," Bala-Tik cut in. "Too much longer."

"—but I've got 'em, and King Prana is just waiting—no, he's *eager*—to pay. Just be a little patient. You'll get your money back, plus the promised profit."

Bala-Tik was growing impatient. "Says you. That is what you said when you borrowed the money. That is what you have been saying via communicator for some time now. Then you went silent. Failed to answer all communications."

"I was busy," an exasperated Han informed him, "collecting rathtars."

"So you say. In the absence of any communication, we did not know what you were doing. With our money. We suspected the worst."

Han smiled afresh. "And now you know the truth. You're here, I'm here, and the rathtars for King Prana are here. You think it's cheap hunting rathtars? I spent that money. I *used* that money. Just let me make delivery and you'll have your investment back. Come with me if you want."

The gang leader's gaze narrowed. "Come with you? Try to follow you in hyperspace? So that you can lose us, take a roundabout route to King Prana, collect all the money, and disappear again? I think not. I don't trust you anymore, Solo." He indicated his men. "*We* don't trust you. So give us our money back. Kanjiklub wants their investment back, too."

Han's reply was replete with frustration. "I told you: I never made a deal with Kanjiklub!"

Bala-Tik gave an indifferent shrug. "Tell that to Kanjiklub." He nodded, looking past Han and Chewbacca.

Both peered back the way they had come. At the other end of the same corridor, another portal opened. An additional clutch of armed intruders appeared, whereupon Han's face lost another bit of color. Though

the newcomers differed greatly in appearance from the Guavians, he recognized them immediately from their patchwork armor and heavy gear.

Kanjiklub cohorts.

Their leader, a long-haired, grim-faced, and thoroughly disreputable individual wanted on at least six worlds, emerged from the group to confront him. For the second time in all too short a while, Han greeted an unwelcome boarder with a smile as wide as it was bogus.

"Tasu Leech! Good to see you!"

Han knew perfectly well that Tasu Leech would never deign to speak Basic, so he was not surprised when the man replied in another language—one with which Han was, fortunately, familiar. "Wrong again, Solo. It's over for you, and for your associate." Raising the weapon he held, Leech aimed it down the corridor.

Chewbacca growled a response, causing Han to mutter under his breath.

"Not *now*, Chewie! That won't help." Han took a deep breath. "Guys! You're all gonna get what I promised. The merchandise is here, the buyer is waiting. I just need to make the delivery. Have I ever not delivered for you before?"

Moving his hands deliberately and slowly, Tasu Leech made a show of activating his weapon. "Twice."

Han frowned. Leech was correct, of course, but Han wasn't about to admit it. "Twice?"

"Your game is old," Bala-Tik called out from the other end of the corridor. "You've played it too many times. Your excuses wore thin many years ago. So many times, so many excuses. Everyone knows them now. I stand here before you and can recite in my head the excuses you are going to make before you yourself can speak them. You are tired, Han Solo.

Tired and old, just like your game. There is no one in the galaxy left for you to swindle."

"Nowhere left for you to hide," added Leech, not to be outdone. "Usually a senile old fool knows when to retire. But sometimes he simply needs to be retired." He started to raise his weapon.

"Wait!" Something had caught Bala-Tik's attention. Taking a couple of steps forward, he peered between Han and Chewbacca. The short, spherical shape sitting there moved slightly to its right, trying to stay hidden behind the Wookiee. "That BB unit—chatter says that the First Order is looking for one just like it. Accompanied by two fugitives."

Han was remarkably indifferent. "First I've heard of it."

Below, straining for a better look, Rey sought purchase on a transition bar. Unfortunately, it was old and weak. Under her weight, it broke free, fell just out of reach of her fingers, and clanged against the floor.

Everyone on the decking above reacted instantly to the sound. Tasu Leech's second-in-command, an unlovely character named Razoo Qin-Fee, stepped forward.

"Search the freighter," Bala-Tik ordered.

Activating an illuminator, another of the Kanji group started down the corridor, aiming the light into every crack, transparent panel, and opening in the walls and floor.

Rey and Finn started moving fast, away from the searchlight and along the crawl space. "We could die here," Rey said.

"That's possible." Finn kept up with her. "In fact, given the present circumstances, I'd say it's almost likely."

"That's right," she muttered back at him. "Try to be optimistic."

He gestured upward. "We don't have weapons, we're relying on the fast talk of an old smuggler who may or may not have been a Rebellion general, and we're trapped between a bunch of homicidal Kanjiklubbers and a Guavian Death Gang. Excuse me if I don't sound optimistic."

"Keep moving!" she snapped. "Maybe we'll get lucky."

"We'd better," he muttered in reply, "because we sure don't have anything else going for us."

Initially prepared to shoot Solo down where he stood, Bala-Tik now found himself desirous of the answers to a few questions. There was no rush to kill the smuggler and the Wookiee. They were trapped in the corridor and weren't going anywhere.

"Be cooperative, Solo, and maybe we can work something out."

Handed a lifeline, however short, Han was grateful for a chance to stall for time. "What do you want to know, Bala? Like I said, I don't know anything about the Order's interest in a BB model or some suspected fugitives."

"Okay then," the gang leader replied. "We'll keep it simple. Where'd you get the droid?"

"He's mine, that's where." Han met Bala-Tik's stare evenly.

The gang leader was not intimidated. Nor was he pleased.

"I am afraid that is not a satisfactory answer." He smiled dangerously. "As you say, Han, we have known each other a long while. In all that time I have never known you to frequent the company of droids, of whatever station or model. Certainly not to be so protective of one."

"Who says I'm being protective of it?"

Bala-Tik gestured. "It tries to conceal itself behind you."

Looking back, Han nudged the droid with a leg but failed to shift BB-8 from its position. "I don't care where it puts itself. It doesn't take much to frighten a droid, Bala."

The gang leader nodded agreement. "Especially one that might be wanted by the First Order."

As Han and the gang leader argued, Rey halted her retreat so abruptly than Finn nearly crashed into her.

"Now what?" he asked. "Please tell me you've stumbled over a couple of pulse rifles."

She was staring at a section of wall. "Maybe something even better." She tapped the cover that protected a slight bulge in the wall. "If this is a flow panel for this corridor, I might be able to manually disrupt the programming. That would trip the emergency sequence and drop all the blast doors in this section. We can trap both gangs!"

Finn considered. "Shut the blast doors from down here? Won't that trap Han and Chewbacca, as well?"

She was excited now. "Yes, but they'll be separated from the gangs. We can work out how to get them out *after* we've neutralized the Guavians and the Kanjis. Redirecting the flow should do it. It doesn't matter to what level: All we want to do is bring down the blast doors."

He nodded enthusiastically. "Let's do it. What've we got to lose?"

She opened the panel, exposing the intricate flow-tronics within, and set to work. Tools would have made it easier, but the system was designed to be set and reset as easily as possible. Finn lent a hand, following her lead.

Above, Bala-Tik was out of questions and out of patience. "Enough banter."

"Bantha? Now you want a bantha?" Han asked. "What, three rathtars aren't enough for you?"

"We're going to take that droid," Bala-Tik told him firmly. "And you're going to give us our money back."

"Or your dead body." Razoo Qin-Fee spoke as he continued to ply the corners of the corridor with his illuminator. "Your choice, Solo."

Members of both gangs laughed. Han laughed with them, albeit uncomfortably. Even if he could keep Bala-Tik talking, the Kanjis were notoriously poor listeners. And he was about out of clever things to say.

That was when the lights began to flicker. Laughter faded as Kanji and Guavian alike regarded the now sporadic illumination with uncertainty. Distant components cycling on and off filled the corridor with a clicking and gnashing like the cries of a thousand mechanical insects. Han's eyes widened. With Chewie moaning beside him, he murmured softly.

"I got a bad feeling about this."

Abruptly, the illumination in the corridor returned to life brighter than ever. Below, Rey leaned back from the now modified flow panel.

"Uh oh."

Finn looked from her to the panel and back again. "Uh oh, what?"

She turned to him, slightly pale. "Uh oh, wrong reflow. I didn't close anything. I opened everything."

He leaned close to the exposed panel, studying the interior lines. "Can you put it back the way it was?"

She shook her head rapidly. "I purposely locked the

reset so that if there was a corresponding panel anywhere in the corridor itself, nobody could undo it and
raise the blast doors. Except they're not going to close
now—and everything else is going to raise up."

Finn stared at her, one thought in his mind, one
word on his lips.

"*Rathtars.*"

IX

"ENOUGH OF THIS," BALA-TIK SNARLED. HE looked back at his men. "New plan! Kill them and take the droid!"

Weapons came up. Han and Chewbacca looked around wildly, but in the smooth-sided corridor there was nowhere to run, nowhere to hide. Han closed his eyes.

Which was when something monstrous appeared behind the Guavians. It was so large it could barely fit in the cargo corridor. Tentacles whipped out to snatch up two of the gang, who screamed as their torsos were crushed. Whirling, howling, those who were still able to do so unleashed wild bursts of fire in the direction of their attacker. Those that struck the rathtar barely caused it to flinch. Wisely, Bala-Tik and the survivors scattered.

Han opened one eye. Turning, he expected the burst of Guavian fire that had failed to reach him to be replaced by a similar barrage from the Kanjiklub members. Except that another rathtar had appeared behind them and, roaring deafeningly, was busily taking the aliens apart. Chewbacca let out a series of short, clipped moans.

"No kidding!" Han yelled. "Come on!" Together, they raced for a side corridor. Under the guns and watchful eyes of both gangs, they never would have made it. But all remaining guns and surviving eyes were, at present, otherwise occupied.

As misdirected blasts smashed into the crawl space around them, tearing streaks in the metal and threatening to make it impossible to move across the overheating floor, Finn and Rey found themselves crawling for their lives.

"That was a mistake!" Finn howled, ignoring the pain in his hands and knees.

"*Huge!*" Rey agreed.

Above, Han nearly ran into one of the Guavians. Fleeing from the rathtar behind him while shooting fruitlessly at the monster, the Guavian never saw Han and Chewie—though he did make the acquaintance of Han's fist. Staggering, he tried to bring his gun to bear on the new threat, only to be sent flying toward the rathtar by the strong arms of the Wookiee. One tentacle caught the unlucky gang member before he could hit the ground.

"Other direction," Han blurted. Chewie moaned while BB-8 beeped frantically. Finding instant agreement in three different languages, they took an accessway that was, for the moment at least, devoid of Guavians, Kanjis, and rathtars.

Elsewhere, Razoo Qin-Fee scuttled past a pair of Guavians who were racing full bore in the opposite direction. Their haste gave him pause, which enabled him to hail a fellow Kanjiklub member coming toward him—just before a tentacle emerged in that individual's wake to grab him and wrench him out of sight. Deciding that the two Guavians who had just passed him going like hell in the other direction might have a better handle on the situation, Razoo whirled

and retraced his steps. This brought him back to two surviving members of his own group. A hasty discussion determined they should avoid both ends of the corridor. Accordingly, they turned down another passageway—whereupon the third rathtar grabbed the pair who had just counseled Razoo. He fired at the creature, with the same ineffectual result as before, and raced away.

It was a big ship, he told himself. There *had* to be a place somewhere that was safe from the escaped rathtars. On the other hand, if the rathtars were between him and his own ship, he might never get off alive. Working cooperatively, as a pack, the carnivores would hunt him down along with every one of his companions. That was the thing about rathtars: While they acted like mindless eating machines and didn't have very large brains, they were really good at working together. And fast. It was hard to believe how fast something that size could move.

No, he was dead for sure, unless he could somehow circle around them and back to where his ship was docked. As he ran, terrified of what he might encounter around the next corner or in the next corridor over, his only solace came from the knowledge that that unspeakable sack of treachery Han Solo was certain to meet the same fate, and in the jaws of his own cargo.

It was small consolation, but in his present dire situation, he clung to it.

A tentative Finn flipped open a hatch and looked down the brightly lit corridor. Nothing. Turning, he looked in the other direction. Nothing. No evilly chattering Kanjiklub members, no heavily armed Guavians, and most important, no slobbering multi-limbed rathtars. He climbed out, giving Rey a hand up, and pointed.

"*Falcon*'s this way!"

She hesitated. "You sure?"

"No! But we can't stay here and wait for Kanji-klubbers and Guavians. We've got to try *something*."

He was thankful but hardly surprised to see how easily she kept up with him as they raced for a far corner. Surviving as a scavenger on Jakku ensured that she was in at least as good physical condition as the average trooper.

"These rathtars?" she was asking him. "What do they look like?"

Rounding the corner, they were brought up short by the sight of surviving gang members doing battle with the subject of her query. It was enormous and round, covered in light-sensitive orange orbs, and composed mostly of tentacles and teeth. Raising one hand to her mouth, she caught her breath, simultaneously mesmerized and horrified by the sight.

"They look like that." Finn reached over and took her arm, not caring this time if she objected. Back the way they had come, around another corner—only this time they didn't stop fast enough.

One tentacle whipped around Finn's waist, and moving with incredible speed for something so massive, the rathtar rushed off with the screaming trooper in its grasp.

"*FINN!*"

Though it was too big for her and too fast, she gave chase anyway.

Fighting in a desperate attempt to break free, Finn realized he might as well have been wrestling with a steel cable. Neither pounding on it with his fists nor kicking at it with his drawn-up legs produced the slightest reaction on the creature's part. He even resorted to trying to take a bite out of it. The hard, rubbery flesh proved impenetrable. At that moment

he would have given a limb for a blaster, even though small-arms fire had shown itself to be largely ineffectual against the monsters.

"Finn!"

Not only had Rey lost sight of him, but now the rathtar had moved so far ahead she could no longer hear Finn's shouts for help. It was a futile exercise anyway. Suppose she did catch up? The rathtar had more than enough appendages with which to sweep her into its grasp without letting go of Finn. Still, she kept running, keeping an eye out for anything that could be of use.

SUBSIDIARY BAY CONTROL ROOM

She'd run all the way past the door before the full meaning of the words struck home. Halting, she ran back and slammed an open palm over the access panel. For an awful moment nothing happened and she was afraid that the relevant system was down. Then the door slid aside, admitting her.

Ignoring entire banks of instrumentation, she made her way to a set of multiple monitors. Not only was the system not down, it was fully activated. There were clear views of motionless cargo, empty storage rooms, the *Millennium Falcon,* both the Guavian and Kanjiklub vessels, and . . .

Finn, being dragged down a main corridor by the rathtar. Dragged toward an empty intersection.

One hand over the pertinent control, she leaned toward the monitor, watching, waiting, hoping that it would respond faster than the door that had led to this control room. *Wait,* she told herself, suspecting that if she blew the opportunity she might not get another. Or at least not another where she would have a chance to recover Finn in one piece.

Slowing, the rathtar edged forward, checking both cross corridors. No wonder they were so dangerous, she told herself as she kept her attention locked on the monitor. Reassured, the creature started forward again, dragging the increasingly weakened Finn behind it.

Her hand came down on the control. An indicator flipped from green to red. On the monitor, a blast door descended with gratifying speed. The rathtar reacted almost immediately—but not quite fast enough to prevent one of its tentacles from being severed by the emergency door. The tentacle, she had calculated, that was gripping Finn.

The shriek of pain and fury from the rathtar was horrible to hear. She paid it hardly any attention as she watched a dazed Finn struggle to his feet and commence fighting to extricate himself from the still-clinging piece of amputated limb.

Stunned by his unexpected escape, he was free of it by the time she arrived. "It didn't get you," he said unnecessarily. "It had me!" He turned around. "But there was a blast door, came down at just the right moment . . ."

"Lucky," she told him. "Which way did you say the *Falcon* was?"

For a moment he eyed her uncertainly, unable to quite escape the feeling that there was something she wasn't telling him. No time for questions now, though. He pointed.

"That way—I hope."

In another corridor Bala-Tik was talking to one of his gang's surviving members. "That thing's taken two of my men." As he said it, a tentacle slipped forward to wrap itself around another screaming associate. "Three of my men," the Guavian corrected himself.

If they didn't do something soon, he knew, none

of them would get off this cursed freighter alive. Even as he retreated, firing behind him, he could not keep from wondering how Solo, that worthless dispenser of devious schemes, had managed to pull it off. Capturing even one rathtar was considered a near-impossibility. Impounding *three* and then getting them aboard a ship alive and in good condition stretched all bounds of believability.

Probably, an increasingly desperate Bala-Tik thought as he let off yet another ineffectual blast, Solo had done it by talking all of them into a state of complete insensibility.

At the far end of the main cargo corridor, the object of the Guavian's curses had taken cover together with Chewbacca and BB-8. Demonstrating unexpected determination in the face of rathtar-inspired bedlam, several members of both gangs had continued to pursue. Their persistent fire prevented human, Wookiee, and droid from crossing the cargo-crowded open bay to reach the waiting disc-shaped ship on the other side.

These guys must *really* want their money back, Han thought as he and Chewbacca returned fire with weapons they had recovered from where rathtar-munched Guavians and Kanjis had dropped them.

Having come this far, he was not about to be denied. Sidling around behind the Wookiee, he gestured across the bay deck. "I'll get the door. Cover us."

Moaning assent, Chewbacca let loose a ferocious barrage as Han, also firing, darted across the open space toward the *Falcon*. BB-8 went with him, judiciously choosing to keep the human between himself and the intruders' fire. Once back at his ship, Han methodically activated the portal via the external emergency controls. For the first time in quite a while he felt some relief, as the ramp lowered smoothly.

Turning, he yelled back toward the corridor terminus.

"Chewie, we're in! Come on!"

Letting out a bellow that signified both recognition of Han's call and defiance of their remaining enemies, the Wookiee turned and raced for the waiting ship— only to be hit in the back of a shoulder by a lucky shot from one of the pursuing Guavians. The impact sent him crashing to the deck.

Uttering a quiet curse, Han left BB-8 behind and raced back toward his injured copilot, firing as he ran. A single well-placed shot took down the Guavian who had hit Chewbacca.

"Get up! Chewie, get up!" Striving to divide his attention between the wounded Wookiee and the gang members who were trying to break out of the far corridor, Han got one arm underneath Chewbacca and strained with all his might. It was like trying to lift a mountain. A big, heavy, hairy, smelly, and badly bleeding mountain. One that he would no more leave behind than he would his ship or himself.

Had the gangs been intact, he and Chewbacca never would have made it back to the *Falcon*. There would have been too many guns, too many blasts to avoid. But the intruders had been drastically reduced both in number and capability. The shot that had struck the Wookiee had really been as wild as the others.

Together, Han still supporting the stumbling Chewie, the two of them started up the ramp. At that moment, the last thing either of them expected to hear was a recognizable, friendly voice.

"Han!"

Dodging the greatly reduced fire from the surviving gang members and keeping to cover as much as possible, Rey and Finn made it across the open deck to

reach the *Falcon*. As they raced up the ramp, a grimacing Han gave orders.

"You shut the hatch behind us!" he instructed Rey, who nodded a swift response. To Finn he snapped, "You take care of Chewbacca!" Half slipping free of his burden, half throwing the wounded copilot in Finn's direction, Han charged up the ramp.

Nearly collapsing beneath the Wookiee's weight, Finn manfully did his best to help the moaning Chewbacca stay upright as the two of them staggered the rest of the way up the ramp.

"How do I do that?" the trooper called after the pilot. To no avail. Han didn't answer.

Chewbacca, on the other hand, groaned, bellowed, and chuffed suggestions. Understanding none of them, a willing Finn nonetheless nodded amenably in response to each one.

"That's right . . . for sure . . . yeah, I'll do that . . . no problem." Wincing as the Wookiee stumbled, Finn had to employ every bit of his strength to keep both of them upright.

If he falls on me, he decided worriedly, *it's all over.* Somehow they made it to the medbay. Helping Chewbacca into the padded alcove that served as a bed, Finn eased the Wookiee in and started digging through the boxes of medical equipment that formed a line on the floor. This was something he could do, he knew, feeling considerably less helpless than he had when trying to assist Rey earlier. Every stormtrooper received training in how to deal with battlefield wounds. Hopefully, the Wookiee's shoulder injury wouldn't present any distinctive surprises.

In the cockpit, Han was hitting one control after another, bringing the *Falcon* back on line. With each green telltale that lit up, a little of his own life did, too. He was startled when Rey arrived and, without

waiting for an invitation, settled down in Chewbacca's seat.

"Hey, what are you doing?" He gestured back in the direction of the lounge. "Passengers back there."

Sliding her fingers over console controls, she spoke while barely glancing in his direction. "Unkar—the guy who last had your ship—installed a fuel pump, too. If we don't prime it, we're not going anywhere." She looked across at him sympathetically.

"I hate that guy," Han muttered. "I don't even know him and I hate him."

"No need." Rey continued to bring instrumentation to life on her side of the cockpit. "I'll hate him on your behalf. Meanwhile, you could use a copilot."

Han frowned at her. "I got one. He's back there." Raising his voice, he yelled toward the lounge. *"Right? I've got a copilot?"* A bellow of pain greeted his query.

"C'mon, Chewie: It's just a flesh wound!" Han heard Finn say. This observation prompted further bellowing, considerably more stressed, and carrying with it overtones of something approaching annoyance.

"Fine!" Han shouted back. *"Be that way!"* Han's hands flew over the controls. "Fuel pump's primed. Watch thrust from your end: We're gonna jump to lightspeed."

She knew a lot about ships, all kinds of ships. But in all her studies she had never come across the maneuver he had just proposed.

"From *inside* the hangar? Is that even possible?"

He was wholly at one with the *Falcon* now, focused intently on the instrumentation. "I never answer that question until after I've done it."

Further discussion regarding the viability of making the jump from stationary position to post-lightspeed

was interrupted by something enormous, ravenous, and bilious landing on top of the ship. Heavy thumping penetrated the cockpit, indicating that something was moving in its direction. This was confirmed a moment later by Rey's scream in response to the appearance of a giant radial mouth that all but covered the forward port. The tooth-filled mouth belonged to a rathtar, which, perceiving the presence of living non-rathtars inside the craft, was chewing its damnedest to get at them. Designed to protect against high-velocity meteoric impacts, the port suffered no immediate damage. Rathtars were notably persistent, however, and frustration only led them to redouble their efforts. Like the rest of them, their mouthparts were exceptionally robust. Design or not, Han had no intention of waiting around long enough to see whether the material of which the port was composed was tougher than rathtar dentition.

"This is *not* how I thought this day would go," he muttered. "Shields up, and angle 'em."

Rey worked the controls. "Got it." She glanced over at him. "Pretty muscular shields for a Corellian freighter."

"The Corellians build 'em the way I like 'em." Under his skillful hands, more instrumentation and equipment came on line. "Of course, I have had a little tweaking done here and there. You may not believe it, but there are some people out there who don't like me."

"Hard to imagine," she murmured.

Seeing that the *Falcon* was powering up, a quartet of gang members took a chance in emerging from cover to fire at the ship. Though their shots were handled by the *Falcon*'s shields, the detonations resonated within.

As far as Han could tell, everything was in readi-

ness. There was nothing more to do but try it. He yelled in the direction of the medbay. "Hang on back there! We're leaving—in a hurry!"

Having dealt with the basics of Chewbacca's injury, Finn was rummaging through the depths of the med-kit he'd found in search of something stronger than a primary painkiller.

"No problem!" he called back, fully aware that, based on the preceding events of the day, there was likely to be one. So while expecting nothing less, he kept searching for something to mitigate Chewbacca's distress even as the ship's shields absorbed additional blasts from the Guavians' weapons.

"Come on, baby," Han was murmuring, "don't let me down." He pulled on the main hyperdrive control.

Nothing.

"What?"

Reaching across to his side of the console, Rey calmly activated a control he had not touched and spoke matter-of-factly. "Compressor."

He glared at her, but only for a moment. As he pulled slowly back on the drive control for the second time, he half smiled at her.

An enormous, overpowering *thunder* filled the cargo hangar as the *Falcon*'s engines came to life. In deciding to rush the ship, the surviving gang members had chosen an unfortunate angle that put them directly behind the engines. When these came on, the Guavians disappeared. So did the corridor behind them, and the walls surrounding it, and a good deal more. In all, a respectable quantity of metal, plasticene, and ceramic alloy, comprising a modest chunk of the big freighter, vanished in the energetic backwash of the *Falcon*'s swift departure. As for the rathtar, it fell apart as the *Falcon* jumped through it, leaving telltale smears behind.

In another part of the vessel, safely sealed off behind the blast doors that slammed shut immediately following the breach of hull integrity caused by the *Falcon*'s unorthodox departure, a battered and infuriated Bala-Tik took time out from bemoaning the loss of his men and equipment to activate a deep-space contact via the freighter's still-functional communications system. Caught in the *Falcon*'s explosive departure, his own vessel was in no condition to pursue. Neither was that belonging to the Kanjiklub. But . . . others might be. If he couldn't collect what Solo owed him, there remained the possibility of a reward for information.

Contact established, he spoke into the pickup. "My name is Bala-Tik. I am a Guavian trader. My personal history is available for general assessment by any who care to research it. My reputation is verifiable. I am letting it be known that the individual Han Solo is likely in possession of the droid that is the subject of a search by the First Order. And that it and Solo together with an unknown number of allies are presently aboard the vessel known as the *Millennium Falcon:* destination unknown. I hereby lay claim to any reward that has been established for information leading to recovery of said droid by the First Order."

He closed the contact. It was out there now: what he knew, and his claim. He could do no more. And until he could either get his own vessel up and running or pay for someone to come out to this hulk of a freighter and pick him up, he was stuck here.

With, he reminded himself uneasily as the sound of a distant banging and tearing of metal reached him, an unknown number of surviving rathtars.

X

THE INFORMATION ARRIVED AT THE RESIS-
tance base on D'Qar coded and encrypted. Ordinary
transmissions were simply ported directly to the relevant parties. Those intended for general distribution
were not even encoded. But when something of specific importance intended for a highly restricted audi-
ence came in, it loaded at only one location. Sometimes
something as simple as mere physical separation provided the best security.

Lieutenant Brance saw the telltale come to life on
his workstation. It took scarcely a second for it to
flip from red to yellow and then to green as the transmission was received, decrypted, and reduced to a
comprehensible hard copy. Pulling it, he scanned the
message. His eyes widened.

Leaving the station, he took off on foot, down one
tunnel, into another corridor, ignoring everyone else
as he searched for the message's recipient. This time
of day he was confident he knew where to find her.
The passages through which he ran were crammed
with all manner of equipment: Sometimes carefully
installed, other times slapped together in haste, it
was nonetheless all functional. Despite the crowding,

Brance knew there was not nearly enough of it. There was never enough. The indigenous growths that pushed their way into the tunnels were only a reflection of the camouflaging forest above the base. Mindless and unthinking though it might be, the native plant life was in its own way an active participant in the Resistance.

He found the general where he expected her to be, conversing quietly with Captain Snap Wexley and an attendant droid. Leia Organa wore a dark vest over a simple blue-gray jumpsuit that was devoid of any indication of rank. Folded sleeves halted at mid-forearm. The color of her boots matched her vest, and a belt of some dark material was threaded neatly through a silvery buckle. Save for a single longer braid, General Organa's gray hair was bound up in a ring that outlined her head. Despite her lack of uniform, no one would mistake the petite woman for anything but what she was: a princess and a general.

All three looked up at his arrival and he passed her the hard copy. He knew that if the general wished to keep the information restricted, she would have said so the instant he had handed it over and would have already dismissed Wexley.

After giving her a moment to scan the content, Brance said, "General, as you can see from the details in this recent transmission, the community on Jakku was wiped out. First Order stormtroopers." Brance glanced at Wexley. "Lor San Tekka was killed."

She did not respond, but instead continued to study the readout. There was additional information: time of the attack, duration, number of assailants, descriptions of the weaponry they had employed—all of it incidental to the sobering consequences. The tactics team would break down the details and note anything useful.

What really mattered was what *wasn't* there.

"If they get to Luke first, we don't have a chance," she murmured. A new thought forced her to ask, "Anything else? Anything I'm not seeing here? What about Poe Dameron?"

"They found his X-wing destroyed. Angle and depth of the blaster marks suggest it was blown up while still on the ground. Definitely First Order: The locals don't have access to that kind of weaponry." His expression tightened. "There's no indication he survived. It looks like we've lost him."

Leia's expression tightened. If they continued to lose fighters like Dameron, the Resistance would have no hope against the First Order. She forced herself to continue reading through the other half of the detailed report. "There's no mention of Beebee-Ate."

Brance nodded at the readout again. "No, General. He wasn't recovered. Our people on Jakku who prepared the report say that he likely perished along with the X-wing."

She looked up. "Never underestimate a droid, Lieutenant." She looked to her right. "While some of them are specialized to an extreme degree—say, in linguistic capabilities—others may converse in simple mechanical languages but possess hidden skills. Beebee-Ate is such an example. In the absence of identifiable remains, we may retain hope." She fixed him with a gaze that had withered the less resilient. "Or are you ready to give up now?"

"No, ma'am," he said zealously.

General Organa turned to the droid in attendance. In sharp contrast to one arm that was a dull red, the bipedal machine's reflective golden torso gleamed from a recent cleaning.

"See-Threepio, you've heard the information from

Jakku. Locate Beebee-Ate immediately— you know what to do."

Nodding slightly and gesturing with the red arm, the protocol droid responded without hesitation. "Yes, General! Of course! The tracking system. Oh dear, this is a calamity!"

In another room, Korr Sella, Leia's personal envoy, awaited the general's arrival. The young woman wore her hair back in a severe bun and her dark green uniform contrasted notably with the general's more subdued attire, as did the badge that identified her as a commander. As usual, Leia did not waste time on small talk.

"You need to go to the Senate right away. Tell them I insist that they take action against the First Order. The longer they bicker and delay, the stronger the Order becomes." She leaned toward the other woman. "If they fail to take action soon, the Order will have grown so strong the Senate will be unable to do anything. It won't matter what they think."

Sella indicated her understanding. "With all respect: Do you think the senators will listen?"

"I don't know." Leia bit down on her lower lip. "So much time has passed. There was a time when they were at least *willing* to listen. And of course, the Senate's makeup has changed. Some of those who were always willing to pay attention to me have retired. Some of those who have replaced them have their own agendas." She smiled ruefully. "Not all senators think I'm crazy. Or maybe they do. I don't care what they think about me as long as they take action."

The emissary nodded. "I'll do all I can to ensure the Resistance gets the hearing we deserve. But why don't

you go yourself, General? An appeal of this nature is always more effective when delivered firsthand."

Leia's smile thinned. "I might make it to the Senate, yes. I might even be able to deliver my speech. But I would never, never get out of the Hosnian system alive. I would have a terrible 'accident,' or become the victim of some 'deranged' radical. Or I would eat something that didn't agree with me. Or encounter someone who didn't agree with me." She composed herself. "I have total confidence in you, Sella. I know you will deliver our message to the full extent of your considerable abilities."

The emissary smiled back, grateful for the confidence the general was expressing.

In a little-used conference room, C-3PO leaned into the shadows to murmur anxiously.

"I've never needed your help more than now—Artoo."

The squat droid he was addressing sat quietly in minimum maintenance mode, without so much as a single telltale blinking.

"How can I have committed such a devastating oversight?" the protocol droid continued. "When we sent Beebee-Ate off, it was my responsibility to perform his final checkout. Which I did, in most excellent and approved fashion. Except—except . . ." If a droid could have fallen to wailing, C-3PO would have done so on the spot. "I forgot to activate his long-range tracking mode! I must have assumed he would always be in the presence of that pilot and that therefore there would be no need. I deserve to have my memory wiped. Oh, Artoo, what am I to do? I wish you'd finally wake up, I need you now."

Only an occasional beep sounded from the smaller droid, indicative of his present dormancy.

"What *would* your advice be? No doubt you'd have an opinion about sending a general alert to all our associate droids, in the hope that one of *them* might encounter Beebee-Ate or his ident signal." Two hands, one gold and one red, rose slightly in realization. "Why, that's brilliant! I will do just that. Artoo, you're a genius!"

Pivoting, he rushed off to implement the concept, leaving behind a very quiet droid.

The fleet of Star Destroyers stood off the white world. Spectacular and isolated, with a mean surface temperature varying from merely cold to permanently arctic, the planet had been altered: its mountains tunneled into, its glaciers hacked, and its valleys modified until it no longer resembled its original naturally eroded form. Those who had remade it had renamed it.

Starkiller Base.

Hollowed out of one snow-covered mountain was a central control facility. At its heart was a great assembly chamber that held hundreds of workstations and their attendant seats. At present, it was occupied by only three figures. One was Kylo Ren. The second was General Hux, who wore his particular mask internally.

Seated on the raised platform that was the focus of the chamber was the blue-tinted holo of Supreme Leader Snoke. Tall and gaunt, he was humanoid but not human. The hood of the dark robe he wore was down, leaving visible a pink, pale face so aged it verged on translucence. Poorly reconstructed, the broken nose added to the asymmetry of the damaged

visage. So did the position of the left eye, which was situated lower than the right. Beneath wispy gray eyebrows, they were a startling cobalt blue. Long since healed over, old cuts and wounds marred the chin and forehead, the latter scar being particularly noteworthy.

Seated in shadow, the tall, slender form loomed over the other two men. Other than the face, only long, spindly fingers showed from beneath the dark robe. "The droid will soon be in the hands of the Resistance," Snoke declaimed, his voice deep, soothing, and very much that of someone in complete control, "giving the enemy the means to locate Skywalker and bring to their cause a most powerful ally. If Skywalker returns, the new Jedi will rise."

Ren sat impassive, neither commenting nor visibly betraying his thoughts.

Hux dipped his head by way of apology and took a step toward the dais. "Supreme Leader, I take full responsibility for th—"

Snoke cut him off. "Your apologies are not a strategy, General. We are *here now.* It is what happens next that matters."

Aware that he had just been spared an unknown but certainly unpleasant fate, the redheaded officer spoke up immediately. "I do have a proposition. The weapon. We have it. It is ready. I believe the time has come to use it."

"Against?"

"The Republic. Or what its fractious proponents choose to call the Republic. Their center of government, its entire system. In the chaos that will follow, the Resistance will have no choice but to investigate an attack of such devastating scale. They will throw all their resources into trying to discover its source.

So they have no choice but to investigate fully, and in so doing . . ."

"Reveal themselves." Snoke was clearly pleased.

"And if they don't . . . we've destroyed them."

"Yes," Snoke said in satisfaction. "Extreme. Audacious. I agree that the time for such measures has come. Go. Oversee the necessary preparations."

"Yes, Supreme Leader." Bowing stiffly, Hux turned and exited the chamber. He took long strides, walking briskly, clearly pleased with himself.

Snoke and Ren silently watched the general go.

When next Snoke spoke there was an intimacy in his voice, a familiarity that stood in sharp contrast to the commanding tone he had used with Hux.

"I have never had a student with such promise—before you."

Ren straightened. "It is your teachings that make me strong, Supreme Leader."

Snoke demurred. "It is far more than that. It is where you are from. What you are made of. The dark side—and the light. The finest sculptor cannot fashion a masterpiece from poor materials. He must have something pure, something strong, something unbreakable, with which to work. I have—you." He paused, reminiscing.

"Kylo Ren, I watched the Galactic Empire rise, and then fall. The gullible prattle on about the triumph of truth and justice, of individualism and free will. As if such things were solid and real instead of simple subjective judgments. The historians have it all wrong. It was neither poor strategy nor arrogance that brought down the Empire. You know too well what did."

Ren nodded once. "Sentiment."

"Yes. Such a simple thing. Such a foolish error of judgment. A momentary lapse in an otherwise exemplary life. Had Lord Vader not succumbed to emotion

at the crucial moment—had the father killed the son—
the Empire would have prevailed. And there would
be no threat of Skywalker's return today."

"I am immune to the light," Ren assured him confidently. "By the grace of your training, I will not be
seduced."

"Your self-belief is commendable, Kylo Ren, but do
not let it blind you. No one knows the limits of his
own power until it has been tested to the utmost, as
yours has not been. That day may yet come. There has
been an awakening in the Force. Have you felt it?"

Ren nodded. "Yes."

"The elements align, Kylo Ren. You alone are
caught in the winds of the storm. Your bond is not
just to Vader, but to Skywalker himself. Leia . . ."

"There is no need for concern." Despite the Supreme
Leader's cautioning, Ren's assurance remained un-
bounded. "Together we will destroy the Resistance—
and the last Jedi."

"Perhaps," Snoke conceded. "It has come to our
notice that the droid we seek is aboard the *Millennium Falcon,* once again in the hands of your father,
Han Solo. Even you, master of the Knights of Ren,
have never faced such a test."

Ren considered his reply carefully. "It does not
matter. He means nothing to me. My allegiance is
with you. No one will stand in our way."

Snoke nodded. "We shall see. We shall see."

It was a dismissal. Turning, wholly preoccupied
now, Ren followed General Hux in exiting the vast
chamber. When he was gone, a grotesque smile twisted
across Snoke's countenance. Then it vanished—along
with the rest of the holo of the Supreme Leader.

● ● ●

I don't know what to do.

Stumbling down the sand flat that wound between towering dunes, the dazed pilot fought to recall who he was, struggled to remember why he presently found himself staggering through what appeared to be an empty desert. His head hurt, and not just from the effort of trying to remember. Reaching up with one hand, he winced as his fingers took the measure of a lump on his forehead that had swollen to the size of a ponnelx egg.

He'd hit his head. Hard. It seemed to him that probably meant something. But what? A concurrence . . . no, that wasn't it. Concussion? Yes! He'd suffered a concussion. How had that happened?

As is often the case with a jolt to the brain case, recent events came flooding back to him in a rush.

Capture. Interrogation. He'd stolen a ship with . . . with . . .

He looked around and began calling the name he remembered.

"Finn! *Finn!*"

Then he recalled that the renegade stormtrooper who had helped him escape had ejected from their stolen TIE fighter as it had plunged out of control toward the surface of . . . Jakku. That was it. He was on Jakku. As for the absent Finn, there was no response to the pilot's anxious shouts. Depending on the angle and speed of ejection, his new friend could have come down anywhere, Poe knew.

His name. That was his name. Poe Dameron, and he was a pilot in the Resistance. But if he was a Resistance pilot, where was his flight jacket?

Probably still pinned in the TIE fighter he had only just managed to set down in one piece. He remembered the crash now. Remembered recovering consciousness just in time to set down more or less intact,

trying to get out of the cockpit before something blew, his jacket caught and holding him back, struggling out of it and then tumbling clear onto the sand—all of it recalled through the haze of his concussion.

He was alive on the surface of Jakku. Alive and alone. There was no way of telling if Finn had been as fortunate. More important, where was BB-8?

The droid could take care of himself, he felt. Poe knew if he could just get offworld and reconnect with the Resistance, a way could be found to recover the droid. All he needed was a ship. He'd already stolen one. Could he steal another?

First, he reminded himself, he would have to locate one. And before that, he would have to find water.

Morning brought neither, only a relentless sun in a cloudless sky. He continued onward because, given his present situation, one direction was as good as another. The salt flat ran between high dunes. It was not a road, exactly, but it was a way, and the hard surface offered much easier footing than the soft, shifting sand that rose above him on either side.

Keep low, he told himself, and you might come across a depression. Where there was a depression there might be dampness, and where there was dampness he could try to dig for water.

He found neither depression nor dampness. Instead, someone found him.

The whine of the approaching speeder was unmistakable. Squinting against the harsh light, he turned. A dark spot appeared between the dunes, expanding rapidly as it came toward him. Flat in front and bulging at the stern, the speeder was an unlovely construct, but to Poe at that moment it had lines as sweet as those of the fastest fighter in the Resistance fleet. Standing in the middle of the salt flat, he began jumping up and down and waving his arms.

At first he thought the speeder was going to keep coming and run right over him. Then it began to slow rapidly, angling to the right. Instead of shooting past, it came to a halt. Emitting a descending whine, it dropped slowly to the ground. A figure little more than half Poe's height promptly descended from the open cockpit.

It was a Blarina. Mirrored eyeshades swept across the broad face above the short, wide snout, and a toothy grin appeared as the speeder's scaly operator closely examined the lone human.

"A bit warm to be out walking by oneself in this country, my friend."

Poe grunted acknowledgment. "It's not by choice, I assure you."

"And where, then, have you come from?" The Blarina's grin grew wider, showing far more teeth than a human mouth. "Or do you just enjoy Jakku's gentle sunshine?"

"I'm lost." That much, at least, was not a lie, Poe knew. "I hit my head and I'm lost."

The Blarina let out a soft hiss. "Lost, indeed. Where's your speeder, my friend?"

Poe thought fast. "Same place I am. Lost."

"I'm Naka Iit. A scavenger of sorts." Once again he looked Poe carefully up and down. "I might just scavenge you."

Poe tensed. He had no weapon, and in the event of a confrontation, he was hardly in any condition to offer much in the way of physical resistance, even to a Blarina who was half his size. The species to which the speeder operator belonged was not especially strong, but they were very, very quick. This one, he reflected, was also fast with words.

Well, with words he could still defend himself.

"It's said that the Blarina are an exceptionally hospitable people."

Naka Iit's grin gave way to a frown of astonishment. "You've heard that? That must be referring to some other Blarina. It certainly doesn't sound like me."

Poe spread his hands wide. "You'd be wasting your time on me. I have nothing worth scavenging."

Raising his eyeshades, Naka stared hard at the pilot out of gold-hued eyes crossed with slitted pupils. "Then what, exactly, are you doing out in this wasteland, with 'nothing'?"

Poe felt himself swaying. He was hot, he was thirsty, he was exhausted, his head hurt, and except for this irritating Blarina he was alone in the middle of nowhere on a nowhere world. He was also possibly a little bit crazy from the heat. Otherwise he likely would not have said what he next said.

"I just escaped from the First Order by stealing one of their advanced TIE fighters, used it to shoot up one of their Star Destroyers, and crash-landed somewhere near here."

Naka stared at the human for a long moment. Then his wide eyes squinted, his scaly cheeks caught the sun as they bunched up, and he burst out laughing. One five-fingered hand wiped at the tears that trickled from the corners of his eyes.

"I'll wet my zinz if you aren't the most barefaced liar I've encountered in twenty years of scavenging on this sandbox!" He extended one lightly clothed arm. "Come with me, my friend. The Blarina *do* say that much good accrues to anyone who helps the mad. Liar or madman, whichever you may be, it amuses me to lend you assistance." Lowering his eyeshades, he turned his gaze skyward. "The spirits have placed you here to alleviate my boredom. Come."

"If it's all the same to you," a sun-addled Poe mum-

bled as he fumbled his way aboard Naka's battered speeder, "I'd be more than happy if you could just give me a drink of water."

Scrunched into a passenger seat designed to accommodate another Blarina, his knees pushed up against his chest, Poe gratefully accepted Naka's offer of a slender metal drinking flask complete with sipping tube.

"I need to get offworld." He spoke between delicious swallows. "As quickly as possible."

"Of course you do," Naka replied soothingly. "Jakku is no place for a madman." He looked to his left. "We're not far from Niima Outpost, but I'm not going to take you there. Local commerce is more or less run by a corpulent sack of slurge who goes by the name of Plutt. I've had words with him in the past and don't wish to confront him again."

Feeling better now that he'd had something to drink, Poe felt that the least he could do was acknowledge his rescuer's predilections. "You're very fond of words."

"As are all Blarina." Naka seemed to grow slightly in his seat. "I once finished fifth in a homeworld soliloquy competition. It is one of our most notable traits."

"Any others?" Poe inquired.

Naka's grin returned, his sharp teeth glistening in the bright sunlight. "We're also famously accomplished liars." He glanced once more at his passenger. "I'll take you as far as Blowback Town. There's a Blarina merchant there named Ohn Gos who is afflicted with the sorry habit of listening sympathetically. I'll introduce you. After that, you're on your own."

The light touch of a claw on a control caused the speeder to accelerate slightly. After that, Naka Iit went quiet. Poe was left to his thoughts—until a gout

of sand exploded from the dune off to their left. Leaning out, Naka looked behind them, uttered a loud hiss, and tromped the speeder's accelerator.

Thrown back in his seat, Poe struggled to regain his balance. "What is it? What's wrong?"

Without turning, a now grim Naka gestured slightly with his head. "Look for yourself."

Leaning to his right and out, Poe peered behind them. Another, much larger speeder was there and gaining. A second shot from it blew a crater in the dune face on his side.

"Strus clan." Naka's tone was bleak. "A motley collection of grunks who can't do salvage, repair, trade, or anything else." The speeder rocked from another near-miss. "So they steal from those who can."

"They're not very good shots," Poe pointed out.

This time Naka did look over at him. "Idiot madman. If they blow us up, they acquire nothing but garbage. They shoot to disable, not to destroy."

"They're catching up," Poe told him. "Can't this thing go any faster?"

"I am a salvager, not a podracer! My craft is built for hauling, not speed!"

Poe considered a moment. "Then let me drive." He leaned over.

"What! Are you insane?" Naka batted at the reaching hands. "No, wait—you are. Why should I let you take control of my only real asset?"

"Because," Poe told him as yet another burst slammed into the salt flat almost directly beneath them, "I am the best pilot you ever met."

They wrestled like that for a while before Naka finally gave in. After all, with a Strus clan speeder closing on them, they had little chance of escape anyway. As soon as man and Blarina had switched positions,

Poe turned the clumsy but sturdy craft sharply to the left—and began to slow.

"Giving up already?" Naka's words oozed sarcasm. "I could have done that much myself."

"Indicate that we're going to surrender." Poe was studying the speeder's controls. They looked very straightforward.

"Why not? Isn't that what we are doing?" The salvager sighed. "I'll have to ask Ohn for a loan. I hate starting over." Rising, he began making gestures at the pursuing craft. No more shots were forthcoming.

Watching the bigger speeder come up on them via the rearview, Poe continued to decelerate until their pursuer was near enough for him to make out the faces and assorted appendages of the now-triumphant thieves. When their larger vehicle was as close as he was willing to let it come, he tilted the nose of Naka's speeder sharply upward and gave it full power. It promptly shot skyward.

The sudden explosive burst kicked what seemed like half the dune beneath them upward and back, dumping the gritty shower atop the big speeder that had slowed almost to a stop behind them. Those Strus not wearing protective goggles received eyefuls of hot sand. The bulk of the grit storm instantly sank into every opening. While the Strus speeder's main propulsion system was sealed against such intrusions, not every instrument, not every component, was.

As Naka's craft soared over the crest of the dune, a sharp grinding noise behind them indicated that the Strus craft had ingested just enough sand to render it at least temporarily inoperable. The sound, like the threatening speeder itself, faded rapidly astern.

Beside him, a gleeful Naka was emitting a kind of cackling hiss. Alien though the exclamation was to Poe, the scavenger's delight could not be denied.

"Oh joy, oh pleasurable delight!" A hand reached over to clap Poe on the shoulder. "Saved by a madman!" The Blarina pointed. "Our destination lies that way. I find myself suddenly amenable to letting you drive. Are you really with the Resistance?"

"Yes." Compared to a stolen TIE fighter, the speeder was easy to operate.

"Then you truly are crazy."

Poe glanced over at him. "We of the Resistance prefer the term 'courageous.' "

"I see little difference." Leaning back in the passenger seat, Naka Iit picked at an incisor with one claw-tipped finger. "I owe you, my madman friend. Beyond just picking you out of the desert, I owe you most thankfully. I will intercede with Ohn Gos. One way or another, we will get you off Jakku!"

"I'm grateful," a relieved Poe told him simply.

"Grateful! What matters the gratitude of a madman?" Naka replied.

But he smiled as he hissed it.

Despite their escape, all was not tranquil aboard the *Millennium Falcon*. After having acquired it, Unkar Plutt had paid for only minimum maintenance, with the intention of preparing it fully for flight only if and when he found a buyer, so components that had worked immediately following lift-off from the surface of Jakku were now starting to show the lack of attention, and others were turning balky.

The alarms, however, were functioning quite efficiently.

Finn did his best to ignore them as he continued to work on Chewbacca's injury. This was made difficult by the Wookiee's habit of grabbing Finn by the neck or shoulder and shaking him violently every time a

fresh spasm of pain shot through the hirsute shoulder. Each time, Finn managed to settle the patient down and continue his ministrations. But his neck was getting sore.

Up in the cockpit, it seemed like every time Han and Rey managed to squelch one problem, a new one materialized to take its place. The present difficulty was a matter of degree. Or rather, degrees.

Rey indicated a readout whose numbers were too high for comfort and rising steadily. "Drive containment torus is overheating."

"Yeah," Han grunted. "You know why?"

A second's glance at the copilot's console was sufficient to supply the answer. "Field instability."

"Yep."

He wasn't going to elaborate for her, Rey realized. If this was some kind of test of her competence . . . No, she decided. What was occurring within the hyperdrive system was too dangerous for a test. She frowned at the controls.

"Need to recalculate and readjust the relevant parameters."

"Recalculate?" He eyed his own instrumentation. "Yeah. Hold on—readjusting . . ." A number of telltales suddenly went to red. "Power overload!"

"I can fix that!" Rey's fingers flew over her controls.

"Field instability is approaching critical! If it overshoots, we won't be able to stabilize it!"

She worked frantically. "Maybe there's an autoflux modulation system? That hasn't been activated yet? If it hasn't come online with everything else, try transferring auxiliary power to it."

"Auxiliary," Han yelled at her. "I'm on it!"

A moment later a deafening roar came from the vicinity of the lounge. Rising from the pilot's seat, Han

headed in its direction. "Be right back. You've got the con."

Utterly unaware of the tremendous compliment she had just been handed, she nodded absently while continuing to manipulate controls.

In the lounge, Finn was finishing the bandaging of Chewbacca's injured shoulder. For someone so big, he reflected as he ducked and dodged the bellowing Wookiee's reactions, Chewie was proving to be an uncommonly difficult patient. As a huge, shaggy hand grabbed Finn yet again, BB-8 scurried clear. His voice muffled by an armful of fur, Finn tried to make the Wookiee appreciate the situation.

"Chewie, you've got to let go of me, understand? I can't secure this bandaging properly if I can't see what I'm doing. Or move. Or breathe."

The Wookiee nodded apprehensively.

"Okay then, help me out here. Let go." Chewbacca promptly shook his head *no*. Exasperated—and by now more than just sore—Finn yelled toward the cockpit.

"I need help with this giant fuzz ball!"

As Chewbacca roared anew in pain, a grim-faced Han left what he had been doing and joined them. "You hurt Chewie," he growled, "you deal with me!"

"Hurt *him*?" Finn continued to struggle with Wookiee torso, shaggy arms, and bandaging. "He's almost killed *me* six times!" Reaching out, a massive hand grabbed him by the collar. Finn responded with a hasty smile. "Which is fine. Really."

Han hesitated a moment, eyed his wounded copilot, and then headed back to the cockpit. Dropping back into his seat, he muttered unhappily as he scanned one readout after another.

"The hyperdrive blows, and there'll be pieces of us in three different systems."

Abruptly, all the alarms stopped. A satisfied Rey sat back in her seat. Confused, Han peered over at her.

"What'd you do?"

"Bypassed the auto-flux and recalibrated manually." She nodded toward the console. "Field has stabilized. Toral containment temperature is dropping back toward normal." She let out a long breath and glanced across at him. "Anything else?"

He let out a short, appreciative laugh. "Yeah." He rose once more from his seat and retraced his steps toward the access corridor. "Keep monitoring ship systems and give me a shout if it looks like anything's likely to blow up in the next couple of minutes."

Back in the medbay, he knelt alongside the supine Chewbacca. The Wookiee was still moaning, but not as forcefully now that the analgesic Finn had administered was starting to work. Carefully, Han checked the bandaged wound while reassuring his copilot.

"Nah," he murmured, "don't say that. You did great. They got you with a lucky shot." He smiled. "Can't look everywhere at once in a running fight. Kanjiklubbers, Guavians, rathtars—*rathtars*! Trying to hold 'em all off while covering for me and making it to the ship—I'm surprised any of us made it." He rose. "You're gonna be fine."

He turned to Finn, who, with BB-8 standing beside and watching, was trying to activate the holochess set. Looking on, Han hesitated. This was difficult for him, but it needed to be said. And he meant it.

"Good job on Chewie. I— Thanks."

"You're welcome." Glancing toward the bed alcove, Finn addressed the patient. "Thanks for not breaking my neck." The Wookiee replied with a guttural, modulated rumble. Finn chose to interpret it as an apology of sorts.

Sliding a finger across a flush control brought the

chess set to life. The pieces steadied themselves before
gazing up at Finn. Then, in lieu of any forthcoming
instructions, they started fighting among themselves.
Annoyed by his lack of control, Finn tried to turn it
off, but that apparently required finding and nudging
a different control. Han suppressed a smile.

Peculiar guy, this one, Han thought. *He can deal
with a battlefield wound but not an ordinary chess
set.* He shrugged. The man's capabilities and lack
thereof were none of his business. Instead, he asked:
"So. Fugitives, huh?"

Finn nodded and indicated BB-8. "It's the map he's
storing. The First Order wants it, and they'll kill anyone who tries to keep it from them."

Rey arrived to join them as Finn finally managed to
deactivate the chess set. "Ship systems are stable. I
made sure before I left everything on autopilot." She
indicated Finn and the droid. "They're with the Resistance. And I was with them. So I guess now in the
mind of the Order, *I'm* with the Resistance."

Resistance fighters? Han eyed Finn with new
respect—and not a little skepticism. The younger man
had handled himself well enough in the brawl on
board the freighter, but that only proved he was a
survivor: not a fighter. Further evaluation could wait
until later, Han told himself. Right now . . .

He looked to BB-8. "Let's see whatcha got."

Dutifully, the droid rolled into a suitable position.
A lens brightened, and abruptly the lounge was all
but filled with an enormously detailed and complex
star map. Nebulae, solo stars, translucent splashes of
concentrated dark matter, and entire solar systems
were displayed before them. Even Chewbacca sat up
to have a better look. Finn was impressed and Rey in
awe—but Han found himself frowning.

Moving forward and into the three-dimensional

representation, he tracked system positions and locator stars. One finger traced the outlines of a particularly bright and well-known nebular cluster. Like everything else in the map, it was brilliantly depicted.

It was also only half there.

He turned to the others. "This is accurate, but it's not complete. It's just a piece. I can tell from the location of the breaks and from what's only partially shown." He grunted softly. "Ever since Luke disappeared, people have been looking for him."

Rey spoke while drinking in the details of the marvelous but imperfect chart. "Why'd he leave, anyway?"

Han pursed his lips; thinking back, remembering.

"He was training a new generation of Jedi. There was no one else left to do it, so he took the burden on himself. Everything was going good, until one boy, an apprentice, turned against him and destroyed it all. Everything Luke had worked toward: gone. Luke felt responsible. He walked away from everything."

Finn's tone was respectful. "Do you know what happened to him? Does anyone?"

Han turned to him. "There've been all kinds of rumors and stories. When people don't have access to facts, they invent what they'd like to believe, or what they think others would like to hear. The people who knew him the best think he went on a personal quest, looking for the first Jedi temple."

Rey had been quiet for a while, absorbing everything in awed silence. She could no longer contain herself.

"The Jedi were real?"

Han half smiled, to himself as much as to her. "I used to wonder that myself. A bunch of mumbo-jumbo is what it sounds like. Some magical power holding together good and evil, light and dark." He

paused, his voice fading. "Crazy thing is, it's all real. The Jedi, the Force—it's true. All true." He brought himself back to reality.

"Just as it's true what Finn here said: The First Order will kill all of us for that map."

An alarm sounded, but this one was different from the flurry that had preceded it. Chewbacca started to rise, but Han put out a hand to prevent him.

"No. You relax." He glanced at Finn. "Don't risk the good work of our friend here by stressing what he's done." He headed for the cockpit. "This is our stop."

XI

THERE MAY HAVE BEEN MORE BEAUTIFUL worlds in the galaxy than Takodana, but if so, they were unknown to Han. Verdant and mild, flecked with bands of white cloud and necklaced with small seas and brightly reflective lakes, it appeared before them as the *Millennium Falcon* dropped out of hyperspace. With him in the pilot's chair, Rey copiloting, and Finn and BB-8 standing behind, the cockpit was crowded. Within Finn, expectation mixed with uncertainty as he gazed at the unfamiliar world ahead.

"What are we doing here?"

"You wanted my help, you're getting it," Han told him. "We're going to see an old friend." At the same time he noticed Rey staring fixedly out the foreport. She seemed on the verge of tears.

"Hey—y'okay?"

"I didn't know there was this much green in the whole galaxy," she said in awe.

He watched her for a moment longer, then sent the *Falcon* into a shallow dive, heading for a well-remembered location. Speed stripped away the clouds around them, revealing what looked like endless evergreen forest. As he slowed the ship to suborbital ve-

locity, other features lingered in his passengers' gaze: rolling hills, rivers, and lakes that glistened like sheets of silver foil.

A towering stone castle came into view as he prepared for touchdown. Looking at it, Finn could not tell by whose hands—or other manipulative appendages—it had been raised. The study of architecture was not a subject on which incipient stormtroopers tended to focus. One side of the castle was dominated by a long freshwater lake. Of more interest to him, the other side featured a landing area crowded with small freighters not unlike the *Millennium Falcon*. Like the *Falcon*, the majority of parked craft looked worn and heavily used, but well maintained.

Disembarking, Rey and BB-8 marveled at forest, lake, and castle. Limping slightly but otherwise disdaining his wounds, Chewbacca ignored the rustic panorama in favor of inspecting the underside of the *Falcon*.

Still on board, Han popped a storage unit and began rummaging through the contents. From among the jumble he withdrew one used blaster after another, placing them carefully to one side. He was still at it when Finn came up behind him.

"Solo, I'm not sure what we're walking into here. A few details would be welcome."

Half turning, Han looked back at him, said quietly, "Did you just call me 'Solo'?"

"Sorry—Han. Mr. Solo. Look, I'm not asking for information lightly. I'm a pretty big deal in the Resistance. Which puts a real target on my back. I just need to know that there won't be any conspirators here, okay? No First Order sympathizers? 'Cause they'd be looking out for me now, and I don't need any surprises."

"Surprises," Han echoed thoughtfully. "Yeah, you're

right. No matter where you go, no matter who you happen to run into, the galaxy's just full of surprises." His expression turned serious. "Listen, big deal, you've got another problem. A bigger problem. Much more serious than worrying about First Order sympathizers. It's this: Women always figure out the truth." He handed over a blaster. Finn took the weapon and turned it over in his hands, giving it a professional examination. It was a substantial piece of ordnance. "Always," Han concluded.

Rising, he brushed past the younger man, heading for the exitway. Finn watched him go, wracked with guilt. But there was nothing he could do about it. Not now, anyway.

Outside, Han interrupted the sightseeing. Rey was barely able to contain her delight at their surroundings.

"I can't believe this place is real. It doesn't even smell real."

He nodded understandingly, gesturing at the surrounding forest. "You got all this greenery pumping out all this oxygen. Makes a big change when all you've been sucking is recycled ship atmosphere." He offered her a blaster. "You might need this."

Rey looked down at the weapon, then back at him. "I've been in one or two tough situations. I can handle myself."

"I know you can, and that's why I'm giving it to you." He pushed the weapon toward her. "Take it."

She contemplated the blaster, drawn to it as she was to any piece of new and unfamiliar tech, and finally accepted it, hefting it carefully.

"It's heavy" was her appraisal.

He considered. Had he guessed wrong? "You do know how to fire that?"

"Trigger," she shot back. "You aim it and pull the trigger."

"A bit more to this model than that. Put a little more effort in, get a little more result out. You've got a lot to learn. You got a name?"

"Rey." She raised the weapon and aimed it at an imaginary target, careful to keep the muzzle pointed well away from Han or anyone else.

"Rey," he repeated. "Rey, I've been thinking about taking on some more crew."

She smiled at him. "According to what you told us earlier, that didn't work out so well for them on your last job."

He brushed it off. "Needed a bigger crew for a bigger job with a bigger ship." He pointed to where Chewbacca was continuing his inspection. "Not so much with the *Falcon*. Maybe bring on one more. A second mate. Someone to help out. Someone who can keep up with Chewie and me and who's smart enough to know when to keep out of the way. Someone who appreciates the *Falcon* and her hidden qualities."

She cocked an eye at him. "Are you giving me a job?"

He met her stare without blinking. "It doesn't pay right away and I'm not going to be nice to you and—"

Pleased as well as taken aback, she interrupted him. "You're offering me a *job*."

"I'm just thinking about it," Han corrected her.

"Well . . . if you did, I'd be flattered." Rey paused. "But there's somewhere I need to be."

"Jakku," Han said knowingly.

Rey nodded. "I've already been away too long."

Han put a hand on her shoulder. "Let me know if you change your mind." Turning, he called toward the ship. "Chewie! Check her out the best you can. With luck, we won't be here long." His gaze returned

to the girl standing before him. "You smile too much, Rey."

Rey nodded obligingly. "I'll work on it," she said with a wide smile.

Once Han was satisfied that, if need be, the *Falcon* could depart in a hurry, they started toward the nearby castle. While Chewbacca remained behind to attend to a number of minor fixes and nurse his injury, the rest of them were able to enjoy the forest and the occasional glimpse among the woods of examples of indigenous wildlife. These invariably proved small and nonthreatening. Approaching the impressive structure and its odd, trapezoidal stonework, Finn found himself unable to estimate its age.

"Why are we here again?" he asked as they started up a wide, curving stone staircase.

"To get your droid on a clean ship. Do you think it was luck that Chewie and I found the *Falcon*? If we can find it on our scanners, the First Order's not far behind." Han indicated the soaring walls now rising before them. Colored flags representing numerous cultures and tribes hung from the battlements, some banners more faded and frayed than others. "The galaxy's full of watering holes, but nothing like this place. It's been run by an old smuggler named Maz Kanata for a thousand years. Want to get Beebee-Ate to the Resistance? Maz is our best bet."

Gently but firmly taking the blaster he had given her out of Rey's hands, Han pointedly holstered it for her at the back of her belt. "Not an establishment to walk into holding a gun. First impressions are important.

"The most important thing here is to keep a low profile, stay under the radar. Maz is a bit of an ac-

quired taste. So let me do the talking. And whatever you do, don't stare."

Rey and Finn replied almost simultaneously. "At what?"

"Any of it," Han warned them.

The entrance was open. A corridor led to a sizable open hall of neatly finished stonework where a hodge-podge of humans, humanoids, and distinctly nonhumans were engaged in what struck Finn as a perpetual round of eating, drinking, gambling, scheming, nego-tiating, arguing, and occasionally attempting to split one another's livers. Or some equivalent organ. Lead-ing the way, Han alternately shoved, requested, or cajoled assorted occupants of the hall out of their path, until at last he halted.

The figure standing in front of him and currently blocking the way was short. Very short indeed, and by the look of what skin and flesh was visible, very old. Abruptly, this decidedly unimpressive humanoid whirled, as if sensing something without seeing it.

What could be seen of the hairless pate beneath the simple gray cap was a withered, weathered yellowish-brown. Huge lenses that were as much goggles as glasses folded forward over both eyes. The nose was small, almost petite, and the mouth thin and drawn. She—for Han had told them it was a she—was dressed simply and practically: baggy dark maroon pants tucked into handmade boots. A vest of some charcoal gray material was fitted over a blue-green sweaterlike shirt whose sleeves were rolled up to just beneath the elbows, exposing skin that was almost gold-colored. A buckle of some silvery material fas-tened a leatherine belt from which hung an assort-ment of tech. In contrast to the plain clothing, the collection of bracelets and rings she wore bordered on the ostentatious.

Catching sight of Han, she let out a shriek that reverberated off the walls and belied her size.

"HAAAAAAAN SOLO?"

All activity in the hall immediately ceased as everyone, regardless of species or aural acuity, turned to look in the newcomers' direction.

"Maz . . . ," Han said wearily.

Finn shook his head. "Under the radar," he muttered. "Perfect."

"You still in business?" Han asked her.

"Barely!" she snapped back at the much taller human. "Thanks to a certain mooch who still hasn't paid me back after nearly twenty years. Can you imagine something so horrible?"

"I might be able to," Han admitted.

Whoever she was—*what*ever she was—Finn had already decided that here was someone who could deal with Han Solo on an equal basis, at least as far as casual sarcasm was concerned.

Maz peered up at Han, her goggled eyes wide. "Where's my boyfriend?"

"Chewie's repairing the *Falcon*," Han told her.

Maz nodded. "That's one sweet Wookiee. I'm so sorry," she abruptly said to Finn and Rey.

"For what?" Rey asked nervously.

"Whatever trouble he's dragged you into," Maz said. "Come! Sit! I can't wait to hear what you need from me this time," she said to Han.

The new arrivals headed off, trailing Maz out of the main hall. Being unremarkable specimens of sentient life, they drew only the occasional passing glance.

Among those who watched them go were an enormous hairless mass of slovenly dressed Dowutin muscle called Grummgar and a svelte slice of skin who went by the name Bazine Netal. In contrast to her hulking companion, Bazine was fully human. Exqui-

sitely if severely clad in a long-sleeved dress patterned
in an optical illusion of black and gray, complete with
black leather skullcap, neck piece, shoulder covering, and a belt that held a long, lethal blade, she also
boasted lips and forefingers painted black. Unlike
those whose eyes lingered but briefly on the new visitors, this mismatched couple tracked Han and his
companions until they were out of sight. As soon as
they had disappeared, still following Maz Kanata,
Netal slipped away from the crowd.

The communicator she employed was capable of
sending encrypted messages via the central planetary
communications booster. With that much power at
her disposal, it did not take long to establish a long-
range connection.

"Yes. It's Bazine Netal. *I've got them.*"

It was a very private place. There was no need to
mark it as such. No need for signs or audible warn-
ings or protective devices. Everyone on the ship knew
what it was, who it belonged to, and what lay within.
None would think of violating the sanctuary. That
way lay censure, possibly pain, and quite likely worse.

The lighting within was subdued. There would not
have been much to see even in the presence of brighter
illumination. A pair of consoles dominated by red
lights flanked the doorway. A single projection console
sat in the center, attended by a lone chair. Otherwise
the room was sparsely furnished. The individual who
claimed the space had no need of the usual accoutre-
ments favored by sentient beings. He was content
within himself and with who he was.

The alcove where Kylo Ren was kneeling and speaking was darker than the rest of the adjoining chambers. He kept it deliberately so, as seemed appropriate

for its function. He spoke now in a tone different from the one he usually employed when conversing with others. There were no orders to be issued here, no pathetic underlings to command. The one with whom he was presently communing would understand everything Ren chose to say, in whatever voice he chose to employ. No need here and now for intimidation, for fear. Kylo Ren spoke, and the object of his words listened in silence.

"Forgive me. I feel it again. The pull to the light. The Supreme Leader senses it. Show me again the power of the darkness, and I will let nothing stand in our way."

Alone in the room, Kylo Ren—saturnine of aspect, lithe of build, tortured of mien, and troubled of eye—gazed at the silent recipient of his confession.

"Show me, Grandfather, and I will finish what you started."

Trembling slightly, he rose from where he had been kneeling and strode off to another portion of his private quarters. There was no response from the one to whom he had been talking: neither argument nor agreement. Only silence from the shape that had been the object of Ren's fervor: a ghostly, deformed mask that had once belonged to another. To a figure of rumor and legend and fear.

Misshapen and malformed as it was, no one who had once laid eyes upon the countenance that had belonged to Darth Vader would ever forget it.

While Finn's appetite had been sharpened by a trooper's customary diet of synthsust, it was nothing compared to Rey's. In spite of himself, he could only marvel at the amount of food the girl downed. It was as if she had never eaten real food in her life. Origins

didn't seem to matter, either. She grabbed and consumed examples of anything within reach without bothering to ascertain its genesis. Han also ate energetically, but he was considerably more decorous. Finn found himself envying the nearby spherical form of BB-8, for whom such messy organic calisthenics were merely an excuse to meditate on the superiority of mechanical life.

"A map leading to the first Jedi temple!" Maz was marveling as she puttered about the kitchen. "To Skywalker himself! I've never given up hope for him."

"Well, that's good to hear, because I have a favor to ask," Han said.

Maz looked at him knowingly. "You need a loan. I heard about the rathtars. King Prana's not happy." She stopped and looked at Rey. "How's the food?"

"So delicious," Rey said enthusiastically between bites.

"I need you to get this droid to the Resistance . . . ," Han said.

"Me?" Maz said archly.

". . . and the loan sounds good, too."

"I see you're in trouble," Maz said. "I'll help you find passage—avoid Snoke's hunter squads—but this journey to the Resistance isn't mine to take, and you know it."

"Leia doesn't want to see me," Han said uneasily.

"Who can blame her!" Maz exclaimed. "But this fight is about more than you and that good woman. Han, go home."

"What fight?" Rey asked.

"The only fight: against the dark side. Through the ages, I've seen evil take many forms. The Sith. The Empire. Today, it's the First Order. Their shadow is spreading across the galaxy. We must face them. Fight them. All of us."

Finn snorted. "That's crazy. Look around. There's no chance we haven't been recognized already—I bet the First Order is on their way right—" He broke off as Maz adjusted her goggles, making her eyes grow even larger than usual. "What?" Finn asked indignantly.

Instead of answering right away, Maz's eyes somehow grew even larger within the goggles, impossibly huge. Then she climbed up onto the table and made her way to stand directly in front of Finn. He started to feel nervous in a way he hadn't since entering the castle. "Solo, what's she doing?" he asked.

Han shrugged. "No idea," he said, "but it ain't good."

Maz finally spoke. "I've lived for over one thousand years, son. Long enough to see the same eyes in different people." She adjusted the goggles again, and to Finn's relief the pirate's eyes went back to normal. "I'm looking at the eyes of a man who wants to run," she said solemnly.

"You don't know a thing about me," Finn said in frustration. "Where I'm from. What I've seen. You don't know the First Order like I do. They'll slaughter us. We all need to run."

Maz considered him, then pointed back into the main hall area. "Big head, red shirt, shiny gun. Bright red helmet with ear flares. They're bound for the Outer Rim. Will trade transportation for work. Go."

Awkwardly, Finn rose from his seat. Everything had happened fast. Too fast. The last thing he had anticipated was the fulfillment of his request.

Reaching—slowly—to his service belt, he drew the blaster Han had given him and offered it to its owner. "It's been nice knowing you. Really was."

Han didn't look at him. "Keep it."

Finn hesitated, but there was nothing more to

say. Pointless words wasted atmosphere. Turning, he walked away.

Watching him go, Rey was confused and hurt by the abrupt turn of events. They had been through a great deal together, she and this strange but agreeable youth, and his sudden, somewhat inexplicable leave-taking was hitting her hard.

Though his thoughts were churning, Finn managed to keep them under control as he approached the table Maz had pointed out. There were no humans in the group, save possibly the red-helmeted captain, but they eyed him without prejudice. Even the top-heavy, warty, one-legged Gabdorin first mate waited politely for him to state his business. Having been pushed to this point, Finn didn't hesitate as he ad-dressed the captain.

"I'm told you're looking for help. I'll work for a lift to any civilized world on the Outer Rim."

The first mate replied to him, but Finn didn't under-stand a word of whatever language the Gabdorin was speaking. The captain remained silent.

"I don't know what that was," he responded, "but it's a deal." He smiled, hoping the expression was not found wanting. Or hostile.

The exchange was interrupted by Rey's arrival, ac-companied by an anxious, softly beeping BB-8. She was confused and angry all at once.

"What are you doing?"

Finn smiled anew at the leader of the alien crew. "Give me a second. Or your equivalent time-part." He edged Rey away from the table, leaving the aliens to mutter incomprehensibly among themselves.

"You heard what Maz said," Rey hissed at him. "You're part of this fight. We both are." She searched his face. "You must feel something . . ."

"I'm not who or what you think I am. I'm not special. Not in any way."

She was shaking her head slowly, not comprehending what she was hearing. "Finn, what are you talking about? I've watched you, I've seen you in action, I've . . ."

His voice tightened as he finally blurted out the truth. "I'm not a hero. I'm not Resistance. *I'm a stormtrooper.*"

That silenced her. He might as well have hit her across the face with the business end of a blaster.

"Like all of them, I was taken from a family I'll never know," he continued rapidly. "I was raised to do one thing. Trained to do one thing. To kill my enemy." He felt something that should not have been there, that was not part of his training, well up in him. "But my first battle, I made a choice. I wasn't going to kill for them. So I ran. As it happens, right into you. And you asked me if I was Resistance, and looked at me like no one ever had. So I said the first thing that came to mind that I thought would please you. I was ashamed of what I was. But I'm done with the First Order. I'm never going back." Suddenly he found it hard to swallow, much less to speak. "Rey, come with me."

She shook her head. "Don't go."

"Take care of yourself," he begged her. "Please." He turned and headed back to the group of waiting aliens.

The red-helmeted captain looked up at him. Finn nodded once, hoping the gesture was as universal as he had been told. "I'm ready whenever you're ready." The first mate replied in his stumbling language and Finn nodded a second time. "Whatever."

The crew members rose and headed for the main doorway. As Finn started to go with them, an an-

guished Rey pivoted and turned her back on him, ignoring BB-8's troubled beeping.

Finn had wanted to say something more before realizing anything he could come up with would be worse than superfluous. Better to leave it as it was, he told himself. Clean break, no scene, no yelling and shouting. He went with the members of the alien crew, pausing at the hall exit to glance back just once. She was still walking away, not looking in his direction. Just as well, he thought as the doorway closed behind him.

That was what he told himself. But it was not what he was feeling.

So preoccupied and bewildered was Rey by Finn's completely unanticipated confession that she failed to notice the lumbering figure and accompanying henchmen who were making their way through the crowd toward her. She was utterly blind to their approach until one thick hand reached out to grab her. A second later BB-8 noticed what was happening and let out a series of alarmed beeps.

"Hello, Rey."

She recognized the voice before she even saw the face.

Unkar Plutt.

There was no mistaking that repulsive countenance. After sparing a quick glance for his oversize minions, she turned her attention to him, astonished.

"How—how did you find me?"

He smiled. It did not improve his appearance. "The ship you stole. The *Millennium Falcon*. You can't really track a ship while it's in hyperspace—but when it emerges, and particularly after it sets down somewhere, there are ways. Expensive, but in the case of valuable property, often worth it. Definitely worth it in the case of the *Falcon*. It happens to be fitted with

a covert Imperial homing device. Old technology, but still quite functional. To which my presence here can attest. Didn't take much to get the necessary relays working."

No one in the hall was paying them the least attention, she noticed worriedly. In a place where everyone minded their own business, she found herself wishing fervently for someone to butt in. She twisted defiantly in Plutt's grasp.

"I suggest. Kindly. That you let go of me. Now."

Despite her attempts to pull away, he drew her steadily closer. She could not avoid the fact that his breath was a suitably aromatic match for his visage.

"I suggest, less kindly, that you come quietly with me. Otherwise we'll begin right here, where you can provide some entertainment for this galactic rubbish." Putting his face so close to hers that they were almost touching, he lowered his voice. "I'm gonna make you and that wearisome droid pay for what you've done."

This close in, he could see her expression—but not her hands. Whipping out her new blaster, she plonked it right up against his nose. His underlings started forward, only to be waved off by their master.

Rey growled softly. "I'm seriously thinking about adding another hole to your face."

He chuckled unpleasantly, then in a single swooping motion grabbed the blaster and wrenched it away from her. Her expression fell. Before he had managed to grab it, she had pulled the trigger—she was certain she had. But for some reason the weapon had malfunctioned.

He shook his head in mock sympathy as he held up the blaster. "You'd need to take off the safety first." One finger moved toward the almost hidden switch in

question. "Here, I'll show you how. You just flip this little—"

The upraised blaster vanished from Plutt's hand, yanked away by a much bigger set of fingers. Startled, Plutt looked back—and up, into the furry face of a deceptively calm Wookiee.

"*Urrrrrrr . . .*"

Not especially eloquent of Chewie, a relieved Rey thought, but it got the point across.

Plutt wasn't impressed. Noticing the bandaged shoulder, he poked at it with the same hand that had swiped Rey's weapon.

"Half a Wookiee ain't much to worry about." He started to retreat into a fighting stance. "Not against all of *me*." He lashed out.

Grabbing the thrusting arm, a roaring Chewbacca twisted and ripped it off at the shoulder, throwing the dismembered limb clear across the room. Looking down at himself, Plutt let out a scream of agony as his underlings hurriedly fell back.

The arm landed on a table where a group of four-armed, long-snouted Culisettos was gambling. With an annoyed huff, one of them picked up the amputated limb and absently tossed it aside, allowing the game to resume. Nearby, a small bipedal GA-97 droid who had been monitoring the pastime turned curiously to check the source of the excised limb. Though it initially focused on Rey, its attention was immediately drawn away from her and to the rotund droid at her side. Visual recognition ignited a small but very important internal sequence that concluded with the GA-97 sending out a compressed signal that was bounced around, coded, decoded, encrypted, and flashed out into deep space.

Where it very soon was picked up, decoded, and

decrypted, to become the impetus for an electronic shout of joy.

Only on very rare occasions did C-3PO encounter a need for forward speed. This was one of them, but his ambulatory programming restricted him to a gait that was less than satisfactory. If only, he mused, he could move as fast as he could talk.

Despite his motive infirmity he eventually found General Organa deep in intense conversation with a tactical specialist. Ignoring the fact that they were engaged in serious discussion, the droid started speaking without prefacing his arrival.

"Princess— I mean, General!" At the sound of the protocol droid's familiar voice, Leia turned and waved off the tech. "I hate to brag—as you know I was fitted with a humility circuit during my last rebuild, though I cannot imagine why anyone would think I would require such an accessory—but I *must* risk taking a moment of your time to sing my own praises!"

"Threepio!" She didn't try to hide her exasperation. "No one has this kind of time!"

"This kind of time was made for precisely this kind of intelligence, General," the droid insisted proudly. "I believe I have successfully located Beebee-Ate! According to the information I have just received through our scattered but attentive network, Beebee-Ate is presently within the castle of Maz Kanata on Takodana."

Leia let out a gasp of excitement. "Maz—I knew you could do it, Threepio! Good work! You deserve an extra oil bath." Murmuring to herself, she started off, the tactical tech in tow. "This changes everything."

Left behind, the bearer of good news had no one to

converse with except himself. As usual, this did not inhibit him.

"Finally! Appreciation so long overdue." He paused a moment, not thinking but instead checking on something internal, before again murmuring aloud. "Oh dear. I think the humility circuit may be malfunctioning."

XII

"CAN YOU GET THE DROID TO LEIA?"

Still seated at the table, Han had scarcely noticed the commotion on the other side of the crowded hall. When a returning Rey and Chewbacca had not been forthcoming about what had taken place, he had decided not to pursue it. At the moment, he was much more interested in talking to Maz—and getting her to take the troublesome droid off his hands.

"I know how important it is to her," he finished.

Maz's response was somewhat less than helpful. "If it's so important to her, do as I said before and take it to her yourself. Whether you believe that she wants to see you or not. Han, when you first came to me, your most important decision, involving your most meaningful bonds, was yet to come." She shook her head. "I'm surprised, frankly. You were always so good at looking ahead. I think now it's your time to look back. At what—and who—you've left behind."

All the discussion and debate was making Rey weary. Coupled with Finn's confession and his walking out on the rest of them, it made her wonder, not for the first time, what she was doing here. She felt lost and alone.

No different, she told herself, than she had felt on Jakku.

Alone . . . alone . . . It echoed in her mind as she sat there. Under the weight of her loneliness Han's voice seemed to fade, and Maz Kanata's as well, until there was nothing surrounding her but a silence as deep and profound as the distant reaches of space itself.

Then something came, stealthy and unidentifiable, to fill it.

A feeling, unrecognized yet somehow familiar. Drawn to it, she rose. Locked in conversation, Han and Maz ignored her as she made her way away from the table and toward a distant corridor—but BB-8 followed.

There was a stairway there: ancient stonework leading downward. Perceiving her unease, BB-8 asked what was wrong.

"I don't know. I—I have to see." She started down the stairway. Struggling, the droid followed.

The stairway terminated in a deserted, dimly subterranean corridor. Why was she here, she asked herself. When herself declined to answer, she continued onward. Though the passageway was not long, it appeared so to her. At the very end was a single door. It almost seemed to vibrate. BB-8 chirped nervously, but she ignored the droid, drawn forward. There was a seal, a lock, on the door. She reached out, only to draw back her hand when it opened before she could make contact.

It was darker still in the room beyond. Among the stone arches and alcoves she could see crates piled haphazardly and shelves filled with packages heavy with age and dust. A bust of some unknown bearded human sat on the floor next to an antique shield fashioned of an unknown silvery metal. Tarps and cloth covered much of the collection. There seemed no

rhyme or reason to the place, no organization of any kind. Objects of obvious value sat side by side with simple woven baskets and bundles of unknown plants.

Though curious as to their functions and origins, she ignored them all, moving deeper into the room toward a table on which rested a single wooden box. There was nothing especially impressive about the container, nothing overtly valuable or significant. Yet of all the items in the chamber she was drawn only to it. Behind her, not a peep of a beep came from an anxious BB-8.

The box was not locked. She opened it.

A heavy, slow, mechanical breathing filled the room. Turning, she found herself looking down an impressive hallway, its architecture reminiscent of the Old Empire. Peering harder, farther, she saw in the distance a section of the famed Cloud City. Two figures were locked in combat, distant, distant. Someone, somewhere, somewhen, spoke her name.

"Hello?" Wreathed in the irrationality of the moment, she called hopefully, but received no answer.

A boy appeared at the end of the hallway. She started toward him, and the world turned inside out, causing her to trip and fall.

Onto the wall, which had become the ground. Not the adamantine ceramic she had just seen, but dry grass. Nearby, a lightsaber slammed into the ground. A missed thrust, a statement of power—she didn't know, couldn't tell. A hand appeared to pull it upward.

Day became night, sky ominous and filled with rain, cold and chilling to the bone. She was standing, she was sitting, she was looking up—to see someone, a warrior, take the full force of the lightsaber. He screamed and fell.

Battlefield then, all around her. Putting a hand to

her mouth, she rose and turned. As she turned, she found herself confronted by seven tall, cloaked figures, dark and foreboding, all armed. Soaked and shivering, she stumbled backward, turning as she half fell. Firelight illuminated her, firelight from a distant, burning temple.

The seven vanished. A sound made her turn, and she blinked in surprise at the sight of a small blue-and-silver R2 unit. A new figure appeared. Falling to his knees, he reached out to the droid with an artifice of an arm—metal and plastics and other materials with which she was not familiar. She blinked and both were gone.

Around her now: barren, snowy woods, the sounds of unknown forest creatures, and a conviction that she must be losing her mind. Once more she climbed to her feet, her chilled breath preceding her. From in front of her, not far away, came the sounds of battle: the cries of the wounded and the clashing of weapons. Then behind her, another voice.

That voice.

"Stay here. I'll come back for you."

She whirled, glazed eyes desperately scanning the dark gaps between the slender trees, trying to penetrate the darkness.

"Where are you?" She started running toward the voice.

"I'll come back, sweetheart. I promise."

"I'm here! Right here! Where are you?"

No response. She started forward again, running, only to be brought to a sudden halt by a figure appearing without warning from behind a tree.

She screamed, and screamed again, and fell backward, backward, sitting down hard in—

She was in the underground corridor, sitting on the

cold old stone, her chest pounding as if she had just run from her home all the way to Niima Outpost.

"There you are."

The voice made her jump. But it was only Maz Kanata, standing alone in the passageway between her and the far stairway.

"What was—that?" Rey stammered as she struggled to catch her breath.

Maz looked from her to the open doorway and then back to Rey. "It called to you."

Rey stood unsteadily, her mind still rocked by a succession of rapidly evaporating nightmares. BB-8 rolled out of the room to come to a stop beside her.

"I—I shouldn't have gone in there." Aware that she might well have violated unknown privacies, she hurried to voice amends. "I'm sorry . . ."

"Listen to me." Maz was watching her closely. "I know this means something. Something very special . . ."

"I need to get back." Rey shook her head, as if the simple physical action might somehow clear everything from her memory.

Maz came closer. "Yes, Han told me that." Her voice was gentle now, not at all the hard, sardonic tone she had employed up until this moment. "Whatever you've been waiting for—whomever—I can see it in your eyes, you've known it all along . . . they're not coming back. But there's someone who still could. With your help."

Tears were beginning to trickle down Rey's face. She'd had enough, of all of this. It was too much. "No," she said simply.

"That lightsaber was Luke's. And his father's before him. It reached out to *you*. The belonging you seek is not behind you. It is ahead. I am no Jedi, but I know the Force. It moves through and surrounds every liv-

ing thing. Close your eyes. Feel it. The light. It's always been there. It will guide you. The saber. Take it."

Rey's voice strengthened as she wiped away tears. "I'm never touching that thing again. I don't want any part of this."

Without another word Rey took off running, heading determinedly toward the stairs that beckoned just ahead. Accelerating, BB-8 easily kept pace. Maz watched her go and sighed.

One could teach knowledge. One could teach skills. One could even, she knew, teach something of the Force.

But patience had to be learned alone.

The mass rally was impressive. Those who were present would never forget it. Which is the point of such things.

A thousand or so stormtroopers and their officers fronted assembled TIE fighters and lesser machines of war. Around them rose the central edifices of Starkiller Base. Towering still higher above the buildings were the snowy crags of the surrounding mountain range that simultaneously shut off and shielded the central portion of the base from the world around it.

Glorying in the moment, General Hux stood at the head of the assembly flanked by his senior officers, all aligned atop a raised platform backed by an enormous crimson-and-black banner stamped with the insignia of the First Order. Enhanced by artfully concealed amplification, his voice boomed across the troops assembled on the parade ground.

"Today is the end! The end of a government incapacitated by corruption! The end of an illegitimate regime that acquiesces to disorder! At this very moment, in a system far from here, the New Republic

lives and wheezes, staggering onward, depraved and ineffectual and unable in any way to support the citizenry it claims to serve. Meanwhile a host of systems are left to wither and die—without aid, without care, without hope. Drowning in its own decadence, the New Republic ignores them, unaware that these are its final moments." A hand swept sharply downward.

"This fierce machine which you have built, to which you have dedicated your lives and labor and upon which we now stand, will bring a final end to the worthless Senate and its dithering members. To their cherished fleet. When this day is done, all the remaining systems in their hundreds will bow to the dictates of the First Order. And all will remember this as the last day of the last Republic!"

Turning, Hux solemnly gave the signal as the assembled thousand turned to face the mountainous, snowy landscape. Turned, and waited.

Deep within the mountain, engineers and techs concluded the final firing protocol for the new weapon. A last connection was made.

Above, the rally ground was silent. Then, at a great distance, an impossible blast of light shot into the sky. Despite the remoteness of the actual firing zone, the light was so bright that despite their protective masks a number of the troopers had to cover their eyes. The blast was followed by a terrible concussive roar as a vast column of atmosphere was displaced. In spite of the distance, everyone was pushed back and many were knocked down by the ground tremor that followed. Airborne creatures by the thousands took fright and took flight.

Having been gathered in stages by an immense array of coupled collectors located on the other side of the planet, a tremendously compact volume of a type of dark energy known as quintessence had been

accumulated at the center of the planet. Held in place inside a roiling molten metal core by the frozen world's powerful magnetic field, augmented by the weapons system's own containment field, it grew until there was nothing like it—nothing natural like it—in this corner of the galaxy. Penetrating to within a predetermined distance of the containment field, an immense hollow cylinder permitted a way out while ensuring that when the weapon was unleashed, gigantic ground-quakes would not roil the world's fragile surface. When the weapons engineers fired the device, a breach was induced in the containment field. At incredible velocity and accelerating exponentially, the concentrated volume of quintessence escaped, transforming as it did so into a state known as phantom energy and following the artificial line of egress that had been provided. Assuming that the rotation and inclination of the planet had been taken into account, the released blast of concentrated phantom energy would travel along a perfectly linear path, punching a small Big Rip through hyperspace itself until it left the galaxy—

—or encountered something in its path that was of sufficient mass to intercept it.

Overwhelmed and exhausted both physically and mentally, Rey finally slowed to a halt. Running solved nothing. Besides, she had nowhere to run to, and she could not run from herself. A familiar electronic chirp made her turn.

BB-8 slowed as he approached, beeping inquisitively. She was far too tired to acknowledge the little droid's concern.

"No," she replied, gesturing. "You have to go back." More beeping, and she could only shake her head

tiredly. "I thought I was strong enough. Or tough enough. But I'm not."

Traveling faster than anything ever generated by artificial means, through a torn portion of space-time whose properties were not fully understood, the concentrated glowing ball of energy lit the night sky above Republic City. Leia's envoy Korr Sella was among those who gazed uncomprehendingly at the inexplicable phenomenon. Disturbed space was energized and lit up by its passage. It was as if a minuscule sun had suddenly appeared from nowhere, heading directly for the world on which she stood.

It struck with enough force to penetrate the crust and the mantle. Stunned scientists assumed the globe had been hit by an asteroid. The reality was worse, much worse. So powerful was the orb of phantom energy that as it dissipated within the planetary core, it blocked the free flow of elysium. Gravitons that normally moved freely and harmlessly through the planet suddenly were blocked from doing so. Almost immediately, the resulting graviton flux released enough heat to ignite the core . . .

Turning the planet into what astrophysicists called a pocket nova.

Expanding outward from the explosion, a tremendous burst of heat tore through the Hosnian system's other worlds, searing their surfaces clean of life and incidentally obliterating all settlements, installations, and outposts, as well as the hundreds of ships belonging to the Republic fleet. In its wake, the detonation left behind a blazing, spherical mass. The home of the Republic had become a new binary system: one utterly devoid of life.

• • •

The alerts that sounded within the Resistance base were like no other. Every warning telltale lit; every audible alarm went off. Confusion reigned until monitoring and detection systems finally settled on an explanation. An explanation that was impossible.

From his station, Lieutenant Brance looked over at where Leia stood beside C-3PO, scarcely able to put words to what his instruments were telling him.

"General, the Republic command—the entire Hosnian system—it's all—gone." He stared incredulously at his readouts.

Stunned silence filled the control chamber. Some catastrophes were simply too overwhelming to draw immediate comment. Everyone knew the tragedy could not arise from natural causes: It had happened too quickly. That meant . . .

"How is it possible?" C-3PO's optics allowed him to rove from one readout to the next without having to approach them physically. "There is no record, no data relating to a weapon of such magnitude." He looked to his right, suddenly alarmed, as Leia swayed where she was standing. "General, are you all right?"

Leaning against a console for support, she steadied herself. "A great disturbance—in the Force. Deaths and passings. Too much death, too many passings." Straightening, her expression grim, she walked over to confront the wiry, slight Admiral Statura. Despite his experience in battle, he was left as shaken by the revelation as anyone else in the room. What had just happened could scarcely be comprehended.

"Admiral," she said, "we must find this new weapon's point of origin. As soon as possible and before it can be used again."

Statura nodded tersely. "I'll send a reconnaissance ship immediately."

She acknowledged his response as Captain Wexley called to her. "General, we're ready for you."

It was to be a conference on strategy like no other, she knew. To confront a threat that exceeded everything else that had gone before it. She spared a moment's thought for her envoy, Sella, who had been on the Republic capital world when it had been destroyed. And another moment for all who had perished, regardless of their personal or political beliefs. First Alderaan, now the Hosnian system. No one, she knew, should have to be witness to the death of an entire world.

She had been subjected to two.

It must not be allowed to happen again.

The crowd of visitors who had filed out of the old castle had turned their eyes to the sky. A light had appeared there, a new star bright enough to be visible in the daytime. There was much speculation as to its cause. Someone suggested that a star had gone nova, but there were no nearby white dwarfs in the section of sky in question. The stellar apparition was inexplicable, which in turn led to fear and uncertainty among those gazing upward.

From a pouch, Chewbacca withdrew a ponipin and handed it to Han. Activating the compact device, Han aimed it at the light in the sky. Automatically, it linked to the much more powerful stellar navigation instrumentation on board the *Millennium Falcon*, providing a real-time reading of the bit of starfield under scrutiny. Within the ponipin's lens, statistics and readouts combined to create a picture of what was happening in the chosen corner of the cosmos.

Before he could voice an opinion, his fears were confirmed by someone behind him.

"It was the Republic. The First Order—they've gone and done it." A concerned Finn looked past him. "Where's Rey?"

That immediately changed Han's focus. "Thought she was with you."

A voice interrupted them, familiar yet now turned uncommonly forceful. They turned to see Maz approaching.

"You three come with me. There's something you must see."

The subterranean corridor in the castle was one Maz had visited not long before. It was also a place to which she had not expected to return for some time. Circumstances, however, had changed.

A familiar door opened to admit her and those behind her. Dark, treasure-filled, and in the distant dark, a box on a table. "You will need this."

From the box she removed a lightsaber. Finn eyed it uncertainly, but even in the poor light, Han recognized it immediately.

Luke Skywalker's lightsaber.

"Where'd you get that?" Han demanded.

"Long story. A good one—for later." Surprising them all, she handed the weapon not to Han or Chewbacca, but to Finn. "Your friend is in grave danger. Take it—and find Rey."

Finn stared at the device. It felt comfortable in his hand. Lighter than a blaster. Was he worthy of such a gift? Only time and circumstance would tell.

Something potent and loud slammed into the castle, causing dust and rock to fall from the ceiling.

"Those beasts," Maz said. "They're here."

● ● ●

For such a small droid, BB-8 was remarkably persistent. Kneeling beside him, Rey continued to argue.

"No, you can't. You have to go back. You're important. Much more so than I am. They'll help you to
fulfill your mission, more than I ever could. I'm
sorry."

She would have continued but for the thrum overhead that drowned out her words as well as BB-8's
startled beeping. The fleet of First Order ships thun-
dered overhead, dropping toward the castle. The
castle—where her friends still were.

Racing through the trees and back toward the castle,
Rey slowed at the top of a slight rise. Wide-eyed, she
could only hope that her friends had managed to
flee the complex before the attack began in earnest.
Swooping TIE fighters were methodically reducing the
stone walls and towers to dust, while others strafed
smugglers and traders who were frantically running
for cover. Their panicked flight was futile, as they
were quickly intercepted by squads of stormtroopers
who had landed nearby.

Turning to run in the other direction, she caught
herself just in time as a shuttle touched down nearby.
Without the slightest hesitation, the cloaked figure of
Kylo Ren emerged and strode forward to join the
battle. A stunned Rey could only track him with her
eyes. She had seen this man before, in a daydream. In
a nightmare.

Beside her, a tree erupted in flame as splintered
branches flew. One of the patrolling squads of troopers had spotted her and opened fire. Taking cover, she
drew her blaster, aimed, and pulled the trigger. The
moment of panic that ensued when it failed to fire
vanished when she remembered to slip off the safety.
Once activated, the weapon proved as accurate as it
was functional, taking down two of the troopers and

giving the rest reason to pause their pursuit. Calling to BB-8, who was at her side in an instant, she started back into the woods and away from the scene of combat.

"Keep going, stay out of sight," she told the droid. "I'll fight 'em off." A querulous beeping prompted a brave, defiant reply: "I hope so, too."

Emerging from behind the rocks and trees where they had taken cover from the devastatingly precise fire that had hit two of their number, the troopers resumed the search—but more cautiously than before. Spotting Ren moving through the debris, one trooper hurried to report.

"Sir, we're still searching for Solo, but the droid that's wanted was spotted heading west, with a girl."

At this Ren said nothing, but instead looked sharply in the indicated direction.

XIII

AS THE ALIEN WOODS CLOSED IN AROUND her, Rey jumped at every sound, glanced sharply at every wind-rustled branch and falling leaf. Holding tightly to the blaster, she held off firing defensively in the direction of every movement for fear of alerting her pursuers to her location. Sensing something just ahead, she slowed and brought the blaster up. A figure stepped out from behind a tree.

It was the nightmare, and he was wielding a light-saber unlike any she had ever seen in the stories she had read. Its beam was an intense, burning red like a controlled flame, and near the hilt, a pair of shorter beams shot outward, perpendicular to the main shaft.

She fired, again and again. Each shot from her blaster he deflected with the lightsaber's beam. Almost as if it were a game, she thought in terror as she continued to fire. He was playing with her.

Until, evidently, he tired of it. He raised a hand, held it toward her, palm outward. As she inhaled sharply, her hand froze on the blaster. She tried to turn, to run, but her legs refused to respond. She could only stand there among the trees, taking in slow, measured breaths, as he came toward her.

Halting an arm's length away, he studied her face from behind his mask. When he finally spoke, he sounded at once impressed and surprised. "You would *kill* me. Knowing nothing about me."

Finding that her mouth and lips worked, she replied defiantly. "Why wouldn't I kill you? I know about the First Order."

"I would say otherwise. But that is a small thing. Simple ignorances are easily remedied." As he spoke, he walked slowly around her paralyzed body. Frightened, she tried to follow him with her eyes, but her head would not turn. "So afraid," he murmured. "Yet I should be the one who should be scared. You shot first. You speak of the Order as if it were barbaric. And yet, it is I who was forced to defend myself against you."

Having circled her, he moved even closer, peering into her face, her eyes. Then the red lightsaber he held came up: close to her flesh, close enough to cast a red glow on her skin.

"Something." He sounded mystified. "There is something . . . *Who are you?*"

Reaching the outdoors after having worked their way through mounds of debris, Han and the others kept to the cover of collapsed stone walls as they took stock of their surroundings. Maz turned to Finn.

"Go. Find the girl and the droid."

He looked back the way they had come. "Lost my blaster. I need a weapon."

Displaying surprising strength for one so small, Maz grabbed the wrist holding the lightsaber and raised it up. "You have one!"

He stared down at her, then at the saber. Did she really expect him to use the old ceremonial weapon?

Blasters he knew, and pulse rifles, but he had never held a lightsaber in his life. Nor did he know anyone who had. Still, if Maz Kanata had that kind of confidence in him . . . He activated the device, admiring the lethal beam.

It made an excellent target for the stormtroopers who opened fire on them. Taking cover, Han and Chewbacca returned fire. No one noticed the troopers who had come up behind them—except Finn. Charging, he surprised one trooper with the glowing blade of the lightsaber, then another. A third came at him with a close-quarters weapon and the two locked in combat. Despite lack of any training with a lightsaber, Finn was athletic and courageous. In tandem with such traits, the saber made him a formidable fighter.

Shutting down and belting his lightsaber, Ren contemplated his immobile captive. Reaching up slowly, he touched her face. The pressure he applied was not physical. Refusing to meet his gaze, she looked away, straining with the agony of resistance, hardly daring to breathe. If only she could get a hand free, a leg—but no part of her body responded to her commands.

Surprised by what he was finding, Ren lowered his hand. Relieved of the mental intrusion, she sucked in great, long draughts of air. His brows drew together and a reluctance to believe his own findings colored his comments.

"Is it true, then? You're nothing special after all? You're just a—Jakku scavenger?"

How did he know that? she agonized as she stared back at him. Surely she hadn't thought it! She'd tried to keep her mind blank, her memory locked, and still he had wormed his way in. He touched her anew.

This time the pain of trying to stave him off brought tears streaming down her face. He was within her mind and her thoughts, and there was nothing—*nothing!*—she could do to keep him out. To resist. But she kept trying, trying . . .

"Hmm . . . ," he murmured softly. "You've met the traitor who served under me. A minor annoyance grown larger than he deserves. You find him more than tolerable." He drew back slightly, bemused. "You've even begun to care for him. A weakness, such distractions."

Suddenly he put his face so close to hers that they were almost touching. "You've seen it! The map! It's in your mind right now . . ."

She could hardly swallow as she strained to pull away from him, anything to pull away, to get him out.

She wanted to scream, but he would not allow it.

The trooper who had engaged Finn was big, strong, and agile. Finn realized the fight would have long since been over if not for the trooper's regard for the lethal potential of the lightsaber. That didn't stop him from finally knocking Finn to the ground and raising his own weapon for a killing strike—only to fall backward, shot before he could deliver the blow.

Rolling over, a relieved Finn saw Han racing toward him, blaster in hand, with Chewbacca not far behind. The older man reached down and an unexpectedly powerful grip helped Finn to his feet.

"You okay, big deal?"

Finn had to grin at that. "I'm okay, yeah—thanks."

They were interrupted by the sudden appearance of a dozen stormtroopers, acting in concert and with weapons aimed, atop a nearby mass of debris. Han

started to bring his gun around, hesitated. The odds sucked.

"Drop the weapons!" the lead trooper ordered. *"Now!"*

Surrounded by blasters, they had no choice but to comply. One trooper made a beeline for the lightsaber and picked it up. Han's thoughts were racing as a second squad of troopers appeared behind them.

"How are we gonna get out of this one? There's too many of 'em," he muttered to Chewbacca. When no reply was forthcoming, he added, "Any ideas?" The Wookiee moaned a terse reply, to which Han responded with a half sneer. "Very funny."

"Hands on heads. Let's go." The lead trooper gestured in the direction of a parked transport. "Try anything and I'll shoot your legs off."

They didn't try anything. There is a time to take chances and a time to wait for opportunity, Han knew. What he didn't expect was that the latter would put in an appearance so soon.

He had never been so happy to see a squadron of X-wings.

Accompanied by other attack craft, the familiar shapes came in low and fast, roaring over the lake and the forest as they blew apart the First Order ships whose pilots, feeling themselves secure, had nearly all landed their craft in the vicinity of the destroyed castle. A perplexed Chewbacca barked his surprise at the unexpected appearance of the non-Republic ships.

"It's the Resistance!" Han yelled, as hope surged within him.

Marked in black, one particular X-wing swooped in dangerously low, attacking at treetop level. Blast after blast took out parked TIE fighters, clusters of troopers, and support vehicles. Whoever was piloting

was skilled enough to fire repeatedly without wasting a single energy burst.

As the captives dove for cover, another blast scattered their captors as they tried to fight back armed only with hand weapons. When the dust cleared enough for them to see, the three rose, and Han and Chewbacca recovered their weapons. Reaching for a trooper's blaster, Finn hesitated. It took him a moment of searching to find the dropped lightsaber. Turning his gaze skyward, he followed the black-stained X-wing as it looped around in an impossibly tight arc, coming back for another run.

"That's one helluva pilot!" he commented.

"Yeah," Han yelled as he beckoned to the younger man. "How about you appreciate the maneuvers from behind cover before you get your admiring self shot?"

At the sound of nearby explosions, Ren ceased his probing, but he did not remove his hand from Rey's face as he turned toward the now ruined castle. She remained standing before him, unable to move, gazing blankly into the distance. A clutch of stormtroopers, breathing hard, came toward him through the trees.

"Sir," the leader gasped, his alarm and dismay evident, "Resistance fighters!"

Ren considered. Though he was not technically in charge of battlefield decisions, no officer would attempt to overrule any decision he chose to make.

"Pull our troops out. We have what we need."

The squad leader saluted, lingered a moment to look on in fascination as at a gesture from Ren the young woman standing motionless before him collapsed, and then he hastened to relay the command

lest his interest in something that was none of his business be noticed. He had no wish to join the woman on the ground in a state of oblivion.

The black-marked X-wing swooped low to take out yet another TIE fighter still on the ground. The retreating stormtroopers, rushing to board their transports, were easy targets for the castle's survivors.

Two, running from the furious defenders, were taken out by Finn, using a recovered blaster. As he looked around for more stragglers, Finn found his attention drawn to a singular figure striding through the edge of the forest. He almost looked away before catching sight of and identifying the burden the cloaked officer was carrying into a shuttle of atypical design. Finn's spirits plunged.

"REY!!!"

Ignoring the fire of retreating stormtroopers, paying no attention to the blasts that gouged the dirt around him, Finn raced toward the shuttle—only to watch helplessly as it lifted off and rose toward the clouds. Irrationally, he tried to follow the dark spot as it rose higher into the sky, running beneath it until it shrank to a dot and then finally disappeared.

"No, no, no, no . . . Rey, *Rey*!"

Ascending, other First Order ships formed up in the wake of the shuttle, creating a tight escort to seal it off from any pursuit. Utilizing oculars far more sensitive than those of any human, BB-8 tracked the battle group until it had receded even beyond his sight, lost at the edge of space. The droid paused for a moment, pondering.

Out of breath, tears glistening on his cheeks, Finn slowed as he drew alongside Han.

"He took her!" Finn managed to gasp. "He took her! Did you see that? She's gone, Rey's gone!"

Reaching out, Han shoved Finn aside without meeting the younger man's gaze. "Get outta my way!"

Knocked off balance, Finn slowed to a stop, stunned, his eyes fixed on Han's retreating back. He was too shocked to know how to respond. As he stood staring, he noticed Maz a short distance away, speaking to BB-8.

"Yes, it's true, they have Rey now," Maz said. "But we can't give up hope." She looked down at the droid, who beeped forlornly. "Go," she told the droid. "Share what you have with your people. They need you."

Finn walked over to her, and together Maz and Finn watched the droid roll off. "Looks like I've got some cleaning up to do, hmm?" Maz said. Then the diminutive smuggler looked up at him and smiled in satisfaction. "Oh wow . . . I see something else now."

"See what?" Finn asked.

"I see the eyes of a warrior."

Han waited until the Resistance transport had settled itself completely before approaching the main access. His attention fixed on the portal, he looked away only to nod down at the round figure of BB-8, who had rolled up beside him. The droid's presence confirmed Han's expectations. He would be surprised if either of them had guessed wrong as to who was going to exit the transport first. However, he was willing to be surprised.

He wasn't.

Husband and wife stood regarding each other for the first time in years. Amid the smoke and drifting embers, neither said a word. Emerging from behind the figure in the portal, C-3PO walked out into the

scorched field to confront the motionless droid beside Han.

"Beebee-Ate! Come here. I'm here to assist you in translating what—"

It took a moment for the countenance of the man standing beside the spherical droid to register on C-3PO's preoccupied consciousness. A visage changed by time and altered by experience, it required a bit of additional visual processing before the protocol droid was able to link it to the images in his memory.

"Oh! Han Solo! It is I, See-Threepio! You probably don't recognize me because of the red arm." Turning to the woman standing in the transport threshold, he continued excitedly. "Look who it is! Han Solo! Isn't that—Excuse me, Prin—uh, General. Sorry. Come, Beebee-Ate. We need to settle on a procedure for debriefing."

The two droids moved off. Chewbacca found an excuse to study the configuration of a grove of nearby trees that had somehow survived the recent conflagration.

Breaking the awkward silence, Han finally spoke to Leia.

"You changed your hair."

Her gaze dropped from his face. "Same jacket."

"No. New jacket."

Unable to stand it a moment longer, Chewie gave in to emotion. Stepping forward, he wrapped Leia in a warm embrace that momentarily resulted in her disappearance within a mass of fur. Letting her go, he moaned a few words that contained far more depth of feeling than would be apparent to an outsider unfamiliar with the Wookiee language, and boarded the transport.

Left alone again, husband and wife also embraced.

Han murmured over her shoulder, "I saw him. He was here."

Hearing this, she closed her eyes. They let the silence take them.

D'Qar's terrain was green and verdant, with flourishing trees that put those on most worlds to shame in size and appearance.

Careful not to damage a single one of the immense, unique growths, the Resistance squadron put down between them. Grassy mounds camouflaged hangars and other structures. Resistance techs were everywhere in evidence, repairing damaged craft, running cables, cleaning and refurbishing. The base was a hive of activity, nearly all of which was hidden from above. One restoration team was hard at work on the parked *Millennium Falcon,* an ugly duckling among the sleeker X-wings and support craft.

The sight of a singular figure in the cockpit of an X-wing that had just landed sent Finn running. Fast as he was moving, he was no match for BB-8. Rolling at maximum speed, the droid nearly knocked him down as it shot past him in its haste to reach the fighter with the black insignia. Its canopy was already open; the pilot had removed his helmet and was chatting with one of the techs as he descended from the cockpit.

Poe Dameron.

No wonder, Finn thought, he and the others had marveled at the pilot's skill during the course of the counterattack at Maz's castle. This was clearly, indisputably, the best pilot in the Resistance. His presence, however, defied reason.

Finn just stared at him, hardly believing what he was seeing.

Kneeling and chatting with BB-8, the pilot was nodding at something the droid was saying. It took him a moment to look up and glance to his right. The expression on his face when he recognized Finn was no less astonished than that of the ex-trooper. Smiling, he rose and gestured as Finn continued toward him.

For a moment they just stared, each overwhelmed to find the other alive. Finn could only shake his head in wonder.

"Poe," he said. "Poe Dameron. Best pilot in the Resistance. I can attest to that, because I got to see him in action. Hell, I was in action with him!"

"Finn!" the other man shouted with a grin. "Bravest trooper in the— Well, ex-trooper."

They embraced, then stood back from each other.

"You're alive!" Finn's observation was heartfelt.

"So are you," Poe countered, adding the unnecessary.

Finn studied him intently. "You look like you're in one piece. I can hardly believe it. I thought you were dead: shot up in that TIE fighter we stole. I ejected. When I finally found the wreckage, I looked for you. Pulled your jacket out of your ship before it got swallowed by the sand. What happened to you?"

"I wasn't dead, just momentarily out of it," the pilot explained. "Came around long enough to see that you had got out. Pulled out of the dive just long enough to set down—hard. Impact threw me clear. Woke up at night; no you, no ship, no nothing. Went looking—in the wrong direction. Got picked up by some itinerant trader." He grinned. "Tell you all about it sometime." A plaintive beep caused him to turn and look down. "Beebee-Ate says that you saved him."

Finn eyed the droid. "It wasn't just me." A slow

smile spread across his face and his eyes twinkled. "Tell you all about it sometime."

"Either way, you completed my mission." Poe gestured at their surroundings. "Beebee-Ate is here, where he was supposed to come all along. *And* you saved my jacket."

Finn started to slip out of it. "Oh, sorry—here."

Poe grinned anew. "No, no. Just kidding. You keep it. It suits you." He held up an arm. "I've got a new one. Suits me." His tone turned somber. "You're a good man, Finn. The Resistance needs the help of more like you."

"Poe—I need *your* help."

The pilot shrugged. "Anything."

"I need to see General Organa," Finn told him. "Can you manage that?"

Buried deep in the native vegetation, the base command center was staffed by guards at multiple levels. The readily recognized Poe, however, had no difficulty proceeding deeper into the complex or bringing his friend with him.

When they arrived at the conference room, they found Leia conversing earnestly with a number of senior Resistance officers. From his training, Finn recognized among them the prominent admirals Statura and Ackbar. All looked over as the two younger men entered. Without hesitating, Poe moved directly to Leia.

"General Organa. Sorry to interrupt, but"—he indicated his companion—"this is Finn and he needs to talk to you."

Excusing herself, she turned away from the officers and directly to Finn. "And I need to talk to him." She took Finn's hand.

She had, Finn mused as he gazed back at her, dark eyes that had seen too much.

"That was incredibly brave, what you did. Renouncing the First Order is almost unheard of. To do that, and then to compound the risk by saving this man's life, marks you as . . ."

Clearly, she had been fully briefed about Finn's exploits. Not that any of that mattered, not now. Anyway, he had grown immune to compliments he didn't think he deserved. What was important was that every passing moment had become precious to him. Otherwise he could never have imagined interrupting someone like General Organa.

"Thank you, ma'am, but I'm here to talk about a friend of mine who was taken prisoner during the clash on Takodana."

She nodded understandingly. "Han told me about the girl. I'm sorry."

That startled Finn, but before he could comment further, Poe jumped in. There was little he wouldn't do to help Finn, but the needs of the Resistance had to outweigh everyone's personal concerns.

"Finn's familiar with the weapon that destroyed the Hosnian system. He worked on the world where it's based."

Leia's excitement was palpable. "You worked on the weapon itself?"

"No," Finn demurred. "I'm a trooper, not an engineer or a physicist. But I've had some tech training, and in the course of that, everyone was told the purpose of the base. I can't tell you how the weapon functions; the science is beyond me. But I *do* know where it is. Or rather, where it's controlled from."

"No reason to keep that a secret from the people guarding it," Poe pointed out with quiet glee, "since stormtroopers never defect."

"We're desperate," Leia told Finn, "for anything you can tell us. Until the Hosnian system was annihilated, we didn't even know such a weapon existed."

"It's located on the world that serves as the First Order's main base," Finn told her. "I'm sure that's where they've taken my friend. I need to get there, fast."

"I'll try to help you," she replied. "You have my word. I'm sure you understand that because of what happened to the Hosnian system, right now the Resistance has other priorities. But if they happen to coincide . . ." Leia paused, and Finn got the impression that his urgency to find someone was something Leia understood all too well. "Then we'll do our best to find your friend," she finished. She indicated the nearby group of officers. "Right now I need you to tell Admiral Ackbar all you know. Everything you can remember about the First Order base, down to the smallest and seemingly most insignificant detail." She paused again for a moment, lost in thought.

"The girl," she inquired, her voice strengthening. "What can you tell me about her that might help us locate her? What's her name?"

Finn struggled to contain his emotions. "Rey."

A strong voice, not human, rumbled behind Finn. Turning, he found himself staring back at the widely set eyes of Admiral Ackbar.

"Come with me, young man. I wish to hear everything and anything you have to say, and myself, I have a great many questions to ask you."

Sitting up on the scanner bed in the med center, Chewbacca was quiet as Dr. Kalonia worked on the Wookiee's injured shoulder. Dark of hair and eyes with a kindly demeanor, the physician was far more

adept than Finn had been, and the device she was employing could not be felt even while it was in use. As the lingering pain faded, Chewie growled appreciatively at the doctor.

"You're most welcome."

The Wookiee looked over and down at himself. All signs of the wound had nearly been erased, at which sight he groaned softly.

"That sounds very scary," Kalonia commented as she worked. Another series of gentle moans. "Yes, you're very brave."

XIV

THE SEARCH HAD TAKEN BB-8 SOME TIME, BUT he finally found what he was looking for. Or rather, who. Or maybe both, since an intelligent droid technically qualified as both a who and a what. In the dark, dusty storeroom he rolled over to the R2 unit and beeped a greeting, the transmission sequence too rapid and too exhaustive for any human to follow. It didn't matter. There was no response from the immobile R2 unit.

BB-8 tried again, utilizing a different droid language. When that also failed, he moved forward and gave the other mechanical a forceful nudge. Like everything else, that too failed to generate a response.

Observing the unsuccessful interaction, C-3PO came forward out of the shadows.

"You're wasting your time, I'm afraid. It is very doubtful that Artoo would have the rest of the map in his backup data." When BB-8 queried the protocol droid, C-3PO responded without hesitation.

"He's been locked down in self-imposed low-power mode. He just hasn't been the same since Master Luke went away."

A new voice, that of a human this time, called to them. "Beebee-Ate!"

In response, the spherical droid reluctantly rolled over to the officer who had interrupted.

"General needs you!"

Beeping a polite farewell to C-3PO and a final thought to the silent R2-D2, BB-8 followed the officer out of the storage area. Behind them, C-3PO bent over his old friend.

"Oh, do try and cheer up, Artoo. This enforced immobility is no good for you. Your cognitive circuits will atrophy from lack of use."

His affable urging proved no more effective than had BB-8's authoritative querying. The R2 unit remained as it was: silent, unmoving, and unresponsive.

In the main conference room, C-3PO worked on BB-8's flank while Han and several officers looked on. Complying with the protocol droid's orders, BB-8 obediently opened a locked and sealed port on its side.

"Ah, thank you. That's it."

Reaching in, C-3PO removed a tiny device. Turning, he inserted it into a matching slot in the multi-sided table-projector that dominated the center of the room. Immediately, a three-dimensional map filled the space above the flat-topped apparatus with stars, nebulae, and other stellar phenomena. Leia studied the display intently. But though her eyes roved knowledgably through the compacted cosmos, she failed to find what she was looking for. Her dissatisfaction was unmistakable.

While he was in his own way equally disappointed, C-3PO was not programmed to display it. Instead, he merely expressed a rational regret.

"General, while I have already completed a preliminary analysis, I'll inform you of my final determination only when I have finished comparing the information available in this map to that in our full database. There. I've finished. Unfortunately, I have to conclude that this map contains insufficient data with which to make a match to any system in our records."

From a corner, Han spoke up. "Told you."

Leia ignored him. "What a fool I was to think we could just find Luke and bring him back."

He moved toward her. "Leia . . ."

She growled at him. "Don't do that."

It stopped him cold. "Do what?"

Her voice was flat. "Be nice to me." Whirling, she stomped off. More than a little bewildered, he followed. Though he caught up to her easily, she didn't stop, nor did she look in his direction.

"Hey, I'm here to help," he told her.

She continued to march forward, her gaze set straight ahead. "When did that ever *help*? And don't say the Death Star."

Frustrated, he stepped out in front of her to block her path. When he spoke again, his tone softened until he was almost pleading—as much as Han Solo was capable of pleading.

"Will you just stop and listen to me for a minute? *Please?*"

The change in tone did more to mollify her than anything else. She eyed him impatiently. "I'm listening, Han."

"I didn't plan on coming here," he explained. "I know whenever you look at me, you're reminded of him. So I stayed away."

She stared at him, shaking her head slowly. "*That's*

what you think? That I don't want to be reminded of him, that I want to forget him? *I want him back.*"

What could he say to that? What possible response could he give to a willful denial of reason? "He's gone, Leia. He was always drawn to the dark side. There was nothing we could've done to stop it, no matter how hard we tried." His final words were the hardest to get out. "There was too much Vader in him."

"That's why I wanted him to train with Luke," Leia said. "I just never should have sent him away. That's when I lost him. When I lost you both."

Han dipped his head. "We both had to deal with it in our own way." He shrugged. "I went back to the only thing I was ever good at."

"We both did," Leia admitted.

He met her eyes steadily. "We've lost our son, forever."

Leia bit her lower lip, refusing to concede. "No. It was Snoke."

Han drew back slightly. "Snoke?"

She nodded. "He knew our child would be strong with the Force. That he was born with equal potential for good or evil."

"You knew this from the beginning? Why didn't you tell me?"

She sighed. "Many reasons. I was hoping that I was wrong, that it wasn't true. I hoped I could sway him, turn him away from the dark side, without having to involve you." A small smile appeared. "You had—you have—wonderful qualities, Han, but patience and understanding were never among them. I was afraid that your reactions would only drive him farther to the dark side. I thought I could shield him from Snoke's influence and you from what was happening." Her voice dropped. "It's clear now that I

was wrong. Whether your involvement would have made a difference, we'll never know."

He had trouble believing what he was hearing. "So Snoke was watching our son."

"Always," she told him. "From the shadows, in the beginning, even before *I* realized what was happening, he was manipulating everything, pulling our son toward the dark side.

"But nothing's impossible, Han. Not even now, at this late time. I have this feeling that if anyone can save him—it's you."

He wanted to laugh derisively. If he did, he knew she might never speak to him again. "Me? No. If Luke couldn't reach him, with all his skills and training, how can I?"

She was nodding slowly. "Luke is a Jedi. But you're his father. There's still light in him. I know it."

The complex restraining apparatus held Rey upright against an angled platform in the cell. She woke slowly. Disoriented, at first she thought she was alone. Her oversight was understandable, since the other person in the holding area did not move, did not make a sound, and at times scarcely seemed to breathe.

Though startled by his unsettlingly silent presence, she took a moment to take stock of her surroundings. They were as different as could be imagined from her previous ones. The last thing she remembered was the confrontation in the forest on Takodana, the sounds of battle, and sending away the droid BB-8. That, and then the mind probe. The pain. Her efforts to shut it out, and the contemptuous ease with which her mental defenses had been brushed aside. Even now, there was a lingering ache at the back of her eyes.

The forest was gone. So was Maz's castle. Bereft of a point of reference, she had no choice but to ask.

"Where am I?"

"Does the physical location really matter so much?" In Kylo Ren's voice there was unexpected gentleness. Not quite sympathy, but something less than the hostility with which he had confronted her in the forest. "You're my guest."

With an ease that was more frightening than any physical approach, he waved casually in her direction. A couple of clicks, and the restraints fell away from her arms. She tried to take the demonstration in stride as she rubbed her wrists. The last thing she wanted was for him to think he could intimidate her any more than he already had. Looking around the room, she confirmed that they were alone.

"Where are the others? The ones who were fighting with me?"

He sniffed disdainfully. "You mean the traitors, murderers, and thieves you call friends? Consider carefully now: I could easily tell you they were all killed, righteously slain in battle. But I would prefer to be honest with you from the beginning. You will be relieved to hear that as far as their current status and well-being is concerned—I have no idea."

She stared at him. Though at the moment he was calm, she could not escape the feeling that a wrong word, an unsatisfactory response, might set him off. *Be very careful with this person,* she told herself.

He looked at her as if she had just spoken aloud. For all the chance she had of hiding her emotions from him, she realized, she might as well have voiced her thoughts.

"You still want to kill me," he murmured.

Her true self got the better of her and she replied

tactlessly, despite the danger. "That happens when you're being hunted by a creature in a mask."

She had a moment to ponder his possible reaction and to fear it. But he did not do what she expected. Instead, he reached up, unlatched and removed his mask. She just stared at him in silence.

In itself the narrow face that looked back at her was not remarkable. It was almost sensitive. If not for the intensity of his gaze, Ren could have passed for someone she might have met on the dusty streets of Niima Outpost. But there was—that gaze. That, and what lay simmering behind it.

"Is it true?" he finally asked. "You're just a scavenger?" She didn't respond, and, perhaps sensing her embarrassment, he changed the subject. "Tell me about the droid."

She swallowed. "It's a BB unit with a selenium drive and a thermal hyperscan vindicator, internal self-correcting gyroscopic propulsion system, optics corrected to—"

"I am familiar with general droid technical specifications. I don't need to acquire one: What I want is located in its memory. It's carrying a section of a transgalactic navigational chart. We have the rest, recovered from the archives of the Empire. We need the last piece. Somehow, *you* convinced the droid to show it to you. You. A simple, solitary scavenger. How is that?"

She looked away. How did he know that? By the same means he had used to learn everything else?

"I know you've seen the map," he repeated. "It's what I need. At the moment, it is all that I need." When she maintained her silence, he almost sighed. "I can take whatever I want."

Her muscles tightened. "Then you don't need me to tell you anything."

"True." He rose, resigned. "I would have preferred to avoid this. Despite what you may believe, it gives me no pleasure. I will go as easily as possible—but I *will* take what I need."

She knew that trying to resist him physically would not only be useless but would likely result in unpleasantness of a kind she preferred not to imagine. So she remained motionless and silent, her arms at her sides, as his hand rose toward her face. He touched her again, as he had in the forest on Takodana.

And hesitated. What was that? Something there. Something unexpected.

As she strained to resist the probe, he pushed into her, brushing aside her awkward attempts to keep him out. While he investigated her mind, he spoke softly.

"You've been so lonely," he murmured as he searched for what he needed. "So afraid to leave." A thin smile crossed his face. "At night, desperate to sleep, you'd imagine an ocean. I can see it . . . I can see the island."

Tears were streaming down her face from the effort she was making to withstand him. Increasingly desperate, she did try to strike out. But just as on Takodana, her body refused to respond.

"And Han Solo," Ren continued relentlessly. "He feels like the father you never had. A dead end, that vision. Let it go. I can tell you for a fact he would have disappointed you."

All the rage and terror bottled up inside her came out as she turned to meet his stare.

"Get—out—of—my—head."

It only made him lean in closer, enhancing her feeling of complete helplessness. "Rey—you've seen the map. It's in there. And I am going to take it. Don't be afraid."

Where the strength to defy him came from she did not know, but if anything, her voice grew a little stronger. *"I'm not giving you anything."*

His response reflected his unconcern. "We'll see."

Narrowing his gaze and his focus, he locked eyes with her. She met his stare without trying to look away. She should have looked away. It would have been the rational thing to do. The sane thing to do. Instead, she just glared, trying not to flinch, not to blink.

Ah, he thought to himself. *Something there, of interest.* Not the image of the map. That would take another moment. But definitely something worth investigating. He shifted his perception toward it, seeking to identify, to analyze, to—

The barrier he encountered stopped him cold. And it was he, Kylo Ren, who blinked. It made no sense. He pushed, hard, with his mind—and the probe went nowhere.

A look of amazement replaced the fear on Rey's face as she discovered herself inside *his* mind. Stunned at the realization, she found herself inexorably drawn to—to . . .

"You," she heard herself saying clearly, "you're *afraid*. That you will never be as strong as—Darth Vader!"

His hand pulled sharply away from her cheek as if her skin had suddenly turned white-hot. Confused, rattled, he stumbled back from her. Her gaze followed him. Her eyes were the same, but something else had changed—something behind them, in her stare and in her posture. He moved to leave and, at the last moment, gestured powerfully in her direction. The restraints that had held her wrists snapped back into place, once again securing her to the inclined platform. Then he once again donned his mask and was gone.

In the corridor, a stunned Ren found that he was breathing hard. That in itself was unsettling. He did not know what had just transpired in the holding cell and, not knowing, was left uncertain how to proceed. He was spared further bewilderment when a trooper appeared, coming toward him. Straightening, Ren gathered himself.

The trooper halted. His evident discomfort at having to speak to Ren bolstered his superior's shaken persona.

"Sir! The Supreme Leader has requested your presence."

Ren nodded and headed off in the necessary direction, accompanied by the trooper. The latter did not pay any attention when the tall figure he was escorting looked back over his shoulder.

In the holding cell, Rey relaxed against the platform. That she could relax at all was significant in itself. Something of great consequence had just taken place. How and what, she did not know. Even in her present situation she felt encouraged, though why that should be she was still uncertain. One thing was clear.

She was going to be given time to contemplate it.

In the main conference room of the base on D'Qar, an ongoing strategy session had brought together the leaders of the Resistance. Leia, Poe, C-3PO, Han, and an assortment of senior officers including Statura and Ackbar were assembled around a three-dimensional map of an isolated, frozen planet that up until now had not been worth a hopeful visit from a minor trading ship. Finn was present, too, since it was his information about the world in question that had prompted the gathering.

"The scan data from Captain Snap Wexley's reconnaissance flight confirms everything Finn has told us," Poe announced to the group.

Wexley spoke up. "They've built a new kind of hyperspace weapon within the planet itself. Something that can fire across interstellar distances in the equivalent of real time." His expression showed his incredulity. "I've had my share of technical training, but I can't even imagine how that's possible."

This time Finn responded. "I can't, either, but those of us assigned to the base heard rumors that it doesn't operate in what we'd call normal hyperspace. It fires through a hole in the continuum that it makes itself. Everybody was calling it 'sub'-hyperspace. That's how it can arrive in moments across a distance like that between the base and the Hosnian system. The amount of energy required to do that is . . ." His voice dropped. "Well, we've seen how much energy is involved. All I know is that it involves a lot of zeros following the primary number."

Wexley nodded slowly. "We're not sure how to describe a weapon of this scale. Our people have come up with some ideas regarding the rapid overheating and subsequent implosion of a planetary core, but the mechanism to induce that so far escapes them."

One of the oldest officers in the room gestured sharply, a look of horror on his face. "It's another Death Star!"

Poe's expression tightened. "I wish that were the case, Major Ematt. But in analyzing everything Finn has told us and coupling that with the information we have been able to gather, this is what we are facing." He waved a hand over a nearby control. An image of the Death Star appeared beside that of the frozen world.

"This was the Death Star," the pilot observed. An-

other control and the image shrank, down to near nothing, until it was a small sphere beside the cold planet. "This is what Finn tells us is called Starkiller Base."

Leia stared at the invidious imagery. If not for the harsh fact that tens of millions of deaths were involved, the side-by-side comparisons would have been laughable. Once more, memories of the destruction of Alderaan flooded back and once more she had to force them aside.

"How can they power a weapon of such magnitude?" she asked.

Poe and Ackbar looked to Finn. Unsure of himself, he hesitated. He was no scientist, no engineer, not even a technician. Yes, he had overheard a number of related conversations, but given what was riding on what up until now had been only hearsay to him, he was reluctant to share them.

Sensing his hesitation, Leia was quick to prompt him. "Finn, please speak up."

He looked across at her. "I'm not sure of the authenticity of what I've heard or been told."

"Whatever it is, it's volumes more than anything we know," she assured him. "Tell us, and let our technical people be the judge of your words."

Taking a deep breath, he gestured at the image of the base. "As you already know, I was assigned there. In the course of performing my duties, I was rotated to multiple locations around the planet. One is on the side opposite from where the weapon is discharged."

An incredulous Statura cut him off. "The weapon system is situated on both sides of the planet?"

Finn looked at the admiral. "Not only is it located on both sides, the system actually runs through the planetary core."

Murmurs of disbelief rose from those gathered around the projection console.

"As near as I understand it," Finn continued, "enormous arrays of specially designed collectors use the power of a sun to attract and send dark energy to a containment unit at the core of the planet, where it is held and built up inside that containment unit until the weapon is ready to fire."

"Impossible," Ackbar insisted. "Although we know there is more dark energy in the universe than anything else, and that it exists everywhere around us, it is so diffuse that it can barely be detected. Let alone concentrated."

Finn persisted, despite the discomfort he felt at disagreeing with someone of Ackbar's rank and experience. "It can be, and it is," he responded with certainty.

Statura, at least, seemed ready to believe. "If the engineering could be worked out," he observed, "one would have access to an almost literally infinite source of energy."

Finn nodded. "General Hux told us it's the most powerful weapon ever built. He said that it can reach halfway across the galaxy." Fresh murmurs of disbelief greeted this latest assertion. "And in real time. Because it doesn't reach *across* the galaxy; it reaches *through* it." He shook his head, which was starting to hurt from the effort of trying to explain what he had overheard but did not understand.

Han Solo understood, all right. Understood what had to be done.

"Okay, so it's impossible, and it's big. How do we blow it up?" The attention in the room shifted to him. His expression was knowing. "I don't care how big it is; there's always a way to do that."

Having cut through the science, he waited for suggestions. None were forthcoming.

"We have to wait until the technical staff have run their detailed analysis," Wexley said. "Then, once they've done that—"

Leia cut him off. Han grinned, but not so she could see it. She was good at cutting people off, he knew.

"We don't have time to wait on analyses and scientific hypotheses. Han's right. We have to act, and act *now*." He eyed her in surprise—and concealed that reaction, too.

"This is the moment that counts," she continued. "Everything we've ever fought for is at stake. We can't wait on theories. We need something, anything, so we can fight back!" She straightened. "We have to take this weapon down before it can be used again."

It was not surprising to her that it was Statura, the most senior officer in the room with an actual scientific background, who finally put forth a notion.

"I can't prove this, but for this amount of power to be restrained until such time as it is released, or fired, there has to be some new, advanced kind of containment field." He nodded toward Finn. "Our friend here confirms as much. The question is: What kind of field?"

"I heard that it involved the planet's own magnetic field," Finn told him, "and something more."

"Yes, yes." Statura was deep in thought. "A planetary magnetic field, even a strong one, would not be enough to contain the amount of energy that we have seen deployed. Also as you say, Finn, there is more involved. I am thinking some kind of oscillating field. If it oscillates rapidly enough, much less energy would be required to sustain it than if it was maintained at a steady state."

"I don't know about stuff like that." Finn leaned

into the holographic map and enlarged a section of planetary surface until a massive hexagonal structure came into view. "But this is where the containment and oscillation field control system is located."

Statura was most pleased. "Excellent, Mr. Finn!" The admiral's gaze traveled around the circle of colleagues. "But disabling this, while a relatively straightforward proposition, would not necessarily destroy the weapon—only render it temporarily unusable until the control system could be rebuilt."

"We'd likely get only one shot at it," Poe put in. "What Admiral Ackbar said about keeping it secret would only work as long as its location remains unknown. Once the First Order realizes that we know where it is, they'd throw everything they've got into defending it with ships, mobile stations, and long-range detectors. We might never get close to it again."

Leia nodded agreement. "Then our first attack *must* succeed." She looked across at Statura. "What do you recommend, Admiral?"

"Assuming for the moment that my hurried supposition is reasonably correct, the weapon would be at its most vulnerable when, as it were, it is fully loaded." Once again he regarded the others. "If the containment field oscillator were somehow destroyed at that moment, it would release the accumulated energy not in a line of fire, but throughout the planetary core where it is being held. If it did not result in the complete destruction of the base, at the very least it would permanently cripple the weapon."

His flare of white hair and beard giving him the look of a prophet, Major Ematt spoke up. "Maybe even the entire planet on which it's based."

As the discussion continued, an officer appeared and handed Leia a readout. She studied it intently as the debate swirled around her.

"None of this is possible," a downcast Ackbar postulated. "While the planet in question may at present be deliberately underdefended, the instant we move forces out of hiding and in its direction, the First Order will realize that we know the location of the weapon. They will mobilize everything in the vicinity to protect it. Their fleet is too large for us to fight our way through. Additionally, despite what Poe theorizes, I would wager they must already have at least a minimal planetary shield in place. Plainly, they can access the energy to support such a defense." He looked at Finn, whose reply was not encouraging.

"Yes, such a shield does exist."

"The situation could not be worse," C-3PO murmured.

Raising a hand for attention, Leia held up the readout. "According to this, we don't have time to study the situation even if we decided to do so. Our team has detected an enormous quantity of dark energy surging toward the world Finn has identified for us. That can only mean one thing." She paused for emphasis. "They're loading the weapon again. I think we can all take a good guess as to what their next target will be."

C-3PO lowered his golden head. "I was wrong. It can be worse."

Seeing the downcast expressions of those around him, Poe reached out and indicated the containment control structure. "They may raise their shields, but if we can find a way past them, we can and will hit that oscillator with everything we've got."

Han grinned broadly. "I like this guy."

Ackbar remained pessimistic. "Any plan is pointless as long as their shields are in place. A proper planetary defense system, as this one is sure to have, will not allow for 'a way past them.'"

Han was not so easily discouraged. "Okay, so first we disable the shields." He turned to Finn. "Kid, you worked there. Whatcha got?"

Finn's eyes slowly widened as he thought back. "I can do it. Shut down their shields. I—" He was nodding vigorously, as much to himself as to the others. "I know where the relevant controls are located." Realization dampened some of his initial enthusiasm. "But I need to be there, of course. On the planet, with access to the location."

"I'll get you there."

Gazing at Han, Leia saw something that had been absent from her life for a long, long time: Solo bravado. "Han, *how*?"

He grinned broadly at her. She had missed that, too, she realized.

"If I told you, you wouldn't like it."

An energized Poe took over. "All right, so we disable their shields, take out the containment oscillation controls, and destroy their big gun. Even if it can fire halfway across the galaxy and it's too big for us to destroy, we can make sure it blows itself to pieces. Sounds like a plan. Let's move!"

XV

IN THE VAST, DARKENED ASSEMBLY CHAMBER
of Starkiller Base were only two figures: one tall and
uncertain, the other looming and imperious. For all
their isolation, they seemed to somehow fill the room.

There was as much curiosity in Supreme Leader
Snoke's voice as there was disappointment. "This
scavenger—this *girl*—resisted you?"

"That's all she is, yes. A scavenger from that incon-
sequential Jakku. Completely untrained, but strong
with the Force. Stronger than she knows." His mask
off, Ren replied with what seemed to be his usual assurance. No one else would have sensed a difference.
Snoke did.

The Supreme Leader's voice was flat. "You have
compassion for her."

"No—never. Compassion? For an enemy of the
Order?"

"I perceive the problem," Snoke intoned. "It isn't
her strength that is making you fail. *It's your weakness.*" The rebuke hurt, but Ren didn't show it.
"*Where is the droid?*"

Smooth and unctuous, the voice of General Hux
rang out in the assembly hall before Ren could re-

spond. "Ren believed it was no longer of value to us."
Turning, the quietly livid younger man followed the
approach of the increasingly confident officer.

"He believed that the girl was all we need. That he
could obtain from her everything necessary. As a result,
although we cannot be certain, it is likely that the droid
has been returned to the hands of the enemy."

Though visibly angry, Snoke's tone remained un-
changed. "Have we located the main Resistance base?"

Hux was clearly gratified to be the bearer of good
news. "We were able to track their reconnaissance
ship back to the Ileenium system. We are coordinat-
ing with our own reconnaissance craft in the area
in order to lock down the specific location of their
base."

Snoke replied with cold satisfaction. "We do not
need it. Prepare the weapon. Destroy their system."

Collected and composed as he was, Hux was not
immune to surprise. "The *system*? Supreme Leader,
according to the most recent galographics, at least
two and possibly three habitable worlds circle Ileenium. Following the destruction of the Hosnian worlds,
would it not be worthwhile simply to destroy their
base and claim the remainder for the Order? We will
have the location of the base within a matter of hours
and—"

Snoke cut him off. "We cannot wait. Not even for
hours. Hours that may permit as little as one ship
to depart with the information that will allow them
to find Skywalker. That would be one ship too many.
The more time we give them, the more likely the
chance, however slight, that they will find Skywalker
and convince him to return to challenge our power.
As soon as the weapon is fully charged, I want the
entire Ileenium system destroyed."

Daring to disagree, Ren took a step forward. "No—

Supreme Leader, I can get the map from the girl, and that will be the end of it. I just need your guidance."

"And you promised me when it came to destroying the Resistance you wouldn't fail me." The threatening figure of Snoke leaned toward Ren. "Who knows if copies of the map have already been made and sent out of the system, to other, minor Resistance outposts? But those who are most aware of its significance will all likely be gathered at their main base. Destroy that, destroy them, and we may at least feel a little more confident that the way to Skywalker is eradicated. Even if copies have been made and exported, the annihilation of their leadership will give pause to any survivors who might dare to contemplate further resistance to us." He sat back. "For that reason alone I would order the destruction of the system, even if there was no assurance it would also put an end to this accursed map." He turned to Hux.

"General, prepare the weapon. With the same efficiency you have already demonstrated."

"Yes, Supreme Leader!"

Buoyed by the praise, Hux turned and strode quickly out of the hall. That left Snoke to fix his eyes on its sole remaining occupant.

"Kylo Ren. It appears that a reminder is in order. So I will show you the dark side. *Bring the girl to me.*"

Slightly apart from the rush of activity that filled the Resistance base, an unlikely pair was going through the stages of performing a final checkout on an old but deceptively fast freighter. Chewbacca and Finn moved quickly to comply with Han's orders.

"Chewie, check the horizontal booster." A growling response provoked an equally terse one from the *Millennium Falcon*'s owner. "I don't care what the

onboard readouts say: There's no substitute for a final visual inspection. You know that. Finn, careful with those dentons. They're explosives."

Halting, Finn gaped at the load he was carrying. "They are?" He faltered. "Why didn't you tell me?"

"Didn't want to make you nervous," Han replied. "When you've finished loading those, go talk to some of those X-wing techs and see if you can scare us up a backup thermal regulator."

The voice that joined in was one that had always been able to bring him to a stop whatever he happened to be doing. He turned to see Leia approaching.

"No matter how much we fought," she said, "I always hated watching you leave."

He grinned. "That's why I left. To make you miss me."

For the first time in quite a while, she laughed freely. It was infectious, happy, and, these days, all too rare. "Well, thank you for that, anyway."

He turned reflective. "It wasn't all bad, was it? I know we argued a lot." He smiled affectionately. "Maybe it's because we both have such shy, retiring personalities. Of course, if you'd only done what I said . . ."

"And you'd only done what I asked," she riposted, still smiling.

He chuckled softly. "I mean, some of it was— good."

"Pretty good," she agreed, nodding.

"Some things never change."

"Yep." She glanced downward, remembering, then met his gaze once more. "You still drive me crazy."

"Crazy as in crazy good, or crazy as in borderline insane?"

"Probably a little of both," she admitted.

He put his hands on her shoulders, and thirty years

fell away in an instant. "Leia, there's something I've been wanting to say to you for a long time."

Fighting to hold back tears, she put a finger to his lips. "Tell me when you get back."

He started to object, caught himself. There'd been too much arguing over the years, he knew. This time he really might not come back; the last thing he wanted was to part on even a semblance of a spat. Instead, he took her into his arms, which really was much better than arguing, or even talking. They stood like that for a long moment, holding tightly to each other.

"If you see our son," Leia whispered, "bring him home."

He nodded without speaking. If nothing else, in thirty years he had learned when to be quiet.

What had happened?

Shackled and unable to move, Rey lay on the inclined platform in her restraints, pondering the encounter with Kylo Ren. At first there had been the same pain and fear she had felt in the forest on Takodana. It had intensified as he had probed deeper and she had fought to resist. Then—she *had* resisted. More than that, it was as if her resistance had somehow turned the probing back on him. For a brief instant, *she* had been in *his* mind. She could remember clearly his shock, then concern, and finally a retreat. He had pulled away from her, and out of her mind, with a suddenness that bespoke—not fright; something else. Apprehension, she decided. Whatever she had done had thrown him badly off balance. He had withdrawn: no doubt not only to consider what had taken place, but also to decide how to proceed with

her. That meant, most likely, he would be back. She would do anything to avoid that.

And that is what she proceeded to do.

If she could push him out of her mind and enter his, what else could she do? What might she be able to do with regard to someone else? Someone less skilled, untrained in the ways of the Force? The single guard posted just inside the front of her cell, for example?

"You!"

He turned toward her, patently unconcerned and not a little bored. She studied him closely. As he was about to speak, she addressed him clearly and firmly—and not only with her voice.

"You will remove these restraints. And you will leave this cell, with the door open, and retire to your living quarters."

The guard eyed her silently. He did not look in the least intimidated. Her confidence wavering as she shifted slightly in her bonds, she repeated what she had said with as much authority as she could muster.

"*You will remove these restraints. And you will leave this cell, with the door open, and retire to your living quarters. You will speak of this encounter to no one.*"

Raising the heavy, black-and-white rifle he held, he came toward her. Heart pounding, she watched him approach. Was she going to be killed, freed, or maybe laughed at? Halting before her, he looked down into her eyes. When he spoke again, there was a notable alteration in his voice. It was significantly less confrontational and—distant.

"*I will remove these restraints. And leave this cell, with the door open, and retire to my living quarters. I will speak of this encounter to no one.*"

Working methodically, he unlatched her shackles. He stood and stared at her for a moment, then turned

and wordlessly started for the doorway. Lying in shock on the reclined platform, Rey hardly knew what to do next. She was free. No, she corrected herself: She was free of this cell. That hardly constituted freedom.

But it was a beginning.

As the guard reached the doorway, she spoke hastily. "And you will drop your weapon."

"I will drop my weapon," he responded in the same uninflected voice. This he proceeded to do, setting the rifle down on the floor, then turning left into the outside corridor to depart in silence.

For a long moment she stared at the open portal. Deciding that it was not a joke and that the guard was not waiting for her just outside the cell, she moved to pick up the weapon and leave.

Normally there was something relaxing about traveling in hyperspace, Finn mused. There was no fighting in hyperspace and very rarely any kind of surprise. Hyperspace travel allowed time for reflection, for casual conversation with comrades, for checking out and preparing one's equipment.

Not this time. Not in the course of this jump.

Weary of living with only his own thoughts, he left the lounge and moved forward into the cockpit, where he found Han and Chewbacca in their respective seats, monitoring the journey.

"I haven't asked you," he said to the pilot. "How are we getting in?"

Han explained without looking up from his console. "Any kind of defense will be geared to guard against an attack in force. They shouldn't be prepared for an attempt by a single ship to slip in. That would obviously be suicide."

Finn nodded as he pondered this. "Okay, now I'm really encouraged. Let's say that your optimistic assessment is wrong, and they're even prepared to detect and destroy a single ship. How do we avoid that?"

"No planetary defense system can be sustained at a constant rate. It would take too much power. Besides, it isn't necessary. All planetary shields have a fractional refresh. Instead of being constantly 'on,' they fluctuate at a predetermined rate. Keeps anything traveling less than lightspeed from getting through. Theoretically, a ship could get its nose in when a shield is off. Half a second later, the shield snaps back on and—well, it isn't good for anyone on that ship."

"Okay, I get that," Finn told him. "Which brings me back to my first question: How are *we* getting in? Without being cut in half by an oscillating shield?"

"Easy." The way Han said the word made it sound like the simplest thing in the world. "We won't be going slower than lightspeed."

Unsure he'd heard correctly, Finn gaped at him. "We're gonna make our landing approach at *lightspeed*? Nobody's ever done that! At least, I've never heard of anybody ever doing it."

One did not have to be fluent in the Wookiee language to get the gist of Chewbacca's comment.

Han smiled pleasantly. "We're coming up on the system. I'd sit down, if I were you. Chewie, get ready."

As the wide-eyed Finn scrambled for a seat and harness and found himself wishing for a number of very large, soft pads, Chewbacca groaned his readiness. Han studied the readouts before him. The Wookiee raised a hand over his own console.

"And . . ." Han followed the declining fractions intently. *"Now!"*

Human and Wookiee hands flew over the main console, supplementing as best they could the approach and landing information they had preprogrammed into the *Falcon*'s instrumentation. Not unexpectedly, more than one last-second override was required in order to make the ship do something that was against its nature and perform maneuvers for which it had never been designed.

And just like that, they were inside the shields.

At that point they were traveling at very much sublightspeed, continuing to slow at an incredible rate, and heading above snow-covered ground directly for a forest that was not as tall but was far denser than the one on D'Qar. Chewbacca howled loudly enough for Finn to hear him clearly above the wild, blaring alarms.

"*I am pulling up!*" Han yelled as he fought with the recalcitrant controls.

While the trees were packed more closely together than those that formed a canopy above the Resistance base, they were much smaller in diameter. The *Falcon* went plowing through them as both pilot and copilot struggled to bring the ship up. A moment later it was clear of the ground and shooting skyward—which was an equally undesirable outcome.

"*Any higher, they'll see us!*" Han shouted. Of course, if the vicinity of the First Order base was monitored by ground-scanning satellites, they were likely to be seen anyway. They could only hope that the instruments on board any such reconnaissance craft were aimed out toward space and not down at the landscape.

Down again they went as Han and Chewbacca fought to retain control while trying to level off. They almost succeeded. Back again among the trees, Han

fluttered the sublight drive while Chewie fought to keep the ship functional. They continued to slow. In the end, it was the forest that braked them, as hundreds of trees splintered and flew around them. The descending *Falcon* still kept going. Fortunately, the whiteness through which it plowed was composed of relatively fresh snow, not ice. It finally eased to a stop, half buried.

On the surface, all was cold and quiet once again.

Ren struggled to control himself. A great deal of his education had been devoted to learning how to live and move forward in the absence of emotion. Right now, he needed every bit of that training to stay calm. As bad as had been the girl's expulsion of his probing, worse was the knowledge she had acquired. At the moment, he did not feel powerful.

He felt diminished.

Becoming aware that an officer was waiting patiently for him to acknowledge his presence, Ren waved the man forward.

"We have not found the girl yet, sir. The alarm has been propagated throughout the base and all troopers are on alert."

"Yes." Ren's voice was almost indifferent, as if the bulk of his thoughts were elsewhere. He looked at the officer. "The trooper who was on guard?"

"Still being debriefed, sir. He doesn't remember what happened. One minute he was at his post, at ease. The next, he found himself in his quarters, changing out of uniform. Initial assessment indicates he is telling the truth." The officer hesitated. "If you would wish to try stronger methods I can . . ."

"No—no. Keep questioning him. Just—questioning.

He may remember something." His tone darkened. "The girl. She's here somewhere. There's nowhere for her to go. When you find her, bring her . . ." His voice drifted away, as did his attention.

The officer waited: to be questioned further, to be given additional instructions, to be brusquely dismissed. But Kylo Ren simply stared into the distance, seeing something that was not apparent to the officer, and maintained his silence.

There was no movement in the forest. A few flakes of snow drifting down made no sound. In the midst of the trees, at the terminus of a very isolated and very linear disaster, rose an unnatural mound piled high with whiteness. From somewhere within came a groan, deep, reverberant, and disgruntled.

"Oh, yeah?" The voice that responded was sharp and decidedly non-Wookiee in origin. "*You* try it!"

Beneath the snow and within the mound that was the *Millennium Falcon*, sparks erupted in the passageway behind the cockpit. Having succinctly delivered himself of his opinion of the most recent effort at piloting by the ship's captain, Chewbacca rose from his seat and headed back to deal with the problem, leaving Finn alone in the cockpit with a brooding Han.

"That should've gone better." Han was studying the readouts that were still functioning. He shook his head, leaning forward to examine a particular telltale. "That wasn't supposed to be so rough. Nearly was worse than that."

Seeing that Han was having a difficult time coming to terms with their arrival, Finn tried to reassure him. "Hey, you just performed the improbable by doing

the impossible. It's not like there was precedent to follow. I mean, I'm not a pilot, but I've been around a lot of pilots, and I've never even heard anybody talking about trying what you just did. You did great." He gestured around them: at the still intact cockpit, at the sky visible through that part of the forward port that wasn't covered by snow, and at himself.

"We're down, we're alive, we're all in one piece. I don't understand. What more could you ask for?"

Han's expression didn't change as he rose and moved to help Chewie. "Was a time it wouldn't have been so rough."

Not knowing how to respond to that, Finn, wisely, said nothing.

Within the command center on D'Qar, conversation was muted. Officers spoke in whispers, if at all, as everyone waited for word. When it came—no one said "if"—then talk would resume as normal. But for now, no one dared voice what they were thinking. What they feared.

Confirmation would come via a series of hastily linked encrypted hyperspace relays. It would be necessarily condensed, as well as reduced to a mathematical formula to minimize any chance of it being intercepted on its way out. As more and more time passed, initial hope began to flag.

Then Admiral Statura broke the tension, looking up from his console to smile at Leia. "The *Falcon* has landed, ma'am."

Moving to his side, she looked at his readouts. What they told wasn't much, but it was enough. "I wish there was more information. I wish we knew—" She stopped herself. Slipping through the

First Order's planetary shields and landing safely would be worth nothing if the *Falcon* were discovered. She knew there could be no further communication until they had accomplished their task. "Tell me they'll get the shields down."

Statura's reply was firm. "They'll get the shields down."

"That was only marginally convincing," she told him.

He smiled anew. "That's what we're operating on, ma'am. Margin, and a thin one at that."

She nodded and turned to a controller. "Send off the X-wings."

"Yes, General!" On the heels of contact with the *Millennium Falcon*, the controller managed to muster some genuine enthusiasm. The operator seated beside her conveyed the formal order.

"All fighters cleared for takeoff."

"Go, blue team. Go, red team," the controller added.

Having been standing by and waiting for the word, the first dozen Resistance fighters to depart were away in an instant. Droids calculated and recalculated approach patterns to the First Order base, reducing options to those deemed most likely to succeed, while the pilots did their best to restrain themselves and conserve their energy for the actual attack.

In the lead was an X-wing marked with distinctive black patterning. Poe was intent on the instrumentation, while BB-8 attended to matters better left to a mechanical. Behind them, the surface of D'Qar fell rapidly away.

"All teams, this is Black Leader," Poe said to the cockpit's omnipickup, "altitude confirmed. Distance confirmed. Arrival coordinates confirmed." He acti-

vated several controls, and the X-wing's hyperspace propulsion system prepared to distort space and time. "Hold for jump to lightspeed on my go!"

When he was confident all was in readiness, he gave the signal. Like flames going out, one fighter after another vanished from the present reality in a streak of light.

He had to see for himself. As he strode down the corridor where walls of exposed igneous rock alternated with panels and consoles of metal and spun synthetics, Ren's emotions were boiling. His present mental state contradicted all of his training, but he could not help himself. He had reacted poorly to what had happened earlier, and that had been reflected in the Supreme Leader's judgment. To add to the discomfort, that slimy sycophant Hux always seemed to appear at the most awkward possible moment.

He gritted his teeth, angry at himself. It was a measure of his current weakness that something like jealousy toward an insignificant simpleton like Hux could even enter his mind. It was nothing but a waste of physical energy and mental concentration. Hux—Hux was not worthy of such attention.

The girl, on the other hand . . .

Entering the holding cell, he found it, as expected, deserted. In the center, the single coppery-hued, angled bench stood empty, its multiple curving restraints open and mocking beneath the subdued red illumination from the ceiling. Unable to contain himself any longer, he pulled his lightsaber, thumbed it to life, and launched into a series of wild swings and strikes, methodically reducing the room to rubble.

Hearing his howls of outrage, a pair of storm-

troopers crossing at the far end of the access hallway changed course to investigate. What they saw within the cell as bits and pieces of red-hot debris came flying out caused them to retreat the way they had come—fast.

XVI

THANKS TO THE SNOW AND THE HEAVY FOR-
est cover, the patrol droid did not see them, and the
deformation warp from a heat distorter Chewbacca
carried in a pouch served to mask their thermal signa-
tures. From time to time, Finn had taken the more
primitive but also effective precaution of using a
branch to wipe out their footprints as they advanced.
Where they could, they kept to rocky surfaces, the
better to minimize evidence of their passage. Slung
across the Wookiee's back was a duffel packed with
advanced dentons whose explosive potential greatly
exceeded their size.

Lengthening his stride, Finn moved up alongside
Han and pointed. "There's a flood tunnel over that
ridge. We can get in that way."

Han looked over at him. "You sure it isn't safety
screened? We can cut through ordinary stuff, but . . ."

Finn shook his head. "There's no screen at all. A
screen would defeat the tunnel's purpose."

Han frowned at him. "You said you worked here.
You never told us your specialty."

Finn looked away as he replied. "Sanitation."

Han gaped at him. "*Sanitation?* How do you

know how to take down the shields?" He indicated Chewie's backpack. "We've got enough stuff to do the job, but we have to know where to set it. We've only got one chance to do this right. If we fail to bring their shields down, we might as well pack up and apply for First Order citizenship." His voice lowered. "Also, everyone in the D'Qar system is going to die."

"I don't know how to take out the shields, Han," Finn admitted. "I'm here to get Rey."

Han turned a slow, frustrated circle. "Anything else you've overlooked? Anything else you've forgotten to tell us?" Nearby, Chewbacca added his own groaning comment. "People are counting on us! The *galaxy* is counting on us!"

"Solo," Finn shot back, "we'll figure it out! We got here, didn't we?"

"Yeah? How?"

Finn smiled encouragingly. "We'll use the Force!"

Han rolled his eyes. "Again the Force. Always the Force." His gaze returned to the hopeful Finn. "I haven't got time to explain it to you, kid, but—that's not how the Force works." He looked up and around. "Where's that patrol droid?" Chewie growled back at him. "Oh really? *You're* cold?"

Red borders flanked a ventilation grid that ran the length of the floor as Rey ran down the hallway, her former guard's blaster rifle gripped tightly in both hands. Needing to catch her breath, she ducked into an alcove that provided at least a nominal amount of cover from anyone moving up or down the passage. Though free of the holding cell, she had no destination in mind. A short survey of her surroundings provided one.

A long walkway was flanked on one side by a stone-and-steel wall. Possibly an exterior barrier, it offered no hope of an exit. But on the other side of the walkway . . .

At the far end was a doorway leading to an open hangar. While she couldn't see far beyond, lines of parked TIE fighters suggested the possibility of escape. All that stood in her way was the narrow, railing-free walkway that crossed a vast, open atrium—and at the far end, a group of stormtroopers engaged in idle conversation. No one was looking in her direction.

Edging forward while keeping close to the wall, she soon found herself at the end of the corridor and near the start of the walkway. A cautious glance over the side and down revealed a seemingly bottomless pit; its sides were molded panels that were softly lit with hundreds of lights extending down, down, until even those lights were not sufficient to illuminate the shadowy depths. How to get across without alerting the hangar guards on the far side presented a seemingly insurmountable problem. The walkway itself was flat and completely open, offering no cover to anyone trying to cross.

She couldn't go back. This might be her only chance to get offplanet. And no matter what she had managed to do previously, she doubted Kylo Ren would allow her to manipulate him, or any lesser minds, again.

The decision was made for her. The echo of approaching booted feet made her turn to look back the way she had come. A clutch of stormtroopers was coming up the corridor, heading her way. There was no chance they would fail to notice her standing within the shallow alcove.

Breaking from cover, she ran to the near end of the walkway. But instead of continuing across and cer-

tainly drawing the attention of the troopers on the other side, she slipped over the edge. And just in time: The fast-moving squad coming up the corridor reached the walkway as she dropped down. Hanging there by her fingers, just out of sight, she reflected that what she was doing was no different from climbing the interior walls of derelict starships back on Jakku. The difference was that there it was a lot warmer, and here the passersby were inclined to shoot at you.

If she let go or otherwise lost her grip, of course, it would solve all her problems. Permanently.

How many troopers were there in the squad? she wondered as they continued to pass above her. How long was it going to take them to get across? Hanging there, waiting, she had time to study her immediate surroundings. What she saw suggested another way out, one that would not involve a possibly suicidal attempt to blast her way past a cluster of hangar guards.

Working her way sideways, hand over hand, while methodically locating shallow footholds, she made it across to a service hatch slotted into the wall of the atrium. It opened, silently and without the need to enter a code, at her touch. While still yawning to depths unknown beneath her, the inner workings of the base that she was able to reach through the hatch provided access to better handholds. If she was lucky and didn't lose her sense of direction, much less her grip, she felt she might be able to work her way across to the corresponding service area that ran underneath the TIE fighter hangar, avoiding the guards above. Then she would have to find a way to access the hangar deck itself and without drawing any attention. Assuming she could do so, she could try to steal a fighter.

One simple predicament after another, she told herself.

First she had to get across. Once, she encountered a small service droid coming toward her. She held her breath, but it ignored her, intent only upon its programmed tasks.

Good thing, she thought with relief as she resumed the crossing, that not all droids had the cerebral capacity of one like BB-8.

The stormtrooper who waited for the doorway to open expected to see an empty transport compartment. Instead, he found himself confronting two humans and one Wookiee, none of whom were inclined to engage him in casual conversation. Sensing this, the trooper reacted quickly and reached for his blaster. Reactions still sharp from years of experience, Han fired, sending the trooper to the ground. As Chewbacca dragged the body out of sight, Han and Finn peered warily around the corridor's first corner.

"The less time spent here," Han quickly decided, "the better luck we're going to have. In fact, the less time we linger anywhere, the better luck we're gonna have."

"Yeah, I know." Checking the corridor outside the transport compartment, Finn gestured to his right. "I got an idea about that." He started off, Han and Chewbacca following.

With Finn leading the way, they managed to make it a considerable distance into the base. Spotting a figure coming toward them, Finn's eyes grew wide. The advancing officer's armor was highly reflective and the black, red-fringed cape that hung down the left side very, very distinctive.

"Here comes our key," Finn whispered.

Han took note of the oncoming figure, then glanced at Finn. "You know this one?"

Finn's expression was tight. "Yeah, we've met."

Reading the other man's tone, Han nodded understandingly. "An old friend, huh?"

"Something like that." Finn's expression didn't change. "As much as I'd wish otherwise, we need her alive." He started fumbling with his blaster. "I'm not real familiar with this model. Is there a setting to stun?"

Han grinned. "We've got something else that's always set to stun."

Far down the corridor a squad of troopers came into view and the three intruders tensed. But the troopers did not turn to follow the advancing officer, marching off instead down a separate passage. Preoccupied with other matters, the officer failed to see the hairy mountain that plowed into her until it was too late. His massive arms wrapped around her, Chewbacca dragged his captive into the narrow cross corridor where his companions were waiting. As she struggled in the unbreakable grasp, she found herself turned around to confront a blaster pointed directly at her face.

An unsmiling Finn had to restrain the finger that was resting on the weapon's trigger.

"Captain Phasma. Remember me?" He moved his weapon slightly. "Here's my blaster, ya still wanna inspect it?"

Phasma held on to her dignity. "Yes, I remember you. FN-2187."

Finn shook his head curtly. "Not anymore. My name is Finn. A real name for a real person. And I'm in charge now."

From behind the former trooper, Han spoke up. "We're just visiting. Finn's been giving us a quick tour and it's been real fun, but we haven't seen the planetary shield control room yet." He broke out into a

broad, pleasant smile. "We'd really like to see the planetary shield control room."

"Now," Finn added menacingly.

Phasma sniffed derisively. "Why should I show you anything?" Behind her, Chewbacca let out a threatening moan and tightened his grip. She let out a little gasp.

"Because if you don't," Han told her, "we'll eventually find it anyway. But you won't know that, because you'll be dead." He nodded toward his copilot. "Chewie here doesn't like people who threaten his friends."

She managed a slight shake of her head. "Even a Wookiee can't crush First Order armor." In response, Chewbacca tightened his grip further. Her mask emitted a slight but perceptible wheeze.

"Well," Han said nonchalantly, "there's one way to find out."

"Or," Finn added, pushing the muzzle of the blaster in a little tighter, "I can simply shoot you. I'm well trained, you know. I know exactly where to put a kill shot. Especially at this range."

"What are you up to here?" she countered. "Are you with the Resistance? Independents?"

"Maybe we'll answer your questions," Finn told her. "Later." Taking a step back, he gestured with the blaster as Chewie disarmed her. "Right now, you're our tour guide. Let's go."

They managed to avoid the few technicians and troopers they encountered by ducking back into concealing alcoves or small passageways. There was one guard stationed outside the room they had to enter. Stepping out into the open, Finn waved and smiled as he walked toward the man.

"Hey, hi! When are you off duty, mate?"

"Not for another . . ." The trooper outside the door

peered at the newcomer. "Why are you out of uniform? In fact, why are you even in this sector?" He started to bring up his rifle. "Put your hands out where—"

A single blow from the Wookiee's massive right hand put the trooper down on the floor, out cold. Han gestured with his blaster as he murmured to Phasma, who was standing in front of him. "What was that you said earlier about First Order armor and Wookiees?" The captain did not reply.

The shield control room was not large. With everything functioning normally, there was no need for technicians to be on duty. The instruments monitored themselves. If a problem arose that they could not self-correct, appropriate notification would instantly be flashed to Central Command. If the difficulty could not be fixed from there, a tech or two would be dispatched to deal with the trouble in person. A planetary shield being a fairly straightforward thing, there was hardly ever a problem with the system.

One such problem was about to be artificially induced.

Taking a seat before the main console, Phasma paused. What was happening right now made no sense. Still, with her chest and shoulders throbbing from the Wookiee's attention, she was not about to offer what would amount to pointless resistance. The fools presently holding their weapons on her would meet their inevitable fate soon enough. She felt something hard push against the side of her helmet.

"Do it," Finn ordered her. Chewbacca added a few choice moans and grunts for emphasis.

Reluctantly, she worked the controls. Accompanied by an appropriate succession of sounds, a sequence of telltales came to life. A readout flared, bright enough for everyone to see it clearly.

SHIELDS DISABLE INITIATED

Leaning toward Han, Finn murmured worriedly, "Solo, if this works, and if I remember correctly what they told us about the shield system, we don't have a lot of time to find Rey."

"Don't worry, kid." Han replied without shifting the muzzle of his weapon a millimeter away from Phasma. "We won't leave here without her."

The stormtrooper captain sat back. "I can't do this by myself. It requires two security codes to access the full system and shut it down."

"I've been in the business of dealing with liars and thieves my whole life. I know when someone's telling the truth—and when they're not." Pressing the end of his blaster against one side of Phasma's helmet, Han lowered his voice. "How well can you hear with one ear?"

More telltales came to life. When she was finished, a second message appeared before them.

SHIELDS DISABLED

"You can't be so stupid as to think this will be easy," Phasma said. "My troops will storm this block and kill you all. Whatever you're planning, it won't work."

"I disagree," Finn replied without hesitation. "I was told escape from the corps was impossible, yet here I am. I was told that training prevented anyone from turning against the Order, yet here I am. I was told that I was going to die on Jakku, yet here I am. And here you are." He glanced over at Han. "What do we do with her?"

Han pondered a moment. "Is there a garbage chute? Trash compactor? I have a pretty good idea how they

work." When Finn threw him a quizzical look, Han shrugged. "Let's just say I've had hands-on experience."

Finn nodded. "Yeah, there is."

The warning alert that appeared on the console in the Central Command control room was new to the monitoring technician. Though to the best of his knowledge it had never come to life previously, he knew perfectly well what it signified. After a quick check to make certain it was neither a system fault nor a test, he felt confident in announcing its activation to those officers who were present.

"Main planetary shields have gone out. Not localized: right across the board."

The officer who happened to be conversing with Hux narrowed his gaze. "General, did you authorize this? I certainly didn't, nor did any of my subordinates."

Hux turned to regard the alert. "No, I most certainly did not." He barked at the technician. "Cause? Possibly external?"

"It doesn't show here, sir," the tech replied.

Hux frowned. "Send a tech squad over to shield control. Could be something as simple as a bad relay, or . . ."

"Or, sir?" the officer inquired. The general didn't respond.

In another command and control center, on another planet in another system, there was a spontaneous outburst of excitement, followed by a hurried response.

"General," the head tech cried out, "their shields are down!"

"Oh my." Threepio leaned toward the relevant console. "So they are!"

"You were right," Leia said to Statura. "Send them in!"

"Give Poe full authorization to attack," Ackbar informed a junior officer stationed at another console. "All available ships, no hesitation. He knows he's not likely to get a second opportunity."

"Black Leader," the officer declared to the pickup that would send out the command via the identical set of relays, "go to sublight. Attack, attack. On your call."

It was the order Poe had been waiting for. While unsure it would come, he had nevertheless run over the strike schematics in his head a dozen times. Timing was critical. Having plotted the vector to the planet that was home to the Order's Starkiller Base as an arc, both to deceive any long-range sensors as well as to delay arrival and emergence from lightspeed, now they could revise the route and head straight for the target.

"Roger, base." Hitting the controls necessary to alter course within a lightspeed run, Poe addressed the rest of his flight. "Red squad, blue squad—follow my lead." At his touch, their revised vector entered the flight computer of every ship in every squadron, and the X-wings promptly adjusted as a single unit.

"Copy, Black Leader," Wexley replied, as his own craft changed direction.

Within Central Command on Starkiller Base, there was rising concern. Hux refused to pace, regarding it as a waste of energy.

"The tech squad," he muttered. "Haven't they arrived at shield control yet?"

"Just getting there, sir," replied the officer who was monitoring the situation. He went quiet, listening, and a strange expression came over his face. He looked back at Hux. "Sir, the lead technician reports that the doorway has been sealed."

Hux grimaced. "Sealed? Sealed how? By whom?"

"He doesn't know, sir." The officer listened. "Heat sealed, all the way around the edge. Possibly by a blaster. Should they get a cutter?"

Hux shook his head. "Tell them to blow the door."

"Sir?" The officer's reply indicated he was unsure he had heard the order correctly.

"Blow the damn door!" Hux shouted. "Tell them to get in there!"

"Yes, sir!" The command was relayed. Moments later a reply was forthcoming from the tech repair team. The officer swallowed, hesitating.

"What?" Hux snarled.

"Sir, the team leader reports that there is—some damage to the shield control system."

"How much damage?" an increasingly irate Hux demanded.

A longer pause this time, following which the officer experienced a sudden intense wish to be anywhere other than where he currently happened to be.

"Destroyed, General. The tech team leader reports that the operational capacity of the entire center has been reduced at least ninety percent by blaster fire."

Hux had not achieved his present rank and position by deferring problematic situations to group consultation. "Bypass the shield center. Where redundancy doesn't already exist, port all controls here."

"Yes, sir." The officer's fingers flew over the console. "It will take a moment, sir."

Hux all but scraped skin from the palms of his hands while waiting.

"Shields?"

"Not yet," the officer told him, still working.

"Why not?"

"Have to block any remaining possible directives from the shield center so that they can't override our efforts here—sir."

"Hurry. In the name of the Order, *hurry.*"

"Yes, sir. I should have it soon, sir."

Hux knew there was nothing more he could do. Further haranguing would only rattle the officer and the other techs in the command center. He could barely stand the silence as they worked.

Because he feared it was deceptive.

Set down on the snowy surface, two TIE fighters and a troop transport flanked the battered, half-buried disc of the *Millennium Falcon*. That the ship's landing had been less than precise was plainly evident. Industrious troops were cautiously concluding their inspection of the ship's interior. One never knew when even a seemingly harmless freighter might be rigged to blow up in the face of an uninvited visitor. Eventually a noncom spoke into his comm unit.

"Ship's clear. No one on board. No antipersonnel traps encountered." Startled by the sudden appearance of a tall, caped figure, the trooper stepped aside and came to attention. "Sir!"

Kylo Ren ignored him as he strode past, his eyes raking every corner of the crashed vessel, looking for—he wasn't sure. Something that might speak to him. Something recognizable, perhaps.

There was nothing in the deserted cockpit, but he

delayed leaving anyway, settling down in the pilot's seat. Something . . .

His deliberation was interrupted by a thunderous roar as squadrons of X-wings dropped from the sky, rocketing toward the hexagon-shaped bulk of the containment field and oscillation control system. Rising from the seat, he rushed out in time to see the Resistance fighters drop toward the massive structure—and begin their bombing runs.

Within Central Command, officers looked on in horror as one strike after another shook the hexagonal structure. Didn't the attackers realize what they were risking? Watching the aerial assault on the center's monitors and through its sweeping windows, a grim-faced Hux knew they probably did—and that it didn't make any difference to them. Turning, he snapped at a mid-level officer.

"Dispatch all squadrons. Take out every attacking craft, no matter the cost. When this is over I don't want to see a single X-wing aloft."

"Yes, General," replied the officer.

"And engage seekers."

The officer hesitated. "In an atmospheric skirmish, sir, seekers will have a hard time distinguishing between our fighters and those of the enemy."

Hux didn't bat an eye. "This is no time to worry about collateral damage." His voice was steely. "*Give the order.*"

"Yes, sir."

"Almost in range!"

As he sent his X-wing into a steep dive, Poe knew this was one attack where failure could not be an op-

tion. The entire Resistance was depending on him and those following him in. One way or another, this First Order weapon had to be not damaged, not temporarily disabled, but completely destroyed. Automatic weapons systems, trackers, and controls were all very well and good, but when it came down to it, this kind of all-or-nothing combat boiled down to ships, their pilots, and how good both were.

"Hit the target dead center as many times as possible with as many runs as we can get. *Let's light it up!*"

As he let loose with the X-wing's full complement of armament, he noted that similar bursts of destructive fire came from Snap's vessel. Rebel Alliance veteran Nien Nunb was there, too, with him and blasting away with the full force of his ship's weaponry.

When they finished with the building that housed the oscillator, Poe vowed silently to himself, there would be nothing left but a smear on the wintry landscape.

It was not necessary to utilize scopes within the control room to see what was happening on another, critical part of the base. Huge explosions erupted from the top of the distant oscillator. Further confirmation of the location and strength of the attack arrived in the form of blaring alarms and strobing warning lights.

A flood of activity enveloped the base as the installation's entire complement was mobilized to respond to the assault from above. Black-suited pilots raced to their TIE fighters as in the distance Resistance X-wings swooped around in a tight arc preparatory to making another run. In the midst of the confusion, an officer shouted into the comm.

"Report to your ships. Report to your ships, now,

now, now! All pilots and backup, get your ships off the ground!"

Walls of gray metal lit from within rose above the three intruders as they made their way down the corridor only to be stopped by blast doors that had been closed ahead of them—an unfortunate safety measure because of the battle that was taking place above the containment control center, but one that Finn had anticipated. As Chewie began removing some small but powerful explosives from the duffel he had been carrying, Finn explained what they could expect from that point on.

"We'll use the charges to blow the blast door." He gestured. "The holding cells for prisoners are down that corridor. I'll go in and draw fire, but it's often heavily guarded, depending on who's being held. I'm gonna need cover."

Han eyed him intently. "You sure you're up for this?"

"No," Finn told him. "But this whole gamble is my call, so taking care of it is my responsibility. I'll find Rey." He said it with so much confidence that Han was inclined to believe the ex-trooper just might pull it off. "There's a footbridge that has to be crossed. Troopers'll be on our tail, so we should plant charges on it, too, take it down after we cross. That won't prevent a pursuit, but they'll have to go around to another passage and it'll buy us some time. There's an access tunnel that'll lead us to the main hangar— I think." His expression tightened. "I just hope she's alive."

A movement caught Han's attention. Squinting, he broke out into a smile and pointed. "Something tells me she is."

And there she was, climbing up an interior shaft wall directly toward them. Finn gaped in astonishment, not quite able to accept what he was seeing. Chewbacca moaned his relief at not having to deal with detonating explosives in such tight quarters.

It took her a moment, long enough to bring to bear the rifle she was carrying, before she recognized the trio and lowered the weapon. Her amazement at seeing them was no less than theirs had been when they had spotted her. Running to Finn, she threw herself into his arms. Neither could hug the other hard enough or long enough. The embracing pair finally separated, if only to look into each other's eyes.

"Are you all right?" a relieved Finn asked. "What happened?" His voice darkened. "Did he hurt you?"

"Never mind me," she said. "What are you *doing* here?"

He smiled softly. "We came back for you."

She tried to find something to say to that, something worthy of the sentiment and the risk they had undertaken. She failed miserably. Chewie, however, had something of his own to add. Whatever the Wookiee had uttered caused tears to well up in her eyes. Having never found himself in such a position before, Finn was unsure how to respond. Knowing well her inner toughness, he wondered what Chewbacca had said that could have inspired such a reaction.

"What'd he say?"

She sniffed and wiped at her face. "That it was your idea."

If he had been unable to find the right words with which to respond before, her reply, combined with the look she gave him, reduced him to a state of temporary aphasia.

It was all very sweet and charming, Han mused as

he observed the happy reunion. If only he could forget that they were stuck on a hostile world, in a First Order base, amid squads of roving stormtroopers who were inclined to shoot on sight.

"We'll have a party later," he finally told them. "I'll bring the cake. Right now, let's get outta here."

XVII

Rising from their base, a host of TIE fighters moved to engage the X-wing squadrons. What had been a precisely plotted sequence of attack runs dissolved into chaotic dogfights as one X-wing pilot after another was forced to break from formation to engage his or her own assailants. Where formerly the sky above Starkiller Base had been filled only with the scream of the invaders' engines, the blueness in which they had been operating now gave way to a cyclone of streaking energy blasts and explosions.

Nearly colliding with an oncoming TIE fighter, Poe let fly at another with the full force of his ship's weapons systems.

"Cover for each other! There's a lot of 'em, but that just means more targets. Don't let these thugs scare you!"

"Blue Three," Snap called out, "got one on your tail! Pull up and give us a view!"

"Copy that!" Blue Three's pilot replied. Yanking back on her controls, Jess Pava took her ship up sharply—exposing the area in her wake to Poe's fire,

which immediately reduced her attacker to flaming fragments.

"I owe you one!" she called out as she sent her vessel diving back into the fray.

"Yeah, you owe me another attack run! Try to stick close, all teams! Follow me in!"

Despite being harassed by the swerving, diving TIE fighters that now seemed to be all around them, a clutch of X-wings managed to get low enough to carry out another strike on the containment structure. A series of hits sent flame and smoke billowing in all directions, but as they pulled up and away, Poe saw that the building was still intact. Worse than intact, he noted: It scarcely appeared to have suffered any damage at all.

"We're not making a dent!" he yelled, confident his cockpit pickup would relay his observations to the rest of the squadrons. "What's that thing made of, anyway?"

A telltale on his console began demanding attention. Flicking his attention to the attendant monitor, his eyes widened.

Seekers. *Hundreds* of seekers, rising from launch batteries concealed beneath the soil and snow. Rising toward him and his fellow pilots, giving them little room to maneuver—or escape.

"We got a lot of company!" It was all he had time to shout before being forced to take evasive action himself. Between blasting out of the sky everything in front of him and avoiding those seekers coming up behind him, he stayed in one piece—barely.

Other members of the attacking squadrons were not so fortunate.

One after another they found themselves hemmed in by multiple seekers. One after another the X-wings

went down, along with any TIE fighter unlucky enough to find itself in the immediate spatial vicinity.

Able to follow the battle via hyperspace relay thanks to the two reconnaissance droids still operating above the surface of the planet, those in the Resistance base command center on D'Qar could only exchange looks of dismay.

"We weren't prepared for anything like this," Admiral Statura muttered. "Our pilots will be annihilated."

An exterior access door opened and four figures came racing out into the snow. Their attention immediately drawn skyward, they slowed to a halt. None of them was an expert in aerial warfare. They didn't have to be. The presence of multiple TIE fighters backed by a seemingly endless barrage of seekers allowed anyone to predict the outcome of the battle. Even the most die-hard optimist would have conceded the inevitable.

Han turned to Finn, his expression solemn. But his tone was the same as always: ready for anything. He gestured toward Chewbacca.

"My friend here has a bag full of explosives that we didn't use inside. Be a shame to make him haul them all the way back to the *Falcon*." The Wookiee added a curt grunt of agreement. "What's the best place we could put 'em to use?"

"The oscillator is the only sensible target," Finn told him. "But there's no way to get inside."

"There is a way."

Everyone turned toward Rey. It was Chewie who ventured the question that had to be asked.

"I've seen inside these kinds of walls," she told them as the sky overhead continued to rain destruc-

tion. "The mechanics and instrumentation are the same as the Star Destroyers I've spent years inside salvaging. Get me to a conventional junction station, I can get us in."

Han nodded and smiled at her. "Get us in. If you can do that, we'll be ready."

A hasty search took them to a parking area filled with a smattering of vehicles. From the varied assortment, they settled on an isolated snow speeder. Between Finn's training and Rey's knowledge of machines, they managed to get it fired up. As Han and Chewie headed for the nearest structure, Finn and Rey took off on the snow speeder. Just in time, it developed, as a trooper monitoring the area saw them take off. When his single shot missed the accelerating vehicle by a wide margin, he followed up with a quick report.

"Speeder stolen from Precinct Twenty-eight."

The reply contained more than a hint of disbelief. "Stolen?"

"Yes, sir. Unauthorized departure."

A pause, then, "We're tracking it. Sending a backup unit immediately."

Careening over a snowdrift as Rey struggled to maintain control of the unfamiliar machine, they scattered small local creatures in front of them as they sped toward the containment center. From the ground, the hexagon loomed ahead of them. Occasional bursts of fiery energy flowered against its roof and sides as the X-wings continued their attack. Finn could see that the number of strikes had decreased markedly.

And the sky continued to darken as the curtain of increasingly opaque dark energy was drawn into the collectors that dominated the other side of the planet, blocking more and more sunlight as the containment unit situated at the planetary core continued to fill.

"Snow is *cold*!" Rey squeezed the speeder between a phalanx of willowy alien trees. "It's the complete opposite of Jakku!"

"Try living here," Finn told her. "There are only two seasons: winter, and dead of winter!"

A sudden *boom* and the speeder's course wobbled. They'd been hit! Switching systems around like a card-sharp dealing on a busy night, Rey succeeded in maintaining speed. A second shot barely missed them.

A glance back showed a second snow speeder in pursuit and closing. Finn realized that the way its driver was shooting, if he got any closer, he could take them out with his next burst. They had to do something, and fast. Rey was skilled at driving, and he was skilled at . . .

"Switch!" he yelled.

They made the difficult change only because they had to, with Rey still in control of their vehicle but Finn now in position to accurately return fire. Multiple blasts hit nothing, as Rey slalomed around and between trees while Finn fought to take out their pursuer. *Damn driver knew what he was doing,* Finn thought with grudging admiration. The man might even have been a former squadron mate. He tried not to think of that as he aimed and got off another burst.

This time his shot struck home, sending the trooper flying. Whether he'd killed him or not Finn didn't know, but the pursuer's speeder slammed into the trees and burst into flame.

"Got him!" As he turned forward once more, Finn's gaze was again drawn skyward. Not, this time, to the space above the hexagon, but distant, toward the horizon. Shafts of an intense deep purple light were flowing there, a curtain of energy being drawn down by the weapon's collectors. He leaned toward Rey.

"They're charging the weapon! We're running out of time!"

"We'll get there!" she yelled back at him, but she realized that they had only the slimmest of chances to prevent the destruction of the Resistance base and the entire D'Qar system.

Watching from cover, Han and Chewie waited until a trio of stormtroopers could be seen approaching a wide, heavy-duty service hatch. It was smaller than any of the major portals they had seen thus far. Which meant, Han hoped, that it was likely to be lightly guarded. As the doorway opened, Chewbacca immediately took out the middle trooper with his bowcaster. Startled, the surviving troopers returned fire, only to be cut down by Han's unerring aim. Alarms began to blare, rising even above the cacophony of the nearby aerial contest. Within the open passageway, another stormtrooper darted back out of sight and hurriedly activated his comlink.

"Enemy sighted and engaged at Oscillator Bay Six! Three men down; send reinforcements!"

Rey brought the snow speeder to a stop beside a small black structure. To Finn it looked unimpressive. But then, he reminded himself, remove a trigger from a gun and while the trigger itself would look decidedly unimportant, its absence would render the gun useless.

After opening a maintenance panel, Rey scrutinized the interior briefly before setting to work. One part after another was disconnected by her deft fingers.

"Been doing this all my life. Never thought about it much until now. It was just something I did every day,

to survive. A routine, like breathing." As if to demonstrate to herself that she was more than a little familiar with the components in question, she closed her eyes while continuing to disassemble the interior of the box. When she opened them again, she was gratified to see that she hadn't missed a single connection.

"Nice piece of instrumentation," she commented absently. "I would have got at least three portions for this."

"What?" Absorbed in the spectacle of the ongoing battle overhead, the enormous streams of dark energy pouring down upon distant, unseen collectors, and a sky that continued to darken around them, Finn hadn't been following her reminiscence.

"Never mind." She continued with the work. "I was just pointing out how one small piece can be important. Like *this,* for example." With her left hand she pulled hard, and a small length of brightly colored flow fiber came away in her fingers.

Now inside the complex, an increasingly anxious Han allowed himself to breathe a sigh of relief as the service hatch they had been monitoring finally parted to reveal a deserted corridor beyond. There was no sign of the single remaining trooper who had reported their presence. Outnumbered, that individual had sensibly retired to wait for the requested reinforcements. As the two intruders rushed forward and stepped inside, Chewbacca let out an agitated moan.

"Yeah," Han agreed. "No kidding."

A quick check of the vicinity indicated that no one, organic or droid, was waiting in ambush. While grateful, Han knew that their surroundings were unlikely to remain peaceful for long. Hurriedly, he and Chewie divided the duffel's explosive contents.

"Let's plant 'em at every other support column we can find," Han suggested. When Chewie responded with a series of emphatic moans, Han reconsidered.

"You're right. Better idea." He indicated the nearest of the building's massive support structures. "We don't have the kind of munitions necessary to bring down more than one. I only hope we brought enough to do that much." He gestured. "We'll put everything we've got on that one column. You take the top. I'll go below. We'll meet back here."

Unintentionally, their eyes met—and the stare held. Man and Wookiee realized it might be for the last time. Nothing more was said. Nothing more needed to be. There never had been, over the years, an excess of superficial chatter between the two whenever there was work to be done. Each knew his job and did it.

That did not keep Han from pausing a moment to look back. When he did, he discovered Chewbacca gazing in his direction. *Same ethic, different species, same thought,* Han mused.

He pointed stiffly. "Go! Before things get messy."

Chewie complied, this time without looking back. Han watched him for a long moment. Then he, too, turned and raced off.

There was a lot on his mind, but when one is emplacing explosives it's usually a good idea to concentrate on the task at hand. Everything else would have to wait until they were done. He checked an install, then moved down to another level.

In contrast to Han's single-minded efforts to place the explosive charges, Kylo Ren's thoughts were focused wholly on locating the as-yet-unknown intruders. Approaching the main entrance to the hexagon, he ignored the squad of backup troopers waiting there

even as they snapped to attention in response to his arrival. Without waiting for an order, one enterprising trooper hit the controls that activated the main portal. At a gesture from Ren, he and his companions followed their leader inside.

The squad's presence was greatly diminished by the daunting interior of the complex. Around them, instrumentation and components hummed smoothly, ensuring that the expanding mass of dark energy that was accumulating at the center of the planet continued to be held safely in stasis until it was time for it to be released.

Halting, Ren slowly scanned his surroundings. Even though they knew what he was doing, the troopers still marveled at the display. After a long moment of deliberation, he motioned them toward the upper levels.

"They're here. Find them. Up there."

The squad immediately went into action, moving off rapidly in the direction he had indicated. Once they were out of sight, Ren turned slowly—and headed downward.

Weapons at the ready, the squad ascended, following prescribed search procedure and covering for one another as they advanced. Blind corners received special attention and added caution.

From the shadows Chewbacca watched them pass, admiring the precision with which they progressed even as he kept still. Once they were out of sight, he emerged to plant another charge.

Below, Han had finished setting a charge and was preparing to climb a bit higher to place one more when a sound made him hesitate. The working structure was full of unidentifiable sounds, but this was different. Taking no chances, he slipped behind a

wide vertical support. Either the sound would not be repeated, or . . .

A glance around the edge of his cover revealed its source, and his countenance underwent a grave shift.

The figure that had paused to look over a railing and down into the farther depths of the structure was known to him.

Here, Ren told himself with increasing certainty. *He is here.* Raising his gaze, he focused on one support column out of many. Slowly he advanced toward it, prepared for whatever might ensue.

Nothing did. There was no one behind the column.

From concealment in a narrow chamber set into a wall, Han watched the caped figure stride past. His lips moved as he watched and he mouthed a single word. Or perhaps it was a name. As he looked on, Ren moved out onto a walkway that spanned a vast open space. Pausing there, he looked around, hesitant, uncertain, before continuing onward. The sound of his boots—the sound that had alerted Han moments earlier—receded into the distance.

Rising from his hiding place, Han looked back the way he had come. If he left now and managed to control his thoughts and emotions while retracing his steps, there was a good chance he could make it out of the building. If he was really lucky, he would be able to slip outside without drawing the attention of any searching stormtroopers—or anyone else. Outside, if all had gone according to the hastily drawn-up plan, Finn and Rey would be waiting with transportation. A chance, then, to make it back to the *Falcon* before everything on this planet went to hell. A chance later for another reunion, on another world. A face swam before his, its features aged but still soft, the voice that emerged from between so-familiar lips biting yet always affectionate. Forming words that lin-

gered in his thoughts. Forming, at last hearing, a request.

A request that wouldn't go away, he knew. It would never go away. He made up his mind. Instead of retreating, he advanced. Instead of running for safety, he took up the challenge. There was no real choice, he told himself as he advanced to the edge of the walkway. And called out.

"Ben!"

It echoed across the gap, reverberated through the vast open space below.

On the far side, a tall figure turned and retraced his last few steps.

"Han Solo." Kylo Ren stared across at the older man. "I've been waiting for this day for a long time."

"Take off that mask." Han's tone was a mix of command and empathy. "You don't need it. Not here. Not with me."

"What do you think you'll see if I do take it off?"

Han moved forward slightly. "The face of my son."

"Your son is gone. He was weak and foolish, like his father." Ren's reply was replete with pity. And anger. "So I destroyed him. But such a small, insignificant request is easily granted."

Reaching up, he slowly removed the mask. For the first time Han saw the face of his son as a grown man—and it jolted him.

Both men were so intent on each other, so preoccupied with their encounter, that neither noticed the newly arrived presence on a railing overhead. Having slipped inside to search for Han and Chewbacca, Finn and Rey found themselves peering down from up high at the pair confronting each other below.

"That's what Snoke wants you to believe," Han was saying. He wasn't pleading—just stating a fact.

"But it's not true. My son is still alive. I'm looking at him right now."

The exchange drew another onlooker, as on a level above, Chewie moved to watch and listen.

Ren's eyes blazed. "No! The Supreme Leader is wise. He knows me for who I am, and who I can become. He knows you for what *you* really are, Han Solo. Not a general, not a hero. Just a small-time thief and smuggler."

A trace of a grin flashed across Han's face. "Well, he's got that part right."

Similarly drawn by the sounds of conversation and disagreement, a third group of spectators had arrived. Held rapt by the confrontation, the squad of stormtroopers looked on as intently as did Finn, Rey, and Chewbacca. Fearful of taking an initiative that might be frowned upon, they awaited a command from Ren.

Stepping out onto the walkway, Han moved toward his son. There was no hesitation in his stride or in his voice. "Snoke's using you for your power, manipulating your abilities. When he's gotten everything he wants out of you, he'll crush you. Toss you aside. You know it's true. If you have half the ability, half the perception that I know you do, you know that I'm telling you the truth. Because unlike him, I have nothing to gain from it."

Ren hesitated.

"It's too late," he said.

"No, it's not." Halfway across the walkway now, Han continued to move forward, smiling. "Never too late for the truth. Leave here with me. Come home." Without the slightest trace of malice or deception, he cast a dagger. "Your mother misses you."

A strange sensation touched the younger man's cheeks. Something long forgotten. Dampness. Tears.

"I'm being torn apart. I want—I want to be free of this *pain*."

Han took another step, then stopped, waiting. A decision had to be made, and for once it was not his to make.

"I know what I have to do, but I don't know if I have the strength to do it." Ren moved out onto the walkway toward Han. "Will you help me?"

"Yes," Han told him. "Anything."

Halting an arm's length from his father, Ren unclipped his lightsaber, looked down at it for a moment, and then extended it toward Han. For an instant that seemed to extend into forever, nothing happened. Smiling, Han reached for the weapon. Then, as the light from outside was fully blocked by the flow of descending, accumulating dark energy, Ren ignited the lightsaber—and the fiery red beam lanced outward to pierce Han's chest from front to back.

"Thank you," Ren murmured, and truly, the darkness above was mimicked by the darkness in his voice.

From their perch high above, Finn and Rey gasped simultaneously.

"Solo. Solo." Finn put an arm around the girl beside him. "Rey."

"No," she whispered. "No, no, no . . ."

Accepting without quite believing, Han stared back into the face of the creature that had been his son. There was nothing to see there. Only darkness in the shape of a face: alien, unthinking, unfeeling. His knees buckled, the beam tilting down with him as he crumpled. Ren extinguished it. For another moment Han held on to the edge of the walkway. A rush of memories flashed through his mind: worlds and time, friends and enemies, triumphs and failures. Words he wished he had spoken and others he regretted. All gone now, lost in an instant, like the one he would

never again be able to hold in his arms. Then he fell, to vanish into the depths.

On another world far, far away, a woman felt a shudder in the Force that lanced through her like a knife. She slumped into a seat, her head lowering, and started to cry.

Stunned by his own action, Kylo Ren fell to his knees. Following through on the act ought to have made him stronger, a part of him believed. Instead, he found himself weakened. He did not hear the roar of the enraged Wookiee above, but he did feel the sting of the shot from the bowcaster as it slammed into his side, knocking him back on the walkway.

Hostile fire being something the group of storm-troopers could react to without having to wait for an order, they immediately blasted back at Chewie. Returning fire, the Wookiee retreated down a corridor, hitting the switch on the remote detonator as he ran.

First one charge ignited, then two, then four, and finally the rest. Enormous, concerted explosions rocked the interior of the hexagon. Walkways collapsed, plunging to the bottom of the interior cylinder. There was shuddering as the walls trembled, held—and then began to fail as their main support and then subsidiary columns snapped. Amid the rising bedlam and confusion, Kylo Ren struggled to stand. As he did so, his gaze turned upward.

To meet the stares of Finn and Rey, peering down at him.

The shock of recognition helped him to regain his footing. Rising to his full height, he started back along the still-standing walkway, moving with determination. Heading upward.

Taking their cue from their leader, those troopers who were not pursuing Chewbacca began to fire at the two figures on the lower level. A crazed, heart-

broken Rey returned their fire. She would have stayed there, blasting away wildly, had not Finn half dragged, half carried her away.

High above and swathed in the shadow of the curtain of descending dark energy, Poe Dameron saw something. An explosion on the roof of the containment center. By its intensity and configuration he could tell that it was not the result of a hit from one of his X-wings, but instead a blast from within. Swinging around, he found that for the first time he could see the *interior* of the seemingly impregnable structure.

It was an opening. A small one. One opportunity, maybe. Given the way the fight was going, probably a last one.

"All units, this is Black Leader. Target structural integrity has been breached! I repeat: Target integrity has been breached! There's an opening. Now's our chance! Hit it hard, give it everything you've got!"

Led by the black fighter and ignoring both pursuing TIE fighters and arcing seekers, the remaining X-wings broke off from defensive combat and dove as one toward the hexagon. A few strikes missed, detonating harmlessly against the still-intact sides of the building. But the others, most, hit their mark. As Poe and his comrades pulled up and away, one detonation after another shook the great edifice. Gradually, almost in slow motion, it began to collapse, the walls falling in upon themselves. More significantly, gouts of flame began to erupt from below, rising from unseen chambers far underground.

Letting out a yell of triumph, Poe accelerated skyward, heading for the outer atmosphere. Secure in his position behind the cockpit, BB-8 emitted a steady stream of excited beeps.

"All teams, nice job!" Poe said to his fellow pilots. "General, the target's been destroyed!"

Leia's warm voice filled his ears, but the message she delivered was an unexpected one. "Good—now retreat immediately! The planet could be unstable. Get out of there now."

Even with the relay in place, it took a moment for the message to be received. Poe didn't hesitate to reply. "If we retreat, we leave our friends behind!"

Having anticipated Poe's response, Leia was ready with her own. "Poe, outside of those of us here, your group is all that remains of the Resistance that's capable of putting up a fight. If you stay to find them, we lose you all."

"General, with all due respect," he said evenly, "we're not leaving our friends behind. Teams, who's with me?"

He expected a delayed response. He was wrong: It came immediately, from Snap. "We're all with you, Poe. You know that." A concurring yelp came from the ship piloted by the Sullustan, Nien Nunb, followed by the others.

"Then let's go do some good and find them!"

XVIII

WITHIN THE CORRIDORS AND CONFINES, THE administrative rooms and technical control sectors of Starkiller Base, there was panic. Technicians reacted with despair as, despite their frantic efforts, one monitor after another went to red as critical systems began to fail.

"Lower-order cells are overheating," declared one tech in the command center. "Emergency crew can't get to the site. Full system load shutdown." When he turned back to Hux there was a look in his eyes that the general had never seen in any of his techs. "The oscillator is failing. We're losing containment."

"Oscillator has been hit." Another officer struggled to keep the fear out of his voice. "Assessing damage. Attempting to sustain power."

Hux watched it all in silence as he backed away slowly. There was no point in doing anything else, he knew. The tech teams would stabilize the oscillation of the containment field. Otherwise, there would be nothing to back up to.

• • •

"Come on." Seeking a path through the snow, shadows, and increasingly dark forest, Finn finally slowed. Where were they running to? In any event, both he and Rey were out of breath. When he looked over at her, he knew the same realization had struck her. It was good, anyway, to stop. Even in the artificial darkness, in the shadow of the curtain of descending dark energy, the forest felt . . . clean.

At least, it did until a singular figure came upon them and uttered a single word.

"Stop."

The three stood staring at one another: Finn and Rey, Kylo Ren some ten meters away. As Ren reached for his lightsaber, Rey pulled her blaster, stepped forward, and took aim.

Before she could fire, Ren raised a hand, halting her. She strained against him, her anger giving her strength. But she couldn't fire. He was struggling also, against her newly discovered ability, as well as the wound inflicted by Chewbacca's bowcaster. Gritting his teeth, he flung his arm sideways in a single, powerful gesture—and the blaster went flying out of her hand. Inhaling deeply, he gestured again, and this time it was Rey who went flying, to smash into a tree nearby and slide to the ground, dazed and hurt.

"Rey—*Rey!*"

Finn started toward her, but the sound of Ren's lightsaber igniting made him turn. In the darkness, the hum and glow of the gleaming red weapon was mesmerizing. With nothing else to fall back on and unable to reach Rey's blaster, Finn resorted to the only defense at his command: He pulled and activated the Skywalker lightsaber.

For some reason, the sight of it was enough to give Ren pause. He stared at it for a moment before reacting.

"That weapon—is mine."

Finn all but snarled his reply. "Come and get it."

Drawing himself up, a towering figure in the snow, Ren did not even bother to gesture. "I'm going to kill you for it."

He rushed forward.

Despite his fear, Finn raised the beam to defend himself. Ren lunged, struck—and Finn parried. Shards of light flew, illuminating the snow and the surrounding vegetation. Drawing back slightly, Ren considered his unexpectedly determined opponent, then resumed his assault with a vengeance.

Finn blocked him again and again, once letting the other man's beam slide against his own and harmlessly off to one side. He counterattacked, to no avail. The longer the contest continued, the stronger Ren seemed to become. It was as if he was enjoying the challenge. Feeding upon it.

At least, it appeared so until Finn parried, swung, and unexpectedly stabbed, the tip of his lightsaber beam grazing Ren's arm. That made it more than a challenge. Taking a step back, Ren reconsidered his opponent. When he closed the distance between them anew, it was with a purpose that had been previously lacking. Expecting an execution, he had found a contest. Now he had been touched. It was time for play to end.

Advancing relentlessly, he was driven by something that Finn could not even sense, far less counter. Still the ex-trooper fought back, until Ren landed a blow that cut across Finn's chest and sent the lightsaber flying from his hand. It landed in the snow six meters distant.

It was over.

Switching off his own weapon, Ren extended an arm toward the device lying in the snow. It twitched

and then began to vibrate as the Force called to it. Stretching out his hand farther, straining, Ren beckoned powerfully—and the lightsaber rose, to come bulleting toward his outstretched fingers.

And past them.

Taken aback, he whirled—to see the weapon land in the hand of a girl standing by a tree. Rey appeared equally shocked that her reach for the device had exceeded his. She gazed down at the weapon now resting in her grip.

"It *is* you," Ren murmured.

His words unsettled her: Not for the first time, he seemed to know more about her than she did about herself. But she had no time to ponder his comment, nor was she inclined to do so anyway; she was too consumed with rage. Holding the haft of the lightsaber in both hands, she ignited the beam—and charged.

Ren met her with his own weapon alight. Expecting weakness, he encountered only strength. Her skill with the device was raw at best, but it was backed by a fury that was as new to his experience as it was unexpected.

When the beams of their lightsabers crossed, the resulting burst of energy lit an entire section of forest.

Within the base, pandemonium reigned as buildings began not just to crumple, but to collapse into a succession of huge sinkholes as the ground itself surrendered to the slowly failing containment field. Observing the cataclysm out a command center window, a young tech rushed for the presumed safety of the building's interior. A senior officer confronted him, stopped him.

"Lieutenant, back to your station!"

Fully aware that in the present situation rank no

longer meant anything, the tech paused only long enough to reply.

"Look, we won't survive here. Even Hux has gone!"

He pushed past the dazed officer, who this time did not try to stop him.

In the darkness of the cavernous assembly room, Hux stood before the image of Snoke. Try as he would, it was proving increasingly difficult to maintain a semblance of control.

"Supreme Leader, the oscillator is failing. The collapse has begun." He looked downward. "There is nothing that can be done."

Furious as he was, Snoke knew there was nothing he could do. So many plans so carefully laid, so many intentions that must now go unfulfilled . . .

"You will leave Starkiller at once and come to me with Kylo Ren. Leave immediately." He added grimly, "It appears that he may have been right about the girl."

To an observer at a distance, it would have appeared as if a series of small explosions was going off in the depths of the forest. Blow after blow landed as lightsaber struck against lightsaber. Though Ren was bigger and stronger than Rey, their struggle had nothing to do with physical size. What she lacked in mass, she made up for in ferocity.

For a while she actually drove him backward, until he regained his self-assurance and in turn pressed her. The fight continued to shift back and forth; first he gained the advantage, then an enraged Rey took it back.

There was a vast rumbling, as of a continent sighing, and a gigantic chunk of forest behind Rey simply collapsed downward, leaving her fighting on the edge

of a cliff so high that the newly formed surface below could not be seen through the rising cloud of dust.

Ren held his lightsaber, poised to strike. "I could kill you right now. But there is another way."

Breathing hard, Rey looked up in disgust at the man looming above her. "You're a monster."

"No. You need a teacher." He was beseeching and insistent all at once. "I can show you the ways of the Force!"

Slowly she shook her head. "The Force?" That was what this was about? Instead of moving to defend herself, Rey closed her eyes. Ren hesitated, confused by her actions. A long moment passed, in which Ren sensed a change in the air, a change in *her*. Then she opened her eyes and attacked, viciously, in a way she didn't know she was capable of, striking again and again as Ren was slowly driven back. The flaring energy from the interacting lightsabers was more pronounced than ever in the flurry of her attack. And—Ren went down.

He was up again in an instant, but not in time to fully deflect a following blow from Rey's weapon. He succeeded in blocking it, but he still took the full force of the strike against the haft of his own lightsaber. The weapon went flying into the snow. Unarmed, he raised a hand and utilized the Force to fend off one slashing blow after another, until finally her fury penetrated his remaining defenses. Taking a glancing blow to the head and chest, he went down, a prominent burn slashed across his face. Weakened, he reached out toward his lightsaber, trying to draw it to him.

One downward cut, she saw. One quick, final strike, and she could kill him. The landing lights of a shuttle appeared in the distance, coming over the

trees in her direction. She had to make a decision, now.

Kill him, a voice inside her head said. It was amorphous, unidentifiable, raw. Pure vengeful emotion. *So easy,* she told herself. *So quick.*

She recoiled from it. From the dark side.

The world shook beneath her as the ground began to split. Turning away from the injured figure, she ran back to where Finn lay badly wounded. A deep gully formed, separating her from General Hux and the arriving troopers. Utilizing the tiny position sensor emplaced in Ren's belt, Hux had tracked him to this spot. He would have taken Rey and Finn, as well, if not for the command that had been issued by the Supreme Leader. That took precedence over everything. There was simply no time left.

The two renegades were going to die here anyway, he told himself as he followed the troopers carrying Ren into the nearby shuttle. As soon as he was aboard, it lifted off, its occupants desperate to flee the dying planet.

Below them, Rey huddled beside the unconscious Finn. Turning him over, she recoiled from the wound Ren had inflicted with his lightsaber. The blow had cauterized instantly. In the dim light she couldn't estimate its depth, nor if it had passed through any vital organs. Holding the unresponsive body in her arms, she started to cry. There were worse ways to die, she told herself as the ground continued to shake and trees began to topple around her.

No, she corrected herself bitterly. There was only one way to die. She steeled her thoughts.

The glow that enveloped her and Finn did not come from the planetary core. It was too bright, too localized. Raising a hand to shield her eyes from the approaching glare, she squinted into the brilliant light.

It took a moment to resolve itself into the scanning beams of a ship. A ship she recognized.

Rising from the vicinity of the new canyon that had appeared behind Rey in the course of her battle with Kylo Ren, the *Millennium Falcon* came toward them. Considering the general conditions and the unstable surface, its pilot made a surprisingly smooth touchdown.

She would have thrown herself into Chewie's arms had he not stooped immediately to pick up the limp body of Finn.

Given the chance, she would have remained in the medbay, where the Wookiee set his burden down. But despite its added modifications, the *Falcon* still flew better with someone in the copilot's seat. In moments they were beyond the atmosphere of the imploding planet. The jump to lightspeed was accomplished without incident, preventing them from observing the final cataclysm. Which was just as well.

A moment after they fled, Starkiller Base system became a binary.

Poe, having called in his teams in relief after spotting the *Falcon* leaving Starkiller Base, was waiting for the ship as it touched down on D'Qar, settling into a vacant space between the remaining Resistance X-wings. Even before the boarding ramp hit the ground, Chewbacca was emerging, moving fast with the still-breathing Finn in his arms. Medical personnel and officers waiting to meet them escorted the pair inside the complex.

Following in the Wookiee's wake, an exhausted Rey found herself greeted by a cheering crowd. Leia Organa was in the forefront, accompanied by a pair of droids. Rey recognized BB-8 immediately, and

wondered at the identity of the gleaming golden protocol droid at his side. Instinctively, she headed
toward Leia.

No general now, Leia took the young girl's face
in her hands. Though brokenhearted at the deaths
of Han and so many brave pilots, Leia was grateful
for the deliverance of the Resistance. In spite of the
presence of the crowd that was looking on, the two
women embraced without embarrassment or hesitation. Then, with tears falling, they moved inside.

Hours passed without word from the medical center.
When Dr. Kalonia finally emerged from the intensive
care section, Rey nearly fainted at seeing the smile on
her face. The physician's words confirmed Rey's hope.

"Your friend's going to be just fine."

"Thank you." It was all Rey could think of to say.

Kalonia looked down at her. "I don't get to treat
many lightsaber wounds. It's such an old weapon.
People today prefer to fight with rifles and blasters,
from long range." She shrugged. "I suppose it doesn't
matter. Death is death, no matter the mechanism that
is employed to beget it." Her smile returned. "But not
for your friend. Not this time."

Located somewhat apart from the swirl of main activity inside the Resistance base, the conference room
was perfect for a strategic gathering. Leia was there,
as well as Poe, C-3PO, BB-8, a handful of chosen officers, and an assortment of equipment and gear that
was considered important but was little used.

Never one to defer in the presence of superiors, Poe
spoke first.

"Kylo Ren said that the segment held by Beebee-
Ate is the last piece of the map that shows the way to
Skywalker's location. So, where's the rest of it?"

"The First Order has it." Rey looked over at him. "They extracted it from the Imperial archives."

Poe stared at her. "The Empire?"

Admiral Statura nodded in agreement. "It makes sense. The Empire would have been looking for the first Jedi temples. In destroying all the Jedi sanctuaries they would have acquired a great deal of peripheral information."

So intent were they on the current conversation and its possible ramifications that no one noticed that a light had come on atop a small R2 unit shoved back among the rest of the equipment in the room. Nor did they see that its hemispherical head had turned to look in their direction.

"We're still at war with First Order," Leia pointed out. "A war that won't end until either it or the Resistance is destroyed. The next time, without Luke, we won't stand a chance."

The silence that ensued was broken by a flurry of beeping and whistling the likes of which the somber gathering had not heard in some time. In the case of this particular beeping and whistling, not in years.

No one was more surprised than C-3PO when R2-D2 came rolling forward to join the assembly.

"Artoo! What—what is it? I haven't seen you this functional since—" He was interrupted by a fresh farrago of beeping that all but drowned him out. "Slow down! You're giving me data overload!" Whether the mechanical hand that rose to the side of the golden head to indicate a headache truly reflected what the protocol droid was feeling or was simply a gesture for the benefit of watching humans, only C-3PO knew.

An excited Leia moved closer. Of all the organics in the room, no one had a more personal relationship to the little droid than she did.

"What's he saying?" she asked.

The protocol droid explained. "If the information you are seeking was in the Imperial archives, he believes he may have catalogued that data. He's scanning through it now."

Rey stared at the diminutive droid. "Artoo has *the rest of the map*?"

"He's certainly implying the possibility!" C-3PO told her. "I've *never* heard him beep with this much energy before."

Emitting a long, sustained whistle, R2-D2 projected a full three-dimensional image of a huge navigational star chart. No one in the room could fail to notice that it was missing a substantial fragment. In response to the hovering image, BB-8 began beeping excitedly.

"Yeah, buddy, hold on," Poe told him. "I have it."

Moving to the side of the spherical droid, the pilot removed from a sealed compartment in his clothing the tiny and very old data device he had originally received from Lor San Tekka. Inserting it into an appropriate receptacle in BB-8, Poe stepped back. For a moment, nothing happened. Then a lens on the droid's curved side came to life, projecting a large section of starfield. Shrinking it down so that its proportions matched those of the missing piece within R2's map, BB-8 adjusted his position slightly.

The two disparate portions merged perfectly to form a completed chart.

"Oh, my stars!" Threepio's exclamation was no less astonished than those of his organic counterparts. "That's it!"

What caused Leia to sway slightly had nothing to do with the Force and everything to do with heartfelt emotion.

"Luke . . ."

"The map." Rey could only stare in wonder as her eyes wandered over a shining, resplendent portrayal

of a substantial portion of the galaxy. "It's the whole map!"

"Artoo!" C-3PO's tone was that of a proud relative complimenting a member of his family. "Artoo, you've done it!"

Cheers and spontaneous embraces filled the room with so much joy that no one paid any attention to who was hugging what representative of whichever species. Rey and Poe were not excluded, though their sudden, tight clinch of shared excitement led to a moment of mutual awkwardness.

"Uh, hi," the pilot mumbled. "I'm Poe."

She nodded slowly, searching his face and finding that she liked it. "I recognize the name. So *you're* Poe. Poe Dameron, the X-wing pilot. I'm Rey."

"I know." He smiled back, a little more at ease. "Nice to meet you."

Amid all the shouting and spontaneous applause, few noticed a protocol droid as he bent over the now quiet astromech unit.

"My dear friend, how I've missed you."

Within the intensive care pod in the medical center, Finn lay in a medically induced coma, his health and life still very much in the balance. Dr. Kalonia's prognosis had been favorable, even positive, but nothing certain could be said until Finn had fully recovered. When wholly parsed, the phrase "be all right" could mean one thing to a physician and something else entirely to the patient.

Sitting beside him, a deeply concerned Rey noted the hour. It was time to go. Leaning in to him as closely as the pod would permit, she kissed him softly, her words full of determination.

"We'll see each other again. I believe that. Thank you, my friend."

Cleaned up and visibly refreshed from his long period of inactivity, R2-D2 led the way up the *Millennium Falcon*'s loading ramp. Nearby, Chewbacca was performing the usual last-minute checks of the ship's external systems. Ordinarily it was a two-person job, but he insisted on doing it by himself.

Standing at the foot of the ramp, an uncertain and uneasy Leia found herself fiddling with the seals on the front of the jacket Rey was wearing. *Foolish nonsense,* she told herself even as she continued. Unworthy of her status and position. But it felt so right, and so natural, to be doing so.

"I'm proud of what you're about to do," she told the girl.

Rey replied in all seriousness. "But you're also afraid. In sending me away, you're—reminded."

Leia straightened. "You won't share the fate of our son."

"I know what we're doing is right. This is how it has to be. This is how it *should* be."

Leia smiled gently, reassuringly. "I know it, too. May the Force be with you."

She watched until Rey was inside the ship and the ramp had closed behind her. Then she joined Poe, BB-8, and C-3PO in moving to a safe distance.

In the cockpit, Rey headed for the copilot's seat, only to find her way blocked by a massive, hirsute form.

"Chewie, the *Falcon* flies better with two people at the controls, you know that. I've already sat in that seat. I'm ready to do so again."

A series of moans came from the Wookiee. Then he turned—and sat down. In the copilot's seat.

Rey felt herself tearing up. "You're serious, aren't you?"

Chewie groaned and, to make certain she grasped his meaning, gestured to his left. Toward the pilot's position.

Sitting down, she settled herself in. She could do this. If Chewbacca felt she could do it, then who was she to dispute him? As she hesitated, the Wookiee reached over and mussed her hair. Grinning, she made a show of trying to slap his hand away. He had no idea how much this innocent, familial gesture meant to her. Behind them, R2-D2 beeped happily.

Facing forward again, she completed a last scan of the console, assuring herself she knew where everything was. From experience, she knew that the *Falcon* was a forgiving ship. She intended to do right by it. Reaching out, she let her fingers play over the controls. Beside her, Chewie did likewise as he groaned his approval.

The *Millennium Falcon* rose.

The planet was mostly ocean, dotted with a sprinkling of towering islands formed of black rock: the throats of volcanoes whose slopes had long since eroded away. Greenery caped the stony flanks, falling in emerald waves toward the azure sea. Above the calm waters, flying creatures soared on wide wings of translucent white.

A great uproar broke out among the wheeling flocks as something larger and louder than any of them descended toward the surface. The *Falcon* banked toward one of the bigger islands, slowing as it did so.

A wide, flat area at the base of the island's central

mountain provided just enough room for the ship to touch down while avoiding the water. It sat there for a while. Slowly, an assortment of small, furtive land animals began to peer out of the forest that cloaked the mountain, drawn by curiosity to this strange arrival.

The ramp descended and the ship's crew emerged. Wookiee and droid looked on as Rey, her old staff strapped to her back, began working her way up the steep, jungle-clad incline before her. Occasionally she would pause to catch her breath and to look back. Each time, Chewbacca would wave. Had he been equipped to do so, R2-D2 would have done likewise.

So old were the stone steps she ascended that grooves had been worn in the front edges by the tramp of thousands of footsteps. The climb was steep, the air humid, and she felt herself tiring. But the thought of stopping never once entered her mind.

Eventually, finally, she found herself in a small clearing occupied by several modest stone structures. The prospect was unbearably primitive. Within the structures there was no movement save for the hurried retreat of small, covert creatures.

She halted abruptly. There was—something. She turned sharply.

Some distance from her, at the periphery of the forest, stood a figure shrouded in a simple cloak and robe. It did not matter that it was facing away from her. She knew instantly who it was. Yet all she could do was stare in silence.

Whether motivated by her stare or by something unknown, the figure finally turned toward her and pulled back his hood.

Luke Skywalker.

His hair and beard were white, and his countenance was haunted. He did not speak, nor did she.

Remembering, Rey reached into her pack and removed his lightsaber. Taking several steps forward, she held it out to him. An offer. A plea. The galaxy's only hope.

She wondered what would happen next.

H4W

Please return / renew by date shown.
You can renew it at:
norlink.norfolk.gov.uk
or by telephone: 0344 800 8006
Please have your library card & PIN ready

KU-750-702

NORFOLK LIBRARY
AND INFORMATION SERVICE

NORFOLK ITEM

30129 078 847 366